MOON FLOWER
The Seven Books of Lukas

Neil Perry Gordon

Dedication

To Maximilian LionMan, my re-wilded son, whose curiosity, dedication and brilliance, inspire these words.

Book Cover Artwork

– *Datura* by Kate Krasin

A native of New Mexico, Kate Krasin (1943-2010) was a consummate silkscreen artist who rendered the West's monumental landscapes on an intimate scale and created exquisite studies of the region's native plants and flowers. Her work is represented in the New Mexico Museum of Art and many other public and private collections.

Contents

Book 1

Chapter 1

<hr>

August 22, 1675

Tomorrow my memory will be erased like words etched in the sand and washed away by a wave. My mind will be emptied of who I am. But at least for today I can tell you that my name is Lukas Pietersen. I'm eighteen years old and I am writing this journal for future reference. Once I imbibe the ceremonial substance, called Moon Flower, my memories will vanish.

Why would I do this? After what happened to my father, I cannot imagine living any other life than that of a warrior. The Pequawkets have offered me a chance to begin this journey and it starts with seeds from the ceremonial plant, Moon Flower.

This magical brew, administered by the Shaman, has the ability to release me into another realm, a place in the spirit world where a connection to the Great Spirit is possible. All the Pequawket warriors have taken this path.

The Shaman has warned me that most likely my memories will be lost. The effect is temporary, although there is a chance it could result in permanent memory loss.

With that in mind, the Shaman has provided a quill and paper to document what I remember about my life, while I still can. I have three days to write, before all is lost.

I wonder what my words will say to me without my recollection of the experiences behind them. Will they be just empty words? But not all memories are born from personal experiences. Some memories are shared with others, and yet still have meaning for the recipients, like the stories my father told me of his journey many years ago to the new world.

My father was a Jew. His name was Solomon Pietersen and he was born in the small town of Vilna in a faraway country called Poland. The years approaching father's twentieth birthday saw an uprising by a military group calling themselves Cossacks, aligned with the Russian tsar. Their intention was to take power away from the Polish-Lithuanian Commonwealth. This resulted in the destruction of many Jewish communities. The survivors who returned to their homes after the uprising found themselves destitute and unable to earn a living because of the government's policies against them.

Amid these rising tensions against the Jewish people, he and his friend Asser and his cousin Jakob decided to leave their place of birth and travel to a place called The Netherlands, a country they heard was tolerant to Jews. They had no idea if they would find work, but anything would have been better than their continual oppression.

After arriving, they spent a few months trying to figure out what to do with their lives. Then destiny showed itself in a new book authored by a young Dutch attorney-turned-explorer, named Adriaen Van der Donck. Van der Donck's book, *A Description of New Netherlands,* became a sensation in the Netherlands.

It was about his first-hand experiences in the New World. Wherever he explored, he documented practically every observable detail. He wrote about the various types of fish that swam in the rivers, and described the amazing and unusual wild animals, as well as the unique flowers and bountiful fruit trees.

Of great interest to these three young readers was a section describing the manners and peculiar customs of the native peoples in the New Netherlands, in particular the Algonquin speaking tribes, who were exceptionally clever at trapping a creature called a beaver.

Van der Donck wrote: "This furry animal has teeth so sharp it fells giant trees as if cut with an ax. But beware of the beaver, because if provoked they are known to bite."

The Algonquin natives claimed that trapping the beaver offered unusual remedies. One was of taking the oil of the beaver and mixing it with honey, then rubbing it on one's eyes to restore poor eyesight. Another useful application was administering beaver water as an antidote for poisoning. Or, for those suffering from gout, just wearing slippers made of beaver skins provided a cure.

But what was of particular interest to father and his friends was that the beaver had under its long glossy coat of fur, another layer of short, tightly packed hairs. This layer could be processed into a rainproof felt that happened to be perfect for men's hats. Father said that the native trappers and the white man had traded thousands of beaver pelts for years. Apparently, the beaver pelt trade was a good business and to these twenty-year-old men, looking for a direction with their lives, it seemed an excellent reason to emigrate to the New World.

On April 12th, 1654, my father Solomon Pietersen, his first cousin Jakob Barsimon and their childhood friend Asser Levy, set sail on the *Peereboom* from the Port of Amsterdam to the New World, known as New Amsterdam.

Their journey took them through the stormy waters of the North Sea and out into the vastness of the Atlantic Ocean. Father told me about the mighty sails that towered into the sky.

"There was nothing more magnificent, when the first breath of wind engaged the limp canvas sails. The ship was transformed from a slow wood-like cradle bobbing like a toy boat in a bathing tub, into an immense sea creature, skimming across the ocean's surface at speeds even the birds had trouble keeping up with," he marveled.

The Dutch West India Company, a semiprivate corporation somehow connected with the Dutch government, operated the *Peereboom*, as well as a fleet of other ships full of men seeking their fortunes. They transported various goods: slaves from Africa, sugar from Brazil, salt from the Caribbean and furs from the New Netherlands across the great ocean. It was known as the Colombian Exchange, named after the great explorer Christopher Columbus who had discovered the New World more than 175 years earlier.

After nearly a month at sea, the *Peereboom* entered New Amsterdam harbor. Father naïvely thought that the campfires illuminating the docks were there to celebrate their arrival; instead they were lit to celebrate the ending of the Anglo-Dutch War. But that didn't matter. These were prosperous times for the Dutch and exciting times for Father and his friends.

Chapter 2

Father believed that he had seen the last of discrimination against the Jews when they were pushed out of Poland. But within two weeks of their arrival in New Amsterdam, an incident occurred that reminded them of why they left their homeland.

A boat carrying twenty-three Jews docked in New Amsterdam. They had traveled from a Dutch colony in Brazil that was lost to the conquering Portuguese. Since the Portuguese had a similar history of intolerance toward Jews, they decided to try their luck in the New Netherlands.

Upon their arrival, Governor Pieter Stuyvesant wrote to his Dutch West India Company superiors in Amsterdam complaining that these Jewish refugees were "repugnant to the general population and representatives of a deceitful race and should not be allowed to infect trouble into the new colony."

While the Dutch West India Company officials agreed with the Governor's characterizations, they allowed the Jews to remain in the New Netherlands and permitted them to trade and travel like other residents, *provided they did not become a financial burden on the colony.*

This announcement opened the door for Father, Jakob, and Asser to establish their export business, which would provide household goods to native trappers in exchange for beaver pelts to be made into hats.

But they would soon find out that New Amsterdam, just like Poland, was a difficult place for Jews. They tried over and over to obtain a license from the Dutch West India Company for their new business but were denied each time. Some of the officials offered bogus excuses such as: they had not been city residents long enough, or they did not possess the correct documentation.

The three men even tried to set up a meeting with Governor Stuyvesant. They made it as far as his office, but were never granted an audience, as the Governor's assistant claimed he was too busy for such trivial matters.

After months of frustrations Solomon and Jakob decided they had had enough and made plans to travel up the North River to try their luck with the trading of beaver pelts at the source.

Asser was not interested in an uncivilized life, and chose to remain in the city, where he would acquire the goods the natives would be interested in trading for, like guns, cooking utensils and fabrics, which were readily available in the Dutch controlled city. The men agreed that this arrangement in dividing their labors made good business sense.

On a fine summer day, as Father described to me, he and Jakob said farewell to Asser, and ventured up the North River on a *sloop* boat to a jurisdiction recently established by Governor Pieter Stuyvesant, called Beverwyck. Located on the outskirts of Fort Orange, Beverwyck was the locus of trading with native trappers.

Chapter 3

Once settled in Beverwyck, Father and Jakob registered their new enterprise with the local Dutch West India Trading office without trouble. No one seemed to care about the men's religion as they had in New Amsterdam, and their application was accepted. The Vilna Trading & Export Company, named after their place of birth, was officially in business.

After finding a proper office by the shipping docks, they set out on their next task of finding a translator to negotiate with the native trappers.

Their first interview was with a scrappy little man. While his skill with the Algonquian and Dutch languages was adequate, his ragged and dirty clothes, unwashed and unshaven face did not seem suitable for a respectable business enterprise.

One afternoon, while having a beer in the Lovelace Tavern, father heard two men having a conversation about a new translator.

"She's remarkable," said a man with a mouth full of potatoes. Swallowing his next bite, he continued, "Not only does she speak Dutch, English and Algonquian, she also can write contracts in all three languages." He leaned in and smiled. "She's young and pretty too."

Father interrupted the conversation and asked the men who this woman was.

"I'll tell you, but don't go sharing it. Before you know it, she'll be too busy for any of us. You can find her at Ten Beaver Street," he said and then whispered, "Her name is Sara Van Winkle."

In the spring of 1648, eighteen-year-old Sara arrived in Fort Orange with her parents, Albert and Hilde Van Winkle. Albert was sent by Pieter Stuyvesant as an agent of the Dutch West India Company to settle a dispute over the control of Fort Orange and the surrounding settlements. The issues involved several violent confrontations between the Dutch West India Company and the settlers regarding the status of the fort and the rights of the settlers to live around it. As a precaution, Stuyvesant instructed Albert to destroy all the buildings within cannon shot surrounding the fort. In an act of defiance, a local trader shot Albert dead while he was supervising the demolition of the buildings.

With no place to go and no source of income, Hilde and Sara were now on their own, living inside Fort Orange. In an act of kindness, following the loss of his friend, Stuyvesant provided for the women's welfare and even arranged for Sara's education. He sent an educator from New Amsterdam to teach Sara lessons in world history, basic mathematics, how to speak and write in English and—what became most valuable—the Algonquian culture and language.

Upon the completion of her studies, Sara became a professional linguist, fluent in Dutch, English, and Algonquian. With her translation skills in great demand for negotiating trade deals with the natives, she and her mother eventually no longer needed financial support from Stuyvesant.

Sara not only worked as a translator for several traders and trappers, but she also was able to understand the native's unusual ways. Many deals were made because Sara not only understood the spoken word, but she also sensed the intentions behind them.

That is how Father met Mother.

A few months after they met, Solomon asked Sara to marry him. The first few years of their marriage, as Mother told me, were some of their happiest. They had a wonderful, loving relationship as well as a growing business that they were building together. Mother began working exclusively for the Vilna Trading and Export Company. Having a full-time translator on the staff provided a huge competitive advantage for their business, and it prospered.

Not long after Mother and Father married, she became pregnant. On January 19, 1657, a frigid winter day, I was born. With a small child to take care of, and with roads either muddy in summer or icy in winter, Father and Cousin Jakob moved the business into the small building at the rear of the property. This allowed Mother to take care of me and still help Father with his business transactions with the native trappers.

Since there were no proper schools in Beverwyck, Mother homeschooled me in literature, mathematics, music, art and—most important—how to read and write in Dutch, English and Algonquian.

Some of my earliest memories were of the trappers walking past our home to the business office in the back. It was exciting seeing them dressed in furs from the animals they had trapped or hunted. In the summer they wore a simple buckskin loincloth with beautiful moccasins decorated with beads, quills and shells. In winter they would layer animal furs such as bear, raccoon, beaver, otter or moose to keep warm.

I'll never forget meeting my first Mohican. I was about five years old and sitting on the bottom step of our front porch when he appeared. He was a young man, perhaps no more than twenty years old. He wore a loincloth, moccasins and a necklace of bear claws draped around his neck. His head was shaved except for a column of spiked hair running from his forehead to the back of his neck. Woven within his cropped hair were owl feathers falling off to one side.

I asked him in Algonquin, "Are you Mohican?"

He stopped, smiled, and said, "I am. How do you know my tongue?"

"Mother taught me," I said, standing up.

"My name is Keme," he said placing his hand over his heart.

I did the same and said, "My name is Lukas."

"You're a fine boy, Lukas. Tell me, where can I find your father?"

"Come with me. I'll show you," I said, running down the pathway to the office out back.

Chapter 4

Father made the announcement over breakfast when I just turned ten years old. He and Mother must have discussed this beforehand, because she smiled when Father said he had something important to tell me.

"Lukas, how would you like to go with me on a business trip to the falls?" he asked with a sparkle in his eyes I rarely saw.

I answered with the most vigorous yes I could muster. I couldn't believe that I would be going to a native village at the falls. I knew from my studies with Mother, that the natives lived in special homes they built called longhouses. Many families lived together in this large home built with thin branches, bent into a curved shape and woven in and out of larger branches that supported the structure. As a waterproof covering, the natives used sheets of bark stripped from the trees. I lived with only Mother and Father in our small home. How exciting it must be to grow up with grandparents, aunts, uncles and cousins, all under one roof.

Mother also taught me about the Cohoes Falls. It would be about a four-hour walk north along the river up to the place where the Mohawk and the North Rivers met.

When the day arrived, I got myself ready before sunrise and waited impatiently for Father. As I paced the long porch that wrapped around three sides of our home, I thought of the traders who visited Father and Jakob and wondered if these men would be similar to those we would meet at the falls.

Father told me that the natives called the Cohoes Falls, The Place of the Falling Canoe. When I asked why they gave it such a name, he said, "Just wait until you see it, Lukas. Then you'll understand."

We heard the falls before we saw them. The sounds of the water crashing upon the rocks rose in intensity as we approached. When it finally came into sight, I was stunned. A fine mist rose like smoke from a fire.

The cliff where the water cascaded down stretched as wide as the North River and higher than the tallest trees in the forest. The rushing of the water was relentless. I immediately understood the Algonquin name. If a canoe happened to go over these falls, the outcome would certainly be disastrous.

As we approached the encampment, a native man walked toward us. He was not wearing the traditional buckskin and moccasins I had expected. Instead, he wore a white fabric robe tied at the waist with a brown and orange belt decorated in a geometric design. A scabbard with a gold wooden handle hung off his belt and a long, orange cape draped from his shoulders. His straight and shiny black hair was so long it reached the middle of his back.

The man recognized Father and greeted him warmly. "Solomon, so nice to see you, and this must be your son," he said in Algonquin.

Father returned the greeting in Algonquin and introduced me. Father then said to me in English, "This is the great Chief Nicholas, of the Turtle Clan."

The Chief looked at me as I stood there gawking. On his forehead were lines carved into his skin in geometric shapes, and upon his arm was etched an outline of a turtle representing the symbol of his clan.

Father nudged me to speak.

I gathered myself and said in perfect Algonquin, "My name is Lukas. It is an honor to meet you, Chief Nicholas."

The Chief threw his head back and let out the biggest and loudest laugh I have ever heard. I could feel my face turn warm in shame. I looked to Father with wide eyes.

"Oh, Lukas, you are a very special boy. Come—would you like to see our village?"

As we walked with the Chief, Father pointed out the Turtle Clan's camp. It was set up against a cliff formation to shade it from the oppressive western summer sun, and when the southeasterly winds swept across the falls, it blew its mist upon the clan offering a refreshing, cooling effect.

A cluster of longhouses surrounded an area where women, girls and boys worked. As we got closer, I saw they were processing beavers into pelts. The Chief showed Father and me the steps involved. After chopping off the legs with an ax, skilled hands made a cut from the base of the tail up the belly to the mouth. Then the pelt was systematically cut away from the carcass. The next step was to scrape off the fat, muscle and connective tissue from the pelt. Once cleaned it was stretched by nailing its round shape onto a board. The pelt was then left to dry.

"How do you trap a beaver?" I asked.

"I like your curiosity, Lukas. Come I'll show you." The Chief led me away from the longhouses and down a path leading to a stream.

"Can you see that mound over there?" He pointed over to where beavers had dammed up the river with sticks and mud.

Following the direction of his finger I saw a mound of mud about as high as my knees.

"See that brown and pinkish thing on top that looks like pieces of dried meat?"

"Yes Chief, I see it."

"That comes from inside the beaver at the base of its tail. For some reason, the beaver is attracted to its scent and when it climbs up the mound to check it out, a twine slips around its neck. The end of the twine is tied to a rock, which pulls the beaver under the water, drowning it."

With our fascinating tour concluded, the Chief asked Father and me to join him in his longhouse. From the outside all the longhouses looked the same, but as we entered the Chief's I knew I was in someplace special. Woven mats in reds and greens with geometric patterns were bound onto the walls. Simple natural color woven mats covered the ground and brilliant shields woven into a variety of designs hung off the concave covering overhead.

The Chief invited us to sit and talk about business. As we sat cross-legged on the mats, a teenage boy entered.

"This is my eldest, Rowtag," the Chief said introducing his son.

The tall, lean boy smiled as he looked at me. Unlike the Chief who wore garments he traded for with the whites, Rowtag wore a traditional headband made from deer hair dyed a brilliant scarlet red and wore a simple buckskin loincloth tied around his waist. He had the chiseled features of his father, but with softer and more forgiving eyes.

When Rowtag greeted us in Dutch, Father's eyes lit up, and he chuckled. I returned the greeting and added in Algonquin, "Your Dutch is good, where did you learn it?"

Rowtag smiled and looked with surprise at his father, who seemed amused at our dueling language game.

Encouraged at our apparent camaraderie, the Chief excused Rowtag and me from the conversation. Out of respect,

I looked at Father before I stood up. Father nodded and Rowtag and I exited the longhouse.

The moment we stepped out, Rowtag took off in a full run toward the falls. I followed closely behind. I didn't want him to think of me as too slow.

Rowtag showed me his favorite crevices and caves that led us to cliffs where we dove off into the black waters with the mighty falls cascading upon us. It was a magical time.

Eventually we were instructed to return to camp, for it was time for Father and me to go home. As we said our goodbyes, the Chief told me that I was always welcome to visit with Rowtag.

With our wagon full of beaver pelts, we headed back, traveling south along the North River. Not more than an hour into our journey, we came upon two soldiers wearing the redcoat uniform of the English army. They ordered us to stop. Father snarled at the soldiers and demanded the reason for their interference.

"We don't need a reason," said one of the soldiers.

"You have no right to stop us," Father insisted and jumped off the wagon seat to confront them.

The larger of the two soldiers didn't like Father's abrupt manner and shoved him backward. As he stumbled, he tripped and fell to the ground. I jumped off the wagon to help him.

"No Lukas, stay there," Father warned me.

But it was too late. I was already crouching alongside him, helping him to his feet. The other soldier, with a pockmarked face and deep-set brown eyes, started to rummage through our wagon.

"Beaver pelts," he announced with a grin.

Father gently pushed me behind him and approached the instigators, barking, "Take your hands off my goods."

Father grabbed the soldier, who was now admiring one of the pelts, and swung him around, ripping the pelt from his hands. The soldier stood there dumbfounded, staring at Father.

The next thing I heard was a blast and saw my father fall to his knees. He paused there, looking at me with his eyes and mouth wide open, before he fell forward face down to the earth. That was when I saw the blood spreading across his shirt and spilling onto the ground.

I looked up to the tall soldier, pointing his smoldering musket at where Father had been standing. He looked back at me with glimmering, evil, catlike emerald eyes that still haunt me. Just then, as if to emphasize his brutality, he smiled at me, exposing a single gold tooth that glimmered in the sunlight.

Then he signaled, with a casual flip of his hand, that his accomplice should walk away, leaving me there alone to comfort Father in his final moments of life.

Chapter 5

For Mother, the murder of her husband, after her own father had been killed years earlier, was too much to bear. She barely ate and wandered the house at night, unable to sleep. I did my best to comfort her by taking over her chores, in addition to my own. I even tried cooking, which did amuse her briefly, but she mostly just looked at me with her deep-set, hollowed eyes and gave me her best smile, saying she would be all right.

It didn't take long for Father's murder and Mother's depression to ignite an anger inside me. I imagined meeting that murderous English soldier with the gold tooth again and exacting my revenge. I delighted myself by thinking about what I would do if I ever got my hands on him.

I fantasized about meeting this soldier, and taking him on, hand to hand. Defenseless tree saplings became my practice target as I pummeled away, punching leaves off branches.

Over the next few years, I spent more and more time with Rowtag at the Turtle Clan's village. I would be gone for days at a time, and when I came home, Mother acted as if she didn't even realize I was away. I tried to comfort her, but sadness overwhelmed her into unending despair.

One day, during this time, the Chief brought me into his longhouse to speak with me. I sat down across the fire pit from him. He studied me intently before he spoke.

"You must learn how to release this anger you carry, Lukas."

"I'm not angry," I said, though I could hear how defensive I sounded.

"Lukas, you cannot carry this burden for the rest of your life. You must release it, if you want to connect with the spirit of your father."

"What do you mean?"

"Our people view the spirit world as the next step in our greater journey. Death is not the end. We continue to exist, but not the way we do in our physical bodies. Lukas, if you allow your anger to control you, it will create a barrier to the spirit world. You must let go if you want to communicate with your father's departed soul."

"I don't know if I can," I said.

"Lukas, you can learn our ways, if you let us teach you," the Chief said opening his palms to the fire.

I looked at the Chief but could not respond.

Sensing my confusion, he said, "Do you know that one day my son Rowtag will seek the path of all young men of our tribe, and take upon himself the challenges of becoming a warrior?"

I nodded as Rowtag did share with me his aspirations of becoming a warrior of the Turtle Clan. He pointed out the many warriors of the tribe and their incredible stories of reaching such an honored designation.

"Lukas, you possess many of the same fine qualities of our warriors," he said gesturing to the few warriors mingling at the other end of the longhouse. "But you must learn to redirect your anger, or it will destroy you."

"I am not sure how to do this. Where do I begin?" I said looking into the flame.

"Wisdom of my people goes back many generations. You are not the first struggling young man we have guided," the Chief said with a smile.

The fire burned hot and released flames high above us toward the opening in the covering above. I returned my eyes to the Chief and asked, "Is it possible that I too can become a warrior?"

The Chief stood up and walked around the flame, gesturing for me to rise. He placed his hands upon my shoulders and stared into my eyes. "I have a fondness for you that is beyond my understanding. I shared this feeling with the Shaman, and he tells me that it is likely we knew one another in a previous lifetime. That is why I would permit you, a white boy, to attempt the challenges, alongside Rowtag, of becoming a warrior."

I was stunned. Just moments before I saw no direction in my life. Now I had a purpose that I couldn't have ever imagined possible. Tears flooded my eyes, thinking how proud Father would be of me, completing such a challenge.

"It would be the greatest honor of my life," I said.

Later that same day, when I arrived home, I found mother hanging the washed clothes on a line to dry. I popped my head in between two bedsheets and announced, "Mother, I have wonderful news."

She continued to pin the sheets to the taut line and said, without inflection, "What is it Lukas?"

"The Chief has said that I can become a warrior of the Turtle Clan," I said, trying to tone down my excitement.

"That sounds nice, Lukas."

I knew she didn't understand, by her lack of concern, so I said, "Do you know what I need to do in order to become a warrior?"

When I finished my explanation, she dropped the bag holding the clothes pins and charged back into the house.

"Mother, wait," I yelled and followed her inside.

She turned to me, with tears in her eyes and said, "You're not one of them, Lukas. A white boy cannot become a warrior."

"Why not? The Chief seems to think so."

"I can't lose you too, Lukas. Life without your father has nearly done me in. If you were to leave me, I don't think I could continue," she pleaded.

"Mother, please sit down and let me explain."

As she sat, she wiped the tears rolling down her cheeks with a cloth she pulled from her apron.

"Father's murder has been devastating to me, Mother. I watched him die in my arms," I said.

"I know, Lukas," she said, softly touching my cheek.

"But I cannot just sit around here the rest of my life. There is nothing here for me." I pointed out the window to the street. "I need more to my life than trading household goods for beaver pelts."

Mother said nothing, except offering me a slight nod.

"I have grown to love my life with the Turtle Clan. They have provided me with a knowledge of the natural and spiritual world that I could never have learned on my own, and now they want to give me the chance to earn one of their highest honors for a young man, to become a warrior of the Turtle Clan. Mother, you know that I am going to do this, with or without your permission," I said, the past few words passing painfully through my lips.

Mother stood up and hugged me tight. I could feel her wet tears upon my neck. She whispered into my ear, "I understand Lukas, but promise you will return to me. Promise me."

"I promise, Mother."

And with that vow, I left home in late June of 1675 to become a warrior of the Turtle Clan.

Chapter 6

A sweet, smoky scent awoke me from my sleep. My eyes opened to the sight of Rowtag's mother Anna burning a bound stub of sage around the perimeter of the longhouse. I looked over to see my friend also stirring from his slumber.

"It's time for your training to begin," Anna told us.

I sat up on my blanket and saw the Chief sitting cross-legged by a small fire. He motioned for us to join him. Rowtag and I sat on either side of the Chief.

As the fire's glow sent quivering patterns of light against the longhouse's interior coverings, the Chief closed his eyes and held out his open palms, as if gathering wisdom from the flames. "To become a warrior, you must accept your inner cowardice," he announced.

Cowardice was not the word I expected to hear. I glanced over to Rowtag who looked equally perplexed.

"Are we not driven by our fears?" the Chief asked, turning his head side to side to look at us.

When we still did not respond, the Chief continued, "It is shameful and the height of selfishness to be moved by our negative thoughts. To transcend cowardice, you first need to recognize it and embrace it. Can you define what frightens you?"

After allowing the question to linger for a moment, he continued, "Your path as a warrior cannot begin if it is based on a false sense of self-worth. You will find your way, not through what frightens you, but through what inspires you."

I was unsure of what it meant to embrace one's cowardice in order to overcome it, but I knew I wanted to learn how to do it.

The next seven days I spent in meditation trying to identify what motivated my actions. Was my aspiration of becoming a warrior motivated by exacting revenge upon Father's murderer? Or perhaps it was fear of living a life without community, and a connection to the spirit world? Or could my ambition be simply fueled by cowardice, as the Chief suggested?

The waterfalls provided several choice spots to linger and meditate on the Chief's words. As I sat watching the water cascade, its mist washing the village dust down my face and arms, I asked myself: *What does it mean to be a warrior?* Was I looking at it as a way to prove my worthiness to others, or just to myself?

A few of the children were jumping off the rocky cliffs into the swirling waters below. I thought how fortunate these innocent young boys and girls were to know only the lessons of the tribe. They had been taught to live in alignment with the selfless-ways of the warrior. Their minds had not been poisoned, as mine had, by the white man's belief system, which was based entirely on the individual, and his egocentric mindset.

I climbed to the tallest peak of the falls, where I could see far into the distance. Out before me flowed the waters of the Mohawk into the North River. Traders and trappers crisscrossed the landscape. Directly below me I saw the children diving into the bubbling pool. I smiled at their playfulness, but understood that a warrior cannot live his life in such a casual, carefree way. A warrior's life is one of intent and purpose.

But in the meantime I relished a few last moments of the joyful gaiety, and leapt off the rocks.

As I surfaced from the cool water of the falls, I realized that the actions of the warrior are born not of fear, but of love for others. To offer such a gift to those in our lives is what creates a warrior. I would need to subdue my ego and understand that a warrior can stand tall and proud when he stands alongside the tribe, not in front of them.

Chapter 7

Rowtag and I reconvened after our seven days of private meditation. While we saw each other from a distance, we were instructed not to interact. I found the ritual surprisingly enlightening and wondered if Rowtag had a similar experience.

I was still unsure why the Turtle Clan would send us out together in our quest to become warriors. Rowtag was the Chief's son, and I was a white boy who was just introduced to the ways of the Turtle Clan. This seemed like a great dichotomy. But the Chief never showed any doubt in his plans.

Rowtag was given the task of teaching me the skills of surviving in the wilderness. He thought it unusual that I didn't possess the knowledge he took for granted. I told him that my parents did not teach me such things.

Rowtag confessed that he had never been out into the wilderness on his own, and that the skills he learned were only practiced in the confines of the village. But he would share with me what he knew.

"My father told me that the best way to master a skill is to teach it," Rowtag said with pride.

"What can you teach me?" I asked.

"I can show you how to make a fire, build shelter, construct bow and arrows, find water, heal wounds, hunt for food, forage for berries and roots and navigate your way through the nearby forests and mountains to find your way back home."

Meanwhile, our lessons with the Chief continued. We learned how a warrior always speaks from the head, and not from his heart. This meant there would be no deviations in our actions once we stated our intentions.

We were also instructed not to speak well of ourselves.

"This will push you further from the truth, and from your true nature. This allows the coward inside you to flourish," warned the Chief.

I found our lessons easy to understand, but difficult to put into practice. The idea of not speaking well of oneself sounds simple to do, but it was so much against my nature not to boast about my skills. I thought of Mother who would proudly say that I was 'quick-witted'. Yet in the Turtle Clan, this would not be considered a virtue.

What I did notice after a few days was that my lack of bluster had a calming effect. My behavior changed. I listened more, spoke less, and I felt a difference.

This theme of knowing one's inner coward continued. The next lesson brought us out into the forest, led by two young warriors. I'd seen quite a few of these strong, lean men moving about in the camp, with striking sculptured faces and deep-set, piercing brown eyes. Their long, straight black hair fell well past their shoulders. These two warriors were no different.

The slightly taller and more muscular man was known as Askook. The other man told me to call him Chogan. They led us up the rocky incline to the falls. As we got close a hand swept across my face and within seconds a length of cloth was wrapped and tied to completely cover my eyes. Two hands grabbed my shoulders and pushed and directed me down a damp and misty black hole. I figured we must be in a cave under the falls. With each step forward, the misty air and the water's roar intensified.

Suddenly the blindfolds were removed, and I could see Rowtag standing inches away from the precipice of the falls. A small push from Chogan who had both hands on Rowtag's shoulders, would send him to certain death on the rocks many feet below. I instantly evaluated my predicament and discovered myself under the same condition, except with my life in the hands of Askook. I could feel my heart pounding as loud as the deafening falls.

Chogan shouted, "The Great Spirit demands that a life is to be sacrificed today. Whose will it be?"

As I tried to absorb Chogan's meaning, he repeated his question. "Whose life will it be?" he barked.

Was he truly asking us to decide whom he should push off the cliff? I looked over at Rowtag, whose ashen face showed his fear.

"Push me," I shouted, instantly thinking of Father.

There was a moment of silence. Even the roar of the falls vanished as I waited for the push. But it never came. The mood suddenly changed as Chogan, Askook and Rowtag smiled at me.

"Well done my friend," said Rowtag. "The Chief will be proud of you."

"What was that?" I asked, my voice shaking in fear.

No one answered, and they turned and walked back through the cave and out into the sunlight. Logic told me that it must have been the Chief who instructed them to test me. Even more disturbing, was the question, why did I volunteer my life in order to save Rowtag's?

As we walked back to the camp no one would answer any of my questions. I was still shaking from the scare when we stood before the Chief.

"What just happened?" I asked.

The Chief gestured for me to sit, and then spoke. "You are brave, Lukas. Not many would have acted as you had today. But tell me, why were you willing to sacrifice your life?"

"Because Rowtag is your son?"

"You are also a son, Lukas," the Chief reminded me.

"Perhaps if I die today, I can be reunited with Father," I said, surprising myself.

The Chief looked at me with warm loving eyes, that brought me to tears.

"Lukas, you do not need to sacrifice your life in order to find your father again. He is always with you. On your quest into the wilderness, you will find yourself very close to him. If you become a warrior, you will have the ability to bridge the gap between our world, and the next, through the Great Spirit. This journey may be long and will be challenging, but this is how you will find your inner peace."

I ran my fingers through my hair and took a deep breath. "I acted impulsively, without thought," I said, looking at the Chief. "I will seek to connect with Father through the spirit world by becoming a warrior of the Turtle Clan. Thank you for your guidance, Chief."

Chapter 8

The next morning, I arose in the longhouse and stepped outside into the warm morning light. I saw Rowtag speaking with the Chief. They glanced over to me and the Chief nodded and walked away.

Rowtag approached and said, "You are to spend the day with the Shaman. Shadow him and observe what he does for the Clan."

All that I knew about the Shaman was that his role was to serve as a spiritual intermediary between the tribe and the Great Spirit they called the Gitchi Manitou, who they believed had created and inhabited the entire universe. This most important spirit was believed to be present in all people and animals, as well as in rivers, oceans, and the sun, moon and stars.

I walked along with this short, and unimposing man while he attended to the sick. He offered along with a remedy that he pulled from his pouch, a ritual to drive the evil spirit that had invaded the sick person's body. The Shaman taught me that this evil spirit was known as the Wendigo.

A mother asked the Shaman to look at her son who was complaining of a headache. Inside the longhouse the boy was lying down and did not look well. The Shaman touched the boy's forehead with his open palm.

"You're too warm. The evil spirit is inside you," the Shaman said.

He pulled out from his pouch a piece of bark from a tree and handed it to the mother. "Soak this in boiling water and have him drink. The evil spirit will leave the body."

The mother placed her hand over her heart, offering her appreciation.

At midday, the Shaman invited me into his longhouse. I stepped inside, out of the blazing sun turning the once soft green grass of the meadows surrounding the camp into coarse straw, and sat alongside the unlit fire pit. The Shaman sat across from me and looked at me with warm, welcoming eyes.

"Lukas," he began. "In a few weeks you will set forth from the camp on your path to learn from the Great Spirit. The Chief and Rowtag have been preparing for your great challenges ahead of becoming a warrior."

I nodded that this was so.

"It is my duty to prepare you for your greatest test you will face. We have sent many young men out into the wilderness. Most return transformed and ready to serve the Clan. However, there have been some who fall under the spell of the Wendigo. If you lose your way in the woods, and I do not mean being physically lost, I mean if you forget your training and resort to acts of cowardice, you will become a target of the evil Wendigo spirit." As he paused to allow me to absorb his words, I imagined black smoke swirling within my mind.

"Once in a weakened state the Wendigo may appear to you in the shape of a man, perhaps even dressed and acting like a Shaman," he said gesturing toward himself.

"The Wendigo will put a curse on you that will transform you into a violent being. If you find your way back to us, we will have no choice but to burn your body to ashes. This is the only way to extinguish the Wendigo from our presence."

I assured the Shaman that I would do everything in my power to prevent such a possession of my body and spirit.

He laughed at my ignorance. "If you encounter a Wendigo you cannot escape. A Wendigo will sense you from miles away by your panicked heartbeat. By the time you are aware of its presence it will be too late."

I wondered if the Shaman's warning was symbolic— or was there a real, living monster out there in the wilderness, ready to take my soul?

Chapter 9

Sitting by the falls on a lazy afternoon, I saw a woman walking over in my direction. She looked to be the same age as my mother, with long, shiny black hair and a beautifully intricate wampum belt wrapped around her slender waist. Longing for Mother made me queasy for a moment, but that quickly faded when the woman's eyes locked on mine and I realized she was heading my way.

Apart from the Chief's wife, Anna, I had little contact with any of the women of the Turtle Clan. What I saw was that most of their daily activities included gathering plants, nuts and berries to eat, cooking the food and taking care of the children. Yet unlike the women of my world, the females of the Turtle Clan could also hold equal positions to men.

When she reached me, I stood up to greet her properly. She gestured for me to sit as she joined me with the falls cascading behind her.

"Greetings Lukas, my name is Sipatu. I am a representative of the Turtle Clan's tribal council. The council has been discussing the preparations for your seven moon journey," she said, picking up a small stone and tossing it from hand to hand. "The council has concerns that the training will be too vigorous for your white man's constitution."

"I assure you, Sipatu, that I can complete the training," I said.

Immediately I worried that I had answered with too much enthusiasm.

"Lukas, the seven virtues are woven into our future warriors beginning at birth. It is not possible to learn them in just a few weeks' time. The council feels the risks are too great sending you to commune with the Great Spirit," she said.

Listening to her words I wondered if this was another test. The episode in the caves testing my bravery under the falls was certainly one. How would a warrior respond?

I straightened the curve of my spine to sit tall before I spoke.

"The council is wise. It may be true, and I may not be worthy. But tell me Sipatu, if I am to become a warrior shouldn't I be intimately acquainted with fear?"

She nodded and gestured for me to continue.

"I know my fears like a mother knows her children, and I can assure you, and the council that my actions, and decisions yet to come, will not be dictated by my fears. Mine will be motivated by love for the tribe. Is this not the way of the warrior?"

Her gentle smile encouraged me. "The Chief has told me that you are wise beyond your years. I wonder though if you are too wise. Perhaps this wisdom you exhibit is nothing more than a mask. Cowards hide behind masks, Lukas."

These were thoughtful words Sipatu spoke to me. In a way, she was right. *Did* I feel comfortable behind my mask of competency? Was she exposing new fears I didn't yet recognize?

"You are judicious, Sipatu," I said. "I confess that I am afraid of looking foolish or being not deserving of the task set before me."

She stood up and signaled for me to rise as well. When we were both upright she smiled, took both of my hands in hers and squeezed them. I looked into her brown eyes that sparkled from the bright sunlight reflecting off them. She let go of my hands, turned away and left me standing there alone to contemplate today's lesson.

Chapter 10

I blamed the pounding rain and darkened sky for waking up late that fateful morning. When I arose, I wondered where Rowtag would go in such a heavy downpour? I stepped out onto the soft rain-soaked ground and assumed that most of the tribe was still taking shelter inside their longhouses waiting for the rains to subside.

A few warriors were casually patrolling the perimeter of the camp. I saw Chogan and asked him if he knew where Rowtag took off to. He told me that he had gone a short time ago to the meadow by the caves for a ceremony.

"You are to join," he told me, pointing up the hill.

Walking up the rocky path I saw wisps of white smoke rising into the moist sky. As I approached the elevated ground of the meadow, I saw many familiar faces of the Clan standing around the smoldering fire including the Chief, Rowtag and the Shaman who were performing some sort of a ritual.

I soon realized that I was witnessing a burial ceremony. I caught Rowtag's eye, and he cocked his head as a signal for me to stand alongside him.

A body was lying several feet deep in freshly dug earth. The rains continued to fall, and the corpse, wrapped in sheets of birch bark, seemed to be floating in the swelling water gathering beneath it.

I whispered to Rowtag, "Who died?"

"The Chief's uncle, Achak. His father's brother."

While the Shaman chanted a song to the dead, tears and raindrops carved pathways down the widow's ash-smudged face. Several elderly women huddled around her offering their kindness and support.

Buried along with Achak were his most cherished personal belongings, such as his bow and arrows and his skins. As the ceremony continued, the eldest men of the Clan added small tokens, jewels and ornaments to the grave, expressing their eternal friendship.

Rowtag shared with me that many believed the soul of the dead might even be reborn within their own tribe. It was not unusual for a child born immediately after a death to be called by the same name as the recently deceased.

After the ceremony, Rowtag and I lingered at the burial ground. We watched the Chief lead the procession down the soaked pathway back to the longhouses.

We spoke about the native's belief in the rebirth of the soul. Death was not the end of life, just a transformation into a new body, yet to be born. I thought of Father and wondered if it was possible that he may have been reborn. Would I one day meet Father as another being and not know it was him?

As we started down the path, anxious to dry off our rain-soaked clothes, Rowtag asked me a question. "The Chief would like to know if you would be able to sit in on our bargaining with the Dutch traders. He thinks you can provide an advantage with your language skills."

"I'm not a negotiator," I reminded him.

"But you speak Dutch and Algonquin. We rely on the trader's interpreters, and this is clearly not very smart," Rowtag explained.

I had to admit, he had a point.

"Tomorrow we are expecting traders, and the Chief would like you present."

My immediate thought upon hearing this was that I had a chance to demonstrate some of my unique skills for a change, instead of being the naïve student. It would be my first opportunity to use the lessons I had learned from my parents about negotiating.

The next morning, I joined Nosh, the clan's negotiator, by the fire pit where we would be meeting the Dutch traders. Stretched and dried pelts were neatly stacked in several piles on woven straw mats. Apparently Nosh was not keen on the idea of my assistance, and I couldn't blame him. My presence could be considered a criticism of his performance. But I assured him that we would act together in the best interest of the Clan.

As we waited for the arrival of the traders, I asked Nosh what he expected to be offered in exchange for the pelts.

"The usual items like cooking utensils, guns, knives and fabrics. The Chief especially likes the fabrics. You see how he dresses," Nosh shared with me.

Soon we saw the delegation coming toward us along the rocky path. Two horses pulled an open wagon with a large canvas covering their inventory. As they approached I was able to make out the faces. It was cousin Jakob and Mother.

I stood up and took a few steps closer to make sure what I was seeing was accurate. I looked over at Nosh who seemed disinterested. Then I saw Rowtag and the Chief walking over with tremendous smiles. They didn't need me to be the super negotiator after all. That was a ruse, for their amusement.

I ran to the wagon and clutched Mother the moment she hopped off. She wrapped her arms around me, pulling me tight to her, and bringing me to tears.

Mother touched my cheeks with her warm palms and kissed my tears. "Lukas, you look well," she said, looking at the buckskin wrapped around my lean, muscular and tanned body.

The Chief ushered us into his longhouse where we sat, talked and ate for hours. Mother and Jakob seemed impressed with what I had learned so far during my warrior training.

"Rowtag and Lukas will begin their journey to commune with the Great Spirit in a few days," the Chief said.

Mother asked if we were ready and the Chief assured her that I did well with my training. "Lukas is a remarkable boy. He has learned the virtues better than some of those who were born into the Clan."

Jakob asked, "I understand that there are seven virtues and the quest takes seven moons. What is the significance of the number seven?"

The Chief looked at me and nodded as a cue for me to answer Jakob's question.

I explained that the Turtle Clan believes the number seven is known as *the seeker, the thinker and the searcher for the truth*. This means that nothing should be taken at face value. There is always a need to understand and uncover the underlying hidden truths. The journey of seeking the truth is not limited to this lifetime but draws from the seven generations of the past and offers its wisdom upon the seven generations yet to come.

"Your father would be proud of you, Lukas. He spoke often of his life in Poland and his parents and grandparents and the importance of leaving a legacy for future generations. Isn't that right, Jakob?" Mother said.

Jakob nodded and added, "Your father and I are first cousins. We came from the same grandparents. Not only would your father be proud, but I am as well."

We spent the afternoon at the falls lounging on the grassy meadow. They were riveted in every detail of my life with the Turtle Clan.

As we walked back down the path to the longhouse Mother spoke to me.

"I know it's been hard on you since your father's murder, and I haven't been a good mother these past five years. I'm sorry, Lukas. But you don't need to do this. You can come home and be with me. I'm feeling better now. I can take care of you," she said with tears running down her cheeks.

"Mother, we already discussed this. You need to let me go."

She looked at me, and I saw so much love coming from her that I also cried. We hugged tightly for a long time, sobbing on each other's shoulder.

I told her that I would not forget her and would return as soon as I was able.

Chapter 11

The crisp autumn weather felt like a cleansing of my mind, and a chance for a new beginning to life, as Rowtag and I made our final preparations for our adventure into the wilderness. Our supplies were limited to the buckskin loincloths tied to our waists, pouches filled with dried and smoked meats, the moccasins on our feet, and our hunting knives.

We were to head toward the rising sun, so instructed the Shaman. This had nothing to do with anything spiritual, it was mainly to avoid the Mohawk territory to the west. This was not to say that we wouldn't run into any other aggressive tribes, or for that matter the English army, who seemed to be everywhere lately.

Chogan and Askook joined Rowtag and me at the fire and offered us a few words of caution. It was only a few years ago that they went on their seven moon journey into the east.

"You think just because you know how to find berries in the forest or trap a rabbit you'll survive?" Chogan mocked.

I looked over to Rowtag who gave me a brief smile. As we had gotten to know each other, we had grown to instantly understand these kinds of nonverbal signs we exchanged. We would provide Chogan and Askook the respect of listening to their advice without comment.

Askook whispered something to Chogan, who nodded.

"We had an encounter with the Wendigo," confessed Askook. His eyes widened and he straightened his spine, trying to stand taller as if the story he was about to tell required it. He certainly got my attention. "One early morning, just after sunrise, we awoke from our camp high up off the ground on a cliff's ledge overlooking a grassy meadow that ended at a tree line in the near distance. With the morning mist hovering off the wild grasses a white man emerged from the trees, running in clear panic across the field toward us. Moments later," he paused and looked at Chogan, "we saw him, the Wendigo, following in pursuit. In a heartbeat he was on the man."

Askook took a deep breath, then continued, "He didn't stand a chance. The Wendigo towered over his victim by twice his height. Its long, bony arms and claw like hands lifted the man and held him at his head and legs." Askook demonstrated by holding his arms overhead.

"Through the mist we watched its dog-like jaw open and bite deep into the man's chest. After the vicious attack, the Wendigo dropped the dead man to the ground. Blood was running down the sides of its long brown jaw. Its tremendous black antlers angled back, and its shiny dark eyes looked up at us. Stunned and unable to move we sat there until it took a step in our direction. Quickly we gathered our bows and arrows and ran as fast as we could."

"Tell him about the white man," Chogan reminded Askook.

Askook leaned in and whispered, "A moment before we took off, the white man struggled to his feet. We thought he was dead lying beneath the mist, but he rose, stood possessed, and appeared ready to serve his new master, the Wendigo."

I had never heard an actual description of the Wendigo before. The image was certainly not what I wanted to hear on our first day out.

It was a common practice of the Turtle Clan to send two braves together into the wilderness in search of the Great Spirit. Askook and Chogan both succeeded, and upon their return were inducted as warriors into the tribe.

There were stories of one brave making it back alone. This displeased the elders and precluded the surviving brave from earning his place in the tribe as a warrior. Living in such disgrace meant that the failed brave left the tribe, never to be seen again.

Just before sunrise, the clear sky sparkled with stars, welcoming our day of departure. Anxious with last minute preparations, I didn't see the Chief approaching with the Shaman. When I finally noticed him, he was whispering something to Rowtag. They embraced and he smiled. I think more as his father then as the Chief.

Then he turned to me and put both hands on my shoulders and pulled me in with both arms hugging me tight. "Lukas, you must remember the skills you were taught are not the same as the skills you still must learn. Notice everything and trust your instincts. The Great Spirit has a purpose for you. You will never see him, but you will know when he is with you," he said.

"I understand. Thank you again, Chief."

Rowtag and I said our farewells and took our first steps upon the rocky path toward the rising sun.

Chapter 12

Askook and Chogan had told us, "Make sure you construct your bow and arrows right away. You will need to hunt for food, and more important, for furs, and you can't do much with just a knife. Winter will come on fast, and you don't want to freeze to death before you starve to death."

We took these words to heart, and on the first morning out, with a sharp chill in the air, we took our first steps into the wilderness.

"There's no turning back now, my friend," Rowtag said.

I nodded, and gestured to the woods. "Our lives are in front of us."

After a few hours' walk, we found a secluded spot in a hilly area covered with hardy Juneberry trees. They looked like promising candidates for our bows. With our hunting knives, we cut off two suitable branches, and carved them into the tapered shape of a bow, leaving a sturdy center for its grip.

Not too far away grew a healthy cropping of milkweed. Rowtag showed me how to harvest several long stems by cracking open its outer covering in order to expose its long fibers. When we had several strands, we weaved them together creating a tough string for our bows.

Our next task was to find something suitable to construct into arrows. Rowtag said we should look for a tree with red leaves.

"The leaves turn red, just before they fall off," Rowtag said describing the tree we needed to look for. "Its branches provide excellent arrows."

With luck on our side the next day, we came across such a tree standing alone in an open meadow. We stripped the bark off a few straight branches. They were indeed a perfect choice for our arrows.

Of course, an arrow cannot fly straight without feathers or pierce anything without a stone shard attached to its tip. Later that same day we stumbled upon a flock of turkeys.

"Perfect," Rowtag said kneeling down and pointing through the trees to the clearing where they congregated.

The problem was that we had no way to easily capture one of these beautiful birds without the use of a bow. But Rowtag was not discouraged. With his hunting knife tightly clutched in his right hand, he chased a turkey into a cropping of thorny blackberry bushes to prevent the bird from taking flight.

A few minutes later he emerged with dozens of scratches and a tremendous smile. He lifted his arm in triumph with his fingers wrapped firmly around the neck of the slain turkey.

I laughed, and slapped Rowtag on his back. "Well done! That was quite a show."

Rowtag smiled. "We do crazy things when we're hungry."

We harvested the feathers for our arrows and butchered the turkey for its meat.

After enjoying some berries and storing away the turkey meat for our fire, we continued our search for our last item, stones for arrowheads. Our search led us to a cave. The afternoon sun flooded deep into the cavern, washing the rock walls with rainbows of colored light. Sparkling in isolated groupings were crystal formations growing like living plants. This was what we were seeking; deposits of a smoky gray stone that could be chiseled into arrowheads.

With our healthy supply of arrows and sturdy bows, we were finally ready for the hunt.

The approach to the mountains to the east was populated with an abundance of deer and elk, which should not be hard to track. Our intention was to kill at least two, skin them and use the hides for additional protection from the coming winter season.

As a small child Rowtag learned to track deer, a skill that I still needed to master. With little effort he found the path of several heading up an incline where he figured they were searching for berries. We quietly followed the tracks and came upon five deer munching at a blueberry patch.

We steadied our positions behind sturdy pine trees. Just as we were about to release, we heard the swish of arrows that crossed our line of sight and struck three of the deer. We withdrew our bows, and quietly slid down to conceal our positions.

Three warriors from a tribe we did not recognize tended to their kill. We watched them offer prayers to the Great Spirit as they slit the animals' throats, allowing them to bleed out. They spoke cheerfully among themselves.

We dared not move in fear of being discovered. They might have been friendly to our Clan, and probably were, but we needed to hunt and find shelter for the night and could not risk our welfare.

After they carried off the carcasses and disappeared into the tall pines down the hill, we emerged. Without speaking, we headed off seeking new tracks for the hunt. As evening approached, we decided to find shelter, and renew our search in the morning. Our dinner was pieces of turkey meat cooked in a stew, and handfuls of blackberries we gathered.

As we were finishing the last morsels of our meal, I asked Rowtag, "Why were you unsure about those warriors?"

Rowtag patted the corner of his mouth with the back of his hand and said, "Lukas, you keep forgetting you're a white man."

The evening was clear, with a chill that signaled autumn was indeed coming to an end. We dug out shallow areas for our bodies to lie in and covered ourselves with the ground cover of pine needles and fallen branches.

Only a few days into our quest, I looked out into the cloudless sky and marveled at the stars twinkling between the thinning tree cover. The Great Spirit indeed was all around us. I felt his presence, *but when would he feel mine?* I pondered.

We rose before daybreak and resumed our hunt. Just as the sun began to warm our skin, Rowtag spotted two deer grazing in a field of tall grasses. I'm sure my hunger pains enhanced my aim as my arrow struck true into the deer's torso. Rowtag also hit his target and both deer fell instantly.

We skinned the animals and started a fire. With the skins drying in the sun, we enjoyed the roasted meat and discussed our plans of heading into the mountains.

That evening we wrapped the buckskin around our shoulders and tried to sleep. But I couldn't rest, knowing that we would still need to find something more substantial than a skin to warm ourselves in the fast-approaching winter.

Chapter 13

The next morning, as the tall pines swayed in unison along the mountain peaks, I imagined I heard the Great Spirit's voice reverberating within its winds. Or perhaps it was Father reaching out to me from the spirit world. I thought of the words the Chief spoke to me.

"Be aware Lukas, when the Great Spirit offers his presence it will be time to pray."

I prayed for strength, wisdom, and for courage to fight my greatest enemy, the coward within me. But we faced another formidable challenge that needed our immediate attention. The frigid northern winds sweeping across the mountains became our primary concern. We needed to hunt for an animal, to offer us its warm fur.

I asked Rowtag why the Clan hadn't provided us with furs, knowing that winter would be upon us within weeks of our departure.

Rowtag said, "We seek to be warriors Lukas, not coddled children."

"Of course," I said.

"I meant no disrespect Lukas, forgive me," Rowtag said taking notice of my shame.

"There is much I need to learn. Thank you for your friendship and guidance," I said.

"We are both teacher and student. Your strength is my inspiration, Lukas."

Hours passed, and we still searched. I glanced over to Rowtag and gestured with a slight shoulder shrug.

"Be patient," he said. "When the Great Spirit is ready, our beast will show itself."

That was exactly what happened, but not as I would have imagined it.

Before we left camp, we had heard stories from the pelt traders about English armies pushing their way north from their forts. A few of the warriors of the Turtle Clan, who knew this territory, warned us to stay clear of the English, which we intended to do.

With no army patrols in sight, we needed to survive while we attempted to track a suitable beast. But as the snow fell, any hopes of tracking vanished. Fortunately, we found cover in a deep cave where we warmed ourselves by a fire and roasted a squirrel on a spit.

We trapped the squirrel using a deadfall trap. I found this was easy to implement with a large flat stone propped up with branches and rigged with twine made from milkweed stems. When the animal bites into the bait, the trigger pin releases the stone, which crashes down and crushes its skull. The key to enticing a creature into the trap was suitable bait, and earlier that day we trapped a nice fatty eel in a river.

The next morning the sun streamed into the cave, and its warmth washed over us. Our bellies were still in need of something more than a measly squirrel. A cloudless sunny sky greeted us as we stepped out into the pine forest. Just at that moment, a sheet of melting snow fell from the trees, creating a shower of sparkling crystals. Rowtag and I shared a smile, ready for the day's hunt.

Chapter 14

Winter had gripped the mountains hard, and we were desperate for fur. The layers of buckskin did a poor job of keeping the frigid winds from seeping through. Across my chest and arms there were splotches where the cold ate my skin. Rowtag seemed less susceptible to the plunging temperatures, but that didn't make him any less enthused about finding an animal to provide its coat.

Knee-deep powder blanketed our path. This made the woods nearly impossible to traverse and forced us to make our way along the icy banks of a river. That was when we stumbled upon a small herd of bison.

They towered twice our height and sported horns as long as tree branches. I wondered how our measly arrows could penetrate their heavy winter coats of brown and black fur, that looked incredibly warm. There were four of them huddled on the banks of the river directly across from us. Steam snorted out of their black nostrils in large bursts and formed a cloud that hung slightly above them. Rowtag held out his palm facing down as a signal for us to drop onto the ice.

We needed to get closer to have a chance for our lightweight bows and arrows to penetrate such a creature. As we crawled on all fours, the bison paid us no attention.

Quickly we moved along the frozen river and were a few feet from the bison when we rose in unison, drew our bows, and let loose our arrows into the bellies of the beasts.

In hindsight, this was foolish. Did we expect these huge animals to fall over dead from an arrow that barely penetrated their tough skin? Instead, the moment the arrowhead struck, the bison took off, stampeding into the woods, sending the deep snow exploding into clouds of white puffs. We quickly scampered away from the riverbank and followed in pursuit.

The trail, now snow packed by the bison, offered an easy way to track them. An hour later we reached the two wounded beasts alone in a clearing, bleeding out from our arrows, and close to death. We approached with stealth, so as not to frighten them and cause another stampede.

Rowtag whispered an idea, that even when he said it, sounded crazy. We each unsheathed our knives, and on the silent count of three, we leaped upon the backs of the bison. With one hand holding on to its large horn and the other to my knife, I reached around, and slit the throat of the injured beast.

Again, I was not ready for what would happen next. The moment I mounted the bison and plunged the knife into its neck, it took off. Instinctively I held on tightly to its horns, my legs clamped around its massive girth. The beast snorted fiercely, exhaling a spray of snot and blood, and barely missed running into several trees as panic nearly blinded it.

Gradually the animal slowed, losing its strength, and settled to the ground. Behind me I saw Rowtag running away from his own injured prey. But its life gave out moments before it could overrun him.

We stood over the animals watching their last hot breaths melt the snow under their snouts. Rowtag lifted his arms and looked up to the sky and offered a prayer to the Great Spirit.

"Great Spirit, we thank you today.
We thank you for Mother Earth.
We thank you for Grandmother Moon.
We thank you for Grandfather Sun.
We thank you for the four directions – the east, the south, the
west and the north.
We thank you for all my relations – the winged nation,
creeping and crawling nation,
the four-legged nation, the green and growing nation, and all
things living in the water.
We honor the clans – the deer, the bear, the wolf, the turtle,
and today we honor the bison.
Great Spirit, we thank you."

It took us three days to skin and butcher the bison. We worked day and night scraping the sinew and muscle off the large skins. The clear skies provided a warm sun allowing the skins to dry as they hung off sturdy tree limbs.

I had never seen so much meat. If it hadn't been wintertime, it would have spoiled within a day or two. The bison provided us with enough food to last for months, and perhaps too much, we feared. The danger now was for wolves to pick up the scent and attack our bounty. We needed to find a place to store the meat safely.

Rowtag and I built a sled from long branches and tied them with twine made from dead dogbane stalks. With no further need for our buckskin coats, we used them as blankets to cover the meat that we carefully arranged on the sled.

After we had filled our bellies and wrapped our bodies in warm furs, Rowtag lifted the two long-branch arms of the sled and pulled it over the snow.

He turned to me and said, "We need to find a cave to store this meat soon."

I agreed, but in the excitement of our bison hunt we were now lost in the woods. If we were to find a cave, it would be by chance. Nevertheless, we headed east and left behind two skeletal carcasses, and a small offering of meat for the Great Spirit.

Chapter 15

We took turns steering the sled through the sunlit forest, and over hilly mountain passes. Rowtag pointed out a large rock formation beyond an expanse of brilliant green pines. With some effort, we each took a handle, and pulled the packed sled uphill.

There we found, facing the southern sky, a deep chamber that nature had carved out over millions of windswept years. This proved to be an excellent place to safely store our meat and make camp. After we unpacked the sled and started a fire, we sat with a view overlooking the mountains and valleys in all directions. Clouds hung low, settling in on snow-covered peaks.

Rowtag, turning the meat over the fire, turned to me and asked, "You once told me that your father was a Jew. What does that mean?"

I rubbed my chin, unsure of how to answer Rowtag's question. I never thought what being a Jew meant. But I remembered what my father once told me.

"A Jew is a nation of Jewish people from the ancient land of Israel," I said.

"Are Jews a tribe, like the Turtle Clan?" Rowtag asked.

"I suppose they are, and similar in many ways. Jews like the Clan believe in only one Great Spirit. Women do not worship alongside the men, just like your people. Jews believe they are the chosen ones, under the eyes of the Great Spirit."

Rowtag listened and nodded.

"Jews are also similar to native people as they too have been forced to relocate their homes great distances because of hatred against them. My father left Poland because of something called a Pogrom, which forced him to leave, and that is why he came to the New Netherlands."

Rowtag interrupted asking, "What's a Pogrom?"

"Father told me that a Pogrom is a word that means to attack Jews as a way to force them out of their cities and villages."

Rowtag said, "Yes, our people are very similar to the Jews."

I nodded and added, "I never considered myself a Jew, but perhaps I am."

"Oh, I believe you are, Lukas," said Rowtag. "Why do you think you are drawn to the Great Spirit? The Jews and the natives are of one people, worshipers of the Gitchi Manitou."

Rowtag's words surprised me. Was it possible that we were of the same people?

He sensed my confusion and said, "The Shaman told me that the Great Spirit creates and inhabits the entire universe and is present not only in the people of our lands, but in lands far away, lands beyond our reach."

Could it be, that in addition to our connection as friends, Rowtag and I also shared a spiritual relationship that bound us at a deeper level? Perhaps going as far back as our ancestry?

We sat all day looking out onto the mountainous landscape, discussing our supernatural connections to each other, when suddenly an unkindness of ravens landed on the tree branches surrounding us.

Rowtag suddenly stood up and pointed to the birds. "We need to go now, Lukas. The wolves will be here soon. Leave the meat, there's no time now."

"I don't understand. Why would the appearance of the ravens signal a wolf attack?" I asked.

Rowtag pointed to the large black birds sitting on branches directly in front of the cave. "The raven and the wolf work together. The ravens are its scouts. They search for prey, and when they find it, they tell the wolves. We have no time."

Upon these words the ravens took flight, cascaded down the line of trees, and disappeared from view. We gathered everything, but left our cache of meat. I was curious if the wolves would actually show up, but apparently Rowtag needed no such proof.

We were only into our first full moon since we left camp, and spring was more than two moon cycles away. With an abundance of bison meat donated to the wolf pack courtesy of the ravens, we were forced back to hunting.

As I remember now, even with this setback, I felt blessed. Rowtag and I were facing adversity, but without fear. We were evolving into survivors. The next step would be not to just endure, but to actually thrive in the wild.

Without the heavy sled full of bison meat, we moved quickly. Leaving the steep mountain range for a more gentle hilly terrain, was also helpful. We hunted every day. The deadfall traps were reliable for catching squirrels and rabbits. Occasionally we tracked deer or elk, and quickly made our kills.

Our clothing evolved as well. With each kill, we added more ways to wrap fur and buckskin around our limbs, torso, and head. We even created a bedroll to sleep within at night. Rowtag and I were living and moving well. Or so we thought.

Chapter 16

After several uneventful days walking through flat open plains, we saw in the distance a range of mountains. At the time we didn't know the name of these magnificent peaks with towering pines poking through gray and white low-hanging clouds. It was during our encounter later on with the English, that I learned its name.

"We should make camp," Rowtag said, pointing behind us.

I turned and looked east, and saw storm clouds headed our way. We had maybe an hour before a nasty-looking blizzard would reach us.

The foothills of the mountain before us looked like the best place to shelter, but we first needed to cross a wide river. As we looked for a bridge of sturdy ice to cross, we came to a sizable outcropping of rocks.

"Let's make camp here," Rowtag called out over the swirling winds.

We maneuvered around some large boulders and stumbled upon an opening.

"What's this?" I asked Rowtag as we cautiously stepped inside.

What we discovered was a series of caves that appeared to run deep underground. This was an ideal place to hold out until the storm passed.

"We should be cautious before we go too far," Rowtag advised.

I agreed, so we started a fire close to the entrance.

As we sat by the fire, we could hear the winds whistling through the rocks and crevices. Occasional gusts of snow swirled in a whirlwind inside the cave. But we huddled down and found comfort with our supply of dried meats and warm furs.

The next morning never came. At least, we had no idea it was morning. When we eventually awoke, we discovered snowdrifts blocking our escape.

"What now?" I said.

"Looks like we need to find another way out," Rowtag said, pointing into the darkness ahead of us.

The cave led us through a maze of large boulders, and crevices that we needed to duck, crawl or squeeze through. We maneuvered between slivers of rock that opened into a larger cavern. A narrow stream of swift blackish waters ran within the stone that split into a crevice beneath us.

We followed along the underground waterway until the dark stream began to dance with sparkles of light. Rowtag squeezed my shoulder to get my attention and pointed up to show me the source of the light from an opening above us. As I looked up, the sky was not visible, but I saw light being reflected off the snow and ice forming on the rocks that blocked our view to the open sky.

"This could be a way out," I said to Rowtag.

Rowtag smiled and nodded. He walked over to the wall and tested the nooks as a way to climb to the opening, just out of our reach. He easily scaled the wall, pulled himself out of the cave, and disappeared from my view.

I yelled out, "Rowtag, what do you see?"

Moments later his round face appeared with his long black hair draping down like the branches of a willow tree.

"You were right—this *is* a way out, Lukas. But it's still snowing hard. We should wait for the storm to pass," he said.

He lowered himself down, and we propped our backs up against the rock wall, listening to the howling of the winds through the rocks above us. I dozed off, waiting for the weather to clear.

A low growl vibrated through me and interrupted my slumber. When I opened my eyes, I was looking at three sets of illuminated golden wolf eyes staring at me. I nudged Rowtag who had also fallen asleep. He grumbled his annoyance but sat up straight when he realized our predicament.

I slowly reached for my knife and gripped it hard. As I prepared to defend myself, I sensed the souls of the wolves. Their unspoken words filled my mind, telling me that we didn't belong here. I asked for forgiveness of our trespass. But they lacked the ability to do so, and they attacked.

Leading with an open jaw, a wolf lunged for my right thigh. I jumped out of the way, barely avoiding its deadly fangs. I plunged, slicing my knife into the wolf's neck. Blood spurted in a stream and sprayed across my face. The wolf fell hard to the cave floor and died instantly.

I turned and saw the other two wolves ripping into Rowtag's flesh. I moved swiftly, stabbing one of the wolves on its hind. It yelped in pain and limped away into the darkness. The lone wolf gnawed on Rowtag, who was lying in a pool of his own blood, unable to move. I leapt at the wolf, driving my knife into his eye. I stabbed furiously, until the wolf collapsed. There we lay, two dead wolves, Rowtag gurgling in his blood and me, uninjured but exhausted.

I knew Rowtag was near death. It would be impossible to lift him up through the opening above us, and even if I could, he would need immediate care beyond what I could provide.

I kneeled down close to him and said, "I'll go find help. You'll be fine. I'll return as fast as I can."

His eyes responded with kindness, and a sad understanding. I squeezed his hand, covered him with his fur, and stood up.

He looked up at me, and whispered, "Don't come back for me. I'll be with the Great Spirit very soon."

I scaled the rock wall and found my way out into the open air. The storm had cleared, and in its wake left knee deep snow. To the east I faced an imposing mountain, displaying tremendous snow-dusted pine trees. I figured that the only way to save Rowtag's life would be to find an English Army outpost, and the most likely direction would be to the south.

I walked in an open valley. The warmth of the sun reflecting off the snow felt good. But I worried about Rowtag. Would I be able to find help soon, and even if I did, would I find my way back to the caves? I looked behind me, and saw my long singular path carved in the snow. The winds would soon erase the trail, and any hope of finding my friend.

That night I took shelter in an abandoned log cabin. It was tucked against a steep rocky cliff and a stream meandering nearby. I made a fire in a stone fire pit and cooked some of the few remaining pieces of bison meat.

As I chewed upon the morsel, I thought of Rowtag alone in the cave, slowly dying. Tears welled up and released down my cheek. What kind of warrior was I if I could allow my friend to die? I prayed to the Great Spirit to keep Rowtag alive long enough for me to bring back help.

The cabin was perfectly situated to take advantage of the winter's southern sun as well as protected from the frigid northerly winds. It was also well built, and quite secure. Maybe this cabin was not abandoned as I first thought. The next morning proved this assumption correct.

I awoke looking down the barrel of an English musket.

"Who the hell are you?" asked an English army officer.

It took me a moment to comprehend the language. For months I had only spoken Algonquin, while my thoughts and dreams took place in Dutch. Mother taught me English, but I had little practice of the language. But as he asked me again, I struggled to answer.

"My name is Lukas. My friend was attacked by wolves and needs help," I finally managed to answer.

"Get yourself up," the soldier ordered.

Once on my feet, he allowed me to dress. The moment I slipped my bow over my shoulder he shoved me to the door, and out into the morning sun. What I saw astonished me. A company of English soldiers upon their tremendous horses snorted and milled about. Magically the beasts separated, creating a pathway for an officer sporting a tall bearskin hat.

"What have we here?" asked the officer. His striking green eyes complemented his red uniform with a bright yellow band along his collar, jacket's edge and wristbands. His face was remarkably familiar. Did I know this man?

"Hello sir, my name is Lukas Pietersen. I need to get some help for my friend. We were attacked by a band of wolves in caves about a day's walk to the north. He is badly hurt."

He introduced himself as Captain John Lovewell.

He looked at me and I could tell he was perplexed by my dress. "Where are you from, Lukas Pietersen?"

I told him about my quest with Rowtag to commune with the Great Spirit, which interested him greatly. He insisted I join him inside the cabin and tell him more of my story.

It didn't take me long as I sat across the table to realize why the captain's face looked familiar. This was the same soldier who five years earlier murdered Father. The final proof was when the captain smiled, and I saw his gold tooth. The image of that tooth had haunted me all these years.

I could feel my face redden as my body temperature rose. My knife was still sheathed on my belt, and I thought about plunging it deep into the captain's neck. My fingers burned with a desire to grasp the handle. But then I remembered to lead with my head, not my heart. I was in no position at that moment to accuse the captain. If I did so, I would never find my way back to Rowtag with medical assistance.

So, I set aside my murderous thoughts and said, "Please, Captain, can you help me find Rowtag?"

The captain turned to the junior officer and ordered him to find a horse for me, and assign a tracker to help find Rowtag.

"My tracker Matwau is from the Pequawket tribe. He speaks Algonquin, and will help you find your friend. If he is still alive, bring him here for medical treatment. Then we will continue our conversation," he said.

Chapter 17

"Ah, Matwau," the captain said as the native guide approached us.

As he held my shoulder, he continued, "This is Lukas, you are to help him track his friend, who was attacked by wolves and is in need of medical care."

I nodded and greeted Matwau in Algonquin.

His thin, weathered, expressionless face became slightly more animated upon hearing me speak his language. He looked at me with his wide-set brown eyes and said, "We should be going."

For a man of at least forty years of age, he moved swiftly as we mounted our horses, and offered our farewells to the captain.

After our brief conversation at the English camp, we spoke little on the way to the caves, but he did tell me that he served the English captain as part of an agreement with his Chief Paugus, of the Pequawkets.

"The Pequawket tribe's camp is not far from the caves. It's through the mountains," he said, pointing to the hills in the distance.

Matwau knew of the caves where I had left the injured Rowtag. He told me that the three wolves we fought were probably part of a larger pack, and others may return to finish him off.

We moved quickly on horseback, and arrived at the place I exited the caves in less than a quarter of the time it took for me to walk it. I pointed to the boulders that hid the entrance and instructed Matwau to follow.

The path I left in the snow was still there, and marked the way back down into the cave. It took me only a few moments to lower myself back down to the chamber where I left Rowtag.

Rowtag was alive, though just barely. His eyes smiled at me, and he tried to lift his arm, but he had no strength to do so.

"Be still my friend. I have brought help."

Rowtag's eyes looked past mine to Matwau, who was now standing behind me.

"I didn't know he was Algonquin," Matwau said, surprised.

"This is Rowtag, son of Chief Nicholas of the Turtle Clan."

"He is the son of a Chief?" he asked with heightened concern.

"Yes, and we need to get him out of here."

A dark, reddish brown puddle of blood had formed around Rowtag. I cut away the buckskin exposing the deep bite wounds on his belly and right knee. Matwau took out of his pouch an ointment that he applied to the wounds, before he covered them with some dried leaves, and then bandaged them with strips of cloth.

"We must take him to the Pequawket camp," Matwau said. "The English cannot heal him. He needs a Shaman."

Matwau fetched a long sturdy rope from his horse saddle. He instructed me to wrap an end around Rowtag's chest and under his arms. He climbed, and with me holding and lifting Rowtag, we hoisted him up, and out of the cave.

We mounted our horses, and with Rowtag's arms wrapped around my torso, Matwau tied the two of us together.

"Let's go," he said, leading us into the mountains, and to the Pequawket village.

It was hard staying on my horse, as Rowtag shifted constantly, almost throwing both of us to the ground. I asked Matwau if we could construct a sled like the one Rowtag and I made to pull the bison through the snow.

"There's no time, Lukas," he said, and he added some more ropes to stabilize both Rowtag and me on the horse.

With Rowtag's head and chest pressed against my back, I could feel his labored, raspy breath. I was afraid he wouldn't last much longer. Matwau told me that we would reach the camp by sunset, which was not far away as I turned and saw the sun already low in the southwestern sky.

We soon saw the Pequawket camp in the valley below. My first impression was that it was not much different from the Turtle Clan's camp. There was a series of longhouses situated around a central point. Off to the west, on a snow-covered plateau, looked like the place where they grew their crops.

Matwau interrupted my thoughts with a warning. "When you sit across from the great Chief Paugus, know that he has fought many battles against the white man. Your sudden appearance will be suspicious. You should be cautious with your answers."

I nodded, indicating that I understood.

We approached the entrance to one of the longhouses. Matwau shouted to two young braves to assist us. They untied the elaborate spiderweb of knots that locked Rowtag and me together and to my horse.

Matwau instructed the braves to quickly find the Shaman. I followed him, carrying my friend in my arms. He barely had enough strength to wrap his right arm around my neck.

The longhouse was smoky from several cooking fires scattered along the narrow and deep enclosure. Small openings in the roof structure of woven reeds allowed some smoke to escape. Dozens of eyes watched, as Matwau and I walked in between the families gathered in their winter home. The smells of smoke, sweat and urine filled my nostrils. Rowtag started to cough from the stale air.

I'm sure a white man carrying an injured brave like a child cradled in his arms wasn't a sight they expected to see. Children ran up to us to stare. Women chatted among themselves, and the men just looked at each other in wonderment.

When we reached the rear of the longhouse, I saw, sitting on an elevated platform of sturdy logs, a man I assumed to be the great Chief Paugus Matwau had told me about on our journey. He sat upright with his legs crossed. His head was mostly bald except for a small cropping of hair tied into a tight ball on the back of his skull. Yet unlike Chief Nicholas, who was fond of European fabrics in bold colors, Chief Paugus wore a simple loin cloth with leather leggings, and several strands of necklaces adorned with colorful beads hung upon his bare muscular chest.

Sitting to his right was an older man wearing large bands of silver wrapped around his biceps and wrists, that glittered light from the fire burning on the floor below the platform.

Matwau spoke to the chief, explaining who Rowtag and I were, and why we came. The Chief became very animated, when he realized that the injured man lying on the woven mats next to the fire was the son of Chief Nicholas of the Turtle Clan. He instructed the Shaman to attend to Rowtag, and for me to take a seat next to him.

The Shaman had kind eyes and a round face, complemented by his large round earrings. I watched as he lowered himself from the platform, and while he attended to Rowtag I sat alongside the Chief.

From the elevated position I could see through the haze the eyes of the tribespeople looking at me. The Chief had many questions, such as how I had learned to speak their language, and why I was traveling with the son of Chief Nicholas.

I told him how my mother taught me as a young child to speak his language and that Rowtag and I, both warriors in training, were traveling together in the wilderness to seek our connection with the Great Spirit. When the Chief was satisfied with my story, his attention turned to the Shaman.

Rowtag had all of his clothing removed except for his small loincloth. The Shaman first removed the substance that Matwau applied, and cleaned the wound. He then treated it with a mixture of a liquid substance that he prepared in a stone bowl, and covered the wound with dried brown leaves.

Rowtag was lying still, his chest barely rising with each breath. The Shaman opened Rowtag's mouth with his fingers, and sprinkled a powder on his tongue. Rowtag immediately went into a seizure. His body stiffened and then convulsed violently. Instinctively I reacted and rose to my feet. The Chief placed a hand on my forearm and nodded to assure me that the Shaman knew what he was doing.

The episode soon passed, but it took a while for his rapid breathing to calm. Eventually his chest settled, and he slept peacefully.

Chapter 18

While Rowtag slept, the Shaman and four elders formed a circle seated cross-legged around him. Matwau and I were summoned to join them. This, I knew from my time with the Turtle Clan, was what they called a healing circle.

I observed that the ceremony required seven participants, another demonstration of the importance of the number seven. A stump of dried wrapped sage, and strands of woven sweetgrass burned and passed around among us, creating a ring of smoke around Rowtag.

The Shaman, the elders and Matwau recited a prayer in unison.

Great Spirit you are the water, may you cry, cleanse,
flow, and rain
Great Spirit you are the fire, may you blaze, devour,
glow, and ignite
Great Spirit you are the air, may you blow, breathe,
gust and cool
Great Spirit you are the heavens, may you connect,
listen, forgive and heal.

Silently, I added my own prayer to the Great Spirit, hoping he would also hear me and heal my friend.

The next morning I awoke while many of the tribe still slept and quietly exited the longhouse. The chilled clean air filled my lungs. With at least eighty souls living in a poorly ventilated structure, the stench was pungent.

A short walk along a beaten snow-packed path brought me to a large lake where the women of the tribe would harvest fresh water for drinking and cooking. Except for a few braves walking around the perimeter of the many longhouses, I thought I was alone. But a voice whispered my name.

"Lukas, I need to speak with you," said Matwau.

The experienced tracker appeared magically. Surprised at his arm's length presence, I asked, "Hello Matwau. Is everything all right?"

He stared at me for longer than comfortable, before he spoke. "The Chief wants you to go back to the English camp with me."

"I cannot leave Rowtag," I told him.

"Rowtag will sleep for many moons and may never wake up," Matwau said seriously.

"But why do I need to go with you?" I asked.

"The Chief wants you to convince Captain Lovewell to allow the tribe the freedom to hunt these mountains without harassment from the English. There have been several confrontations with our warriors by the English soldiers who have taken our kills," Matwau told me.

This sounded true to what I knew of the captain's nature, and I shared the story of my father's murder with him.

"I am saddened for your loss Lukas, but I am not surprised. The captain is an evil man, but he is also powerful with his well-armed company of Rangers. We must find a way to contain him without stirring his anger."

"How can I convince the captain to restrain his men?"

"Captain Lovewell has lost his translator to cholera. You will offer yourself as a replacement in exchange for an understanding," Matwau explained.

I was flummoxed. Chief Paugus expected me to serve with the English army as a way to protect his hunter's bounty?

"The last thing I want to do is help the captain."

Matwau gave a gentle smile and said, "I understand your pain, Lukas, but now is not the time to seek your retribution. You cannot refuse the Chief. It would be a mistake to say no. You will need to seek your revenge at some other time. For now, you must serve the tribe."

The healing circle ceremony had ceased, and Rowtag was placed upon a woven mat and covered with blankets. His breathing was steady now, though shallow. Perhaps Matwau was right. Maybe Rowtag would never wake up.

Chapter 19

At first, Captain Lovewell questioned my language skills. I told him that my mother taught me Algonquin when I was a child, and he asked, "Why would your mother teach you a native language?"

"My parents traded with the natives for beaver pelts."

"By your accent, I assume your parents were Dutch?"

"My mother is Dutch."

I wondered how far this conversation would go. It seemed unlikely that the captain would remember me, or my father.

"So you speak Dutch, English and Algonquin?"

I nodded.

"Tell me why would Chief Paugus offer such a valuable service to me."

I explained that the Chief had offered my services in exchange for allowing his warriors unimpeded rights to hunt the mountains.

"This seems like a bargain. I accept, Lukas. We welcome you as our translator. I hope you can prove yourself worthy," said the captain.

I didn't have to wait long for my first test. The next morning a junior officer rudely shook me awake. "On your feet you Dutch fuck, we're leaving," he yelled.

By the time I opened my eyes, all I could see was the tail of his red coat leaving my tent. I must have been a strange sight to these English. As far as I knew I was the only white translator they had ever encountered, and on top of that my English had a distinctive Dutch accent, courtesy of Mother. Good thing they didn't know that I was also half Jewish.

Horses snorted and stomped the snow, beating it into a surface as hard as cobblestones. I maneuvered my way to the captain's quarters for my orders. The guards, apparently aware of who I was, allowed me to pass into the captain's house-sized tent.

Captain Lovewell was adjusting the silver-handled sabre on his belt as I entered.

"Ah, Lukas, are you ready?" he asked me.

"Ready, sir?"

"Dammit man, didn't someone tell you? We are heading north to Lake Winnipesaukee. It's time we put a stop to the Sokokis Tribe who have been attacking the King's men," he explained.

I didn't know about this tribe, but I figured they must be Algonquin speaking and perhaps related to Pequawket. The main reason Chief Paugus sent me was to prevent such aggressive actions by the captain.

"Sir, perhaps you can send Matwau and me to speak with them first and try to settle this peacefully," I proposed.

The captain's face turned nearly purple with anger, and I thought he was going to withdraw his sabre and run me through. Instead, he took a step toward me and pointed a finger from his white-gloved hand an inch from my face.

"You are here, Lukas, to serve the crown, not these savages. Don't forget your place," he snapped.

I nodded respectfully and withdrew to ready myself for the expedition. When I got back to my tent Matwau was waiting for me. His eyes were burning in anger.

"Chief will not like this," Matwau whispered.

I nodded in agreement. "But what are we to do?"

"We must warn the Sokokis. Tell them the English are coming."

"How will we do that?" I asked.

Matwau leaned in very close and whispered in my ear, "I will lead the English to their campsite on Lake Winnipesaukee. It will be frozen now. I will show the captain a secluded place to make camp, and that night I will cross the lake and warn the Sokokis."

I felt uneasy about the plan. How would the Sokokis react? Would they attack the Rangers first, or would they just wait, and defend themselves? I was just about to voice my worries when Matwau put a finger to his lips to hush me.

"No more talking," he said, and left me in my tent to worry alone.

Chapter 20

Later that morning, Matwau and I had the honor of riding alongside the captain leading the company of thirty soldiers out of camp. I was curious why the captain trusted Matwau to find the Sokokis longhouses. I would have been suspicious of a native Algonquin guiding an English army into battle against a closely related tribe. But I figured Matwau must not have given the captain any reason not to mistrust him during the past few months that he had served him.

During our trek the captain's temper cooled as the warm sun reflected off the winter landscape. He was curious about my background and how I ended up with the Turtle Clan. I cautiously shared my history.

"Why do you want to become a warrior, Lukas?" the captain asked.

This question from the captain had many possible answers. But I had no choice but to temper my words. After all, the only thing I could say was that the captain was the main reason I wanted to become a warrior and that if he hadn't shot Father, I would not be sitting in front of him now, discussing the reasons.

"It is my intention to lead a life of courage, and devotion to the Great Spirit."

"You know Lukas, your ambition is not much different than mine," the captain offered.

That's outrageous, I thought. *This man who murdered my father is the last person I have anything in common with.* But what he said next offered a softer side to his personality that I would never have thought he could muster.

"I too wanted to be a warrior at a young age. As a child, my father, uncles and grandfather all served in the King's army as distinguished officers. These men were my idols. But I can see how you were drawn to the romantic ideal of connecting with this Great Spirit you speak about. I admire your dedication to a single-minded quest," he said.

I thought that perhaps this was a moment where I could convince the captain there could be another way of resolving the conflict with the Sokokis Tribe.

"Captain, please allow me to speak with the Sokokis Chief. Perhaps we can propose a peaceful solution," I said with conviction.

The captain looked at me, this time with more amusement than disdain. "You're a boy, Lukas, albeit a wise boy. But you know nothing about the enemy. Playing diplomat is not a child's game. Even the most experienced peacemaker would walk away frustrated trying to negotiate a peace. These people are savages, and do not understand the ways of civilized men. Do not ask me this again, Lukas."

So that was that. I hoped only that Matwau would be able to warn the Sokokis when we arrived at Lake Winnipesaukee.

With the sun setting at our backs, we made camp hidden from the Sokokis longhouses. The captain ordered no fires, so as not to alert the Sokokis scouts patrolling the lake. There were many winter nights that Rowtag and I slept without a fire, so this was not a burden. Actually, the weather that night was not cold. A sign that spring was approaching.

As I readied myself for sleep, Matwau suddenly appeared in my tent. His hands were grasping his stomach and as I looked closer, blood was trickling through his fingers and dripping onto the mud below.

"Are you all right, Matwau? What happened?"

"I've been shot," he managed to say as he fell to his knees.

I laid him down on my bedroll and put a hand over his wound. But the bleeding continued. If nothing were done, he would quickly bleed out.

"Who shot you?"

"Stupid English. I think they thought I was a deer or an elk."

"Why would they be hunting now?"

"I don't know," answered Matwau with his breath laboring.

"I need to get you help," I said.

"No, Lukas. You must go warn the Sokokis. I will see the Great Spirit now. This is my time," Matwau said as he struggled for breath.

"I can't leave you," I insisted.

"You must go, Lukas. Go to the Sokokis camp and warn them before it's too late," he said.

I looked at him with tears welling up, and said I would honor his request. As I wrapped my bison fur around my shoulders, Matwau stopped breathing. His eyes looked beyond the mortal world, as the Great Spirit claimed him.

I had no trouble slipping past the guards patrolling the English camp, thanks to their constant chattering and heavy footfalls, and began my trek across the frozen lake under cover of the moonless night.

As I stepped gingerly across the ice, I thought how I would approach the village. Unlike Matwau, I was a white man approaching in the middle of the night, and a warrior might see me as an intruder and shoot me before I had a chance to warn them about the real threat coming from the English army.

The longhouses were set back from the lake a good distance. I could see the camp from the lake's edge, where I hid behind a cover of holly bushes. Warriors stood guard and walked the perimeter. There would be no way to casually enter the camp, and simply ask to speak to the Chief.

The only way would be to surrender to one of these warriors and hope for the best. With my arms raised above my head, I stepped out into the open field separating me from the longhouses.

Seconds later I was knocked to the ground by something heavy to my head. I lay stunned with half of my face buried in the snow.

"I need to see the Chief," I managed to say in Algonquin.

There was talk among several of the warriors. I caught a glimpse of a few of the warriors' faces as I attempted to lift my head. They bickered back and forth, unable to decide what to do with me. Eventually, after much discussion, they agreed to bring me to the longhouse.

My arms were now tied tightly behind my back and my head throbbed in pain. More than just a trickle of blood ran down my forehead. I knew the cut was deep and needed mending. But that was not these warriors' concerns, at the moment. As we entered the longhouse, I became the center of attention. They shoved me forward, forcing me to stumble and fall. I was kicked, punched, and spat at by young Sokokis boys, who were greatly amused by my presence.

After this gauntlet of physical abuse, I made it to the ceremonial post where the Chief and the Shaman waited for me. Blood from my wound ran over one eye, forcing me to close it. My head ached, and I felt dizzy.

I somehow shouted the word "Stop," in Algonquin. A collective gasp was heard from my use of their language in a forceful way. I saw from the corner of my open eye a figure come toward me. I lunged out of the way and avoided another blow.

"Enough," the Chief announced. He motioned to his warriors to sit me down and nodded to the Shaman. The Shaman in turn gestured to a woman behind me who began to treat my wound, as soon as I was sitting cross-legged, looking up at the Chief.

He told me his name was Chief Squandro, and asked why I had come.

"Chief, I have come to warn you. Captain Lovewell and fifty Ranger soldiers are camped across the lake. They plan on attacking you before dawn," I said, breathlessly.

The constant murmur rippling among the tribespeople hushed upon hearing my words. All eyes and ears were upon the Chief, waiting for his reply.

When he finally spoke, he said simply, "We knew this day would come."

My wound was treated and a bandage wrapped around my head. I was given a leaf to chew on, which had the power to revive me. In the meantime, the Chief barked out orders to his warriors, who were now preparing for battle, and also instructed the women and children to gather what they needed so they could hide out in the forest.

Every person knew exactly what to do, and the pace of the activities was frenetic. But the Chief and the Shaman remained steady and did not move, a very reassuring image for the anxious tribe.

The Chief asked me to share my story of how I ended up sitting in front of them. Not sure how far back I should go, I settled upon sharing my encounter with Chief Paugus of the Pequawket tribe, and my mission as a translator with Captain Lovewell.

When I asked why the Sokokis were attacking English soldiers as the captain had asserted, the Chief shared with me a story.

"This past summer," he began, "three English soldiers approached our camp. When they saw my wife Wawetseka, and my infant son Menewee playing by the lake, they decided to test the white man's ignorant belief that a native baby can dog paddle upon birth as do animals." He paused to gather himself.

"These English had some idea this would prove that we are not humans, but savages as they claim. They took my boy, and tossed him into the lake. My wife dived in after him and pulled him out. But not before he swallowed too much water. He never recovered, and died the next day.

"We soon learned that these three soldiers were from Captain Lovewell's Ranger Company. When we demanded justice for their crime, they ignored us. We took our own retribution on those murderous white scum," he concluded.

I sat stunned and saddened by the Chief's story. But now I understood the reason for the escalation of hostilities. Of course, Captain Lovewell would not punish his men for such brutish behavior. On the contrary he probably encouraged it. His arrogance had caused the increase in violence, which he apparently relished.

The captain needed to be stopped. I tried to stand. But a wave of dizziness forced me back down to the mat.

"Easy, Lukas," the Shaman said. "You are not in any condition to go anywhere."

I nodded reluctantly.

While the tribe prepared themselves for battle, I was left to rest and recover. I knew I still had some time to get back across the lake and try to stop this madness. Slowly I got up and found myself steady enough to walk. Casually I joined the women and children who were leaving the longhouses and seeking safety in the woods to the north.

A few steps beyond the tree line I slipped away unnoticed and made my way back to the English camp across the frozen lake.

Chapter 21

By the time I made it back, the Rangers were in marching formation, with the captain and his officers on horseback leading them. I called out to stop. I must have been a ridiculous sight, appearing like a tiny dog barking at the captain, sitting high in the saddle on his massive horse.

"What is it, Lukas?" he asked, holding up his white-gloved hand.

"Captain, please, I know why the Sokokis killed the soldiers. It was retribution for your men killing the Chief's baby son," I pleaded.

"What are you talking about?" he demanded.

"I just met with Chief Squandro who told me about the three soldiers who drowned his son. They were killed in retribution. If we just try to talk, we can avoid all of this," I said, sweeping my arms across the lines of armed soldiers.

"You met with the Chief?" he asked.

I nodded.

"Damn you, Lukas," he shouted. "How dare you undermine my plans?"

The captain turned to an officer and spoke for a few moments. Then he stood up tall, pressing his feet into the stirrups, and announced his orders to his second in command.

"Lukas and I will approach alone across the lake, acting like I am ready to negotiate. You take the company and flank them from the tree line to their north. If the Chief accepts my offer to negotiate, wait until we are in the longhouse before you attack. If he refuses, we will engage them there, and you'll surprise them from the rear," he ordered.

"Let's go, Lukas. You'll ride with me," he said, reaching down with an outstretched arm for me to share his saddle.

He easily pulled me up. I wrapped my arms around his muscular torso, and he kicked his horse, which promptly obeyed. As we rode, I felt sick to my stomach. Both scenarios the captain had proposed meant disaster for the Sokokis. With the warriors preparing for battle at the longhouses, those escaping to the woods would be unprotected, and easily slaughtered by the English.

What would the Chief think upon seeing me riding in with the captain? Would he assume that a negotiated settlement was possible, and invite us into the longhouse, and soon thereafter be under attack from the rear? Or would he be suspicious, and take the captain prisoner, only to find out that his entire clan of women and children were being annihilated? Either way, I seemed only to have made things worse.

The captain led his horse across the same frozen lake that I had just traversed twice. The sun had just begun to brighten the eastern sky, the Rangers were on their way to inflict their murderous intent upon the Sokokis tribe, and there was nothing I could do to stop them.

The captain guided his stallion by its bridle off the ice and onto the embankment. My heart pounded like a war drum. Any moment we would be out onto the opening surrounding the longhouses.

I held my breath in order to hear well. But there were no sounds except for the horse stomping across the muddy approach. The area before the longhouses, where I first surrendered myself, was empty.

The captain tied the bridle of his horse to a sapling and pointed for us to search the longhouses. I followed closely behind, wondering if we would stumble upon the warriors readying themselves inside the structures. As we entered one after another, it was clear that the Sokokis longhouses were abandoned. They left just in time, I thought. But where did they go? Which was exactly what the captain wanted to know.

"What is going on, Lukas?" he demanded.

"I don't know?" I stammered. "They were just here."

"Did you lead me into a trap?" the captain asked, on the verge of rage.

I didn't know what to say. Did the Chief use me as an unsuspecting pawn? But what about the women and children who escaped to the north, were they now under attack from the flanking English army? I soon learned my answer.

We suddenly heard horses outside the longhouse. The captain ran to the entrance and I followed closely behind. The morning sun was now shining through a clear sky, illuminating the captain's men approaching.

Captain Lovewell's face was ashen with fear when he spoke to his officers and they explained that apparently the Sokokis had escaped, and somehow the English soldiers had not stumbled upon the tribe.

But then we heard it. The sounds of the Sokokis warriors' war whoop from all directions.

The captain barked out orders for the men to form a circle in a defensive position. Within the circle, another one formed. While the outer circle fired, the inner one reloaded their weapons.

The warriors came from all directions and moved fast. Arrows flew and struck soldiers who fell into a mix of snow and mud with blood now mingling in it. I was caught in the center of the circles and knew that if I wanted to survive, I needed to escape.

Any opening in the outer circle was either quickly closed or penetrated by a warrior charging through swinging an ax or a knife. Right before me a brawl between a Ranger and a warrior ensued. The warrior slashed the soldier's throat in a lightning quick move and finished with an equally swift scalping.

Rangers were being slaughtered in great numbers. Sounds of gunshots echoed alongside cries of the wounded. I was able to slip out of the circle and run toward the tree line. Once there I turned to see the remaining moments of the devastation I had caused.

I saw the captain, who had narrowly escaped. He was on his horse yelling for his men to retreat. Then I spotted the Chief, who also saw me. For a brief moment the sounds of the battle silenced as we connected. Chief Squandro put his right hand upon his chest and then held it out with his palm facing me and nodded. I returned the gesture and disappeared into the woods.

Chapter 22

I wandered alone through the forest. It took a while for me to settle down from the intensity of the battle. After the near massacre of the English Rangers by the Sokokis warriors, I knew that if I was ever to cross paths with Captain Lovewell again, he would consider me his enemy.

But the sounds around me were soothing. I looked up to the stars through the openings in the forest canopy and decided that I should go back to Rowtag.

Without Matwau, finding the Pequawket winter camp could be a problem. But I recalled that he had offered me some lessons on how to navigate the wilderness by looking into the evening sky and the stars. Matwau had told me that all the stars move except for one.

"This star is called the North Star," he said pointing at the brightest one in the sky. "Now look below that and you will see two more stars."

I followed his finger and found them.

"If you draw a line from the North Star through those stars, no matter where they are in the sky, that will show you true north," he said and paused for me to comprehend.

"To find your way home you must know where you have come from," he instructed and drew a circle in the snow.

He marked the circle in four parts. "North, east, south and west," he said.

"Since we know north, and we traveled to the southeast," he showed me on the drawing, "to return home we must seek northwest," he said, holding out his finger in that direction.

I realized that if I was ever to return to Rowtag and the Pequawket tribe I would need to put Matwau's tracking lesson into practice.

It took seven sunrises before I found my way back to the Pequawket village. Besides using the North Star as my guide, I also recognized landmarks that confirmed I was on the right path.

Tired and unsure of my greeting from the Chief, and the Shaman, as well as the health of Rowtag, I entered their longhouse. All eyes turned to me, and the usual chatter silenced.

The Chief and the Shaman sat high upon their elevated platform and watched me approach. Then I saw Rowtag. He was not lying down. He was sitting cross-legged staring at nothing. I stopped and crouched down to put my face in front of his. I looked into his eyes, but they did not look back at me, but instead through me, and beyond.

"Rowtag, are you all right?" I asked.

He said nothing and didn't acknowledge me in any way.

"Rowtag, it's me, Lukas," I tried again, squeezing his shoulders.

But there was no response. I turned around seeking an explanation.

The Shaman was now standing next to me and said, "His body is present, but his inner light has dimmed."

"What does that mean?" I asked.

The Shaman shook his head, and led me to the Chief, who was waiting for me.

The Chief listened to my adventures without interruption. He offered no indication of sadness or remorse by the death of Matwau, the ambush of Captain Lovewell or Chief Squandro's retribution. But his expression changed when I told him how my actions had been the cause of significant consequences.

"The Great Spirit watches over you, Lukas," he said. "Most people pass through life without so much as a ripple. But you cause great storms in your path."

I nodded regretfully and looked over to Rowtag, the most obvious victim of my actions.

The Shaman noticed my melancholy, and offered, "It is not the agitator who causes sadness, illness or grief. Without disruptions, we languish and decay. Our journey, Lukas, is to strive to know the Great Spirit, and only through provocation can we achieve such communion."

These words released some of the tension I felt coursing through me. I said that my purpose was to seek out the Great Spirit, but I had not yet felt a connection. In fact, I still had no idea of what the Gitchi Manitou was, except for a name.

That was when the Shaman asked me if I was ready to know the Great Spirit.

I nodded that I was.

"The journey to know the Great Spirit is not one of common consciousness. It is not a communion of the flesh, but a communion of your soul," the Shaman said.

My eyes darted back and forth between the Shaman and the Chief, trying to understand.

The Shaman continued, "The path to calling oneself a Pequawket warrior encompasses an odyssey into the celestial world. That is where you will finally unite with the Gitchi Manitou."

Before I had an opportunity to ask what such a journey would require, the Shaman told me about the Moon Flower.

"You must unleash your earthly body and mind, and I can assist you, Lukas," he said.

I looked over to the Chief who nodded his encouragement.

The Shaman continued, "There is a plant we call the Moon Flower. It blooms only at night and reflects the light of the moon itself. I use it to alleviate pain, and to restore life. It has healed your friend's physical wounds," he said, and gestured toward Rowtag.

"But when the Moon Flower is prepared in a certain way, it has qualities that will open your soul to understand the Great Spirit. Once you have taken the potion you will be under my watch for a full moon cycle. During this time your mind will be cleared of your past. No memory will exist of who you were. You will have no mother, no father, and no history. You will start your life anew. This is necessary to connect with the Great Spirit," the Shaman said.

"Will I ever get my memory back?" I asked.

"You may, or you may not. Of all the Pequawket warriors who have taken the Moon Flower, most do regain their memory. But there are those who do not."

I looked around at the warriors sitting with their families, wondering which ones permanently lost their memories.

"But it will not matter if you remember, or not," the Shaman said returning my attention back to him. "Once you have taken to the path, your life will have new meaning. Your past will be nothing more than a story."

When I first started this journey with Rowtag, our quest was to survive the wilderness with nothing more than my knife and a loincloth for seven moons. I understood that this was part of the path to becoming a warrior and to finding communion with the Great Spirit. Yet I admitted that after our numerous adventures, I felt no closer to the Great Spirit than I had that first day I left the Turtle Clan.

As I sat with the quill and paper before me, I attempted to write all I would want to know when I returned from the other side. Perhaps my memories had built a protective wall around my consciousness that would prevent me from connecting with the Great Spirit?

The Shaman said that the mind creates chambers where we hide our fears and secrets, and without the help of the Moon Flower these doors can never be opened.

Was I ready to clear out the prison cells in my mind, and to take this celestial journey and ultimately become a Pequawket warrior? I looked over to Rowtag, who continued to stare into nothingness, and decided that I must continue, for both of us.

As the full moon rose, the Shaman placed me in a large bunk elevated off the earthen ground of the longhouse and draped it with woven cloths to provide me with privacy.

"You will stay here until the next full moon," he said.

I lay upon a comfortable array of woven mats and various furs and skins, wearing only my buckskin loincloth.

"All your needs will be attended to," the Shaman assured me.

I understood this to mean I would not only sleep and eat in this human cocoon, but also relieve my bladder and bowels here as well. Assisted by two elderly women of the tribe, the Shaman began the ceremony.

He handed me a small clay cup filled with a brownish liquid showing a swampy green spiral design forming on its surface. Without taking a moment to examine it too closely, I lifted my head, and swallowed in it one gulp.

Book 2

Chapter 1

---

*M*y belly burns. Glowing embers emerge through my skin and explode into tiny bursts of light above me. These small balls of fire float up to the heavens and glimmer like stars until they explode, and millions of sparks descend and seep back inside me. My body is on fire. I scream. There is darkness.

Mother is serving me breakfast. I hear Father.

"Lukas, are you ready?" he calls out.

"Let him finish, Solomon," Mother says.

"Sara, we need to get going."

I stare into my soup, at the chunks of meat with bread and potato.

Father looks at me. "Come now, Lukas, we need to leave."

I am sitting next to Father on the wagon. I say, "Rowtag is hurt, Father. We must get him and bring him home to the Chief."

"Nonsense, Rowtag is fine. I just saw him," Father insists.

Soldiers are blocking our way. I see Captain Lovewell. His musket is pointing at Father. I hear an explosion; the captain has fired. Blood gushes from a hole in Father's chest.

Father is floating on a sea of crimson blood.

There is darkness.

The wolves have killed Rowtag. He is lying in a pool of blood on the cave floor. I am leaning against a boulder. A lone wolf is before me. His golden eyes speak to me.

"You were warned by the ravens," the wolf says to me.

I stare back, afraid to speak.

"Why did you come here?" the wolf asks.

"There was a storm. We needed shelter," I explain.

"A warrior knows the dangers of a place like this, Lukas."

"I didn't know."

The wolf lunges at me with his jaw open. I see blood trickling between his white fangs.

I close my eyes and drift into the darkness.

"Lukas, you have betrayed me," says Captain Lovewell.

We are standing alone in the empty field where the battle with the Sokokis took place. The captain looms over me, wearing his bearskin hat. The sun's rays reflect off his gold tooth and blind me. I hold my hands up to shield the brightness.

"You killed my father," I say.

"He attacked one of the King's soldiers. That is punishable by death."

"He was stealing our pelts," I yell.

"You walked my army into an ambush, Lukas. That is treason. You will die by hanging."

"It is not treason. You are the enemy. I am a warrior," I announce.

He laughs and laughs, holding his belly with one hand and pointing a finger at me with the other. "You, a warrior? You are a coward, Lukas. You are ruled by your fears." The captain vanishes into the darkness.

"Where is Rowtag?" the Chief asks me.

I am too ashamed to answer.

"Tell me where my son is, Lukas," the Chief asks again.

"I left him. He was attacked by wolves," I say sadly.

"You were told, Lukas, that if you come back alone, you come back in shame. You cannot stay with the clan. You must leave," says the Chief.

I begin to cry. "Please don't make me go. I am sorry. Rowtag is my only friend."

The Chief points behind me, and I turn into the darkness.

"Father is dead," I tell Mother.

She looks at me. Her eyes fill with tears and stream like the waters at the falls.

"I tried to stop them," I say.

"You are just a boy, Lukas. How could you stop the English army?" Mother says.

"I will avenge Father's death," I tell Mother.

"It is too dangerous. I cannot bear to lose you too, Lukas," she says, and continues to weep.

"But I am a warrior, Mother. The captain will pay with his life for Father's death," I say.

Mother looks up to the heavens and falls to her knees. Her arms are spread wide like an eagle, and she wails. Black clouds suddenly appear. Loud thunder shakes the earth, and lightning illuminates the sky. I look back down at Mother, and she is gone into the darkness.

I am lost in the caves. There is no way out. I hear the wolves coming for me. I run deeper and deeper into the dark chambers of the earth. Suddenly a sparkle of light brightens my way. I follow it to a hollow. The light is bright from an opening far above me.

I shout, "Is there someone there?"

A darkened face appears in silhouette. I cannot see who it is. The person speaks.

"Close up the hole," shouts an order from the captain.

I hear a stone scraping against stone, and the hole is sealed.

I hear his laughter. I feel the wolves growl. I see the darkness.

Like soup in a pot over a flame, I feel hot bile in my belly bubble, and boil. Small fires ignite on its surface. Vibrations cause the flames to flicker and dance. The smoldering fire in my belly erupts and escapes upwards like a volcanic explosion.

My eyes open just as I spew an evil concoction skyward. I see the substance strike the woven mats above me, and cling to it like river mud slung against a boulder.

I collapse back to my bed. Hands attend to my mess. I drift away back into the darkness.

I wrap the bison fur across my face to protect me from the winds slicing through the forest. My bow and arrows are tucked in tightly. Dusts of snow swirl around me. Cold is snapping at my fingers and toes, causing them to go numb. Trees creak in pain from the storm. I hear the howls of wolves.

Though it is daytime, the gray sunless sky offers no illumination to the forest floor. Shadows dance like ghostly figures. The wails intensify. Wolves do not make such sounds. It's nothing I can identify. But whatever it is, it's getting closer.

Black clouds roll in. My heartbeat vibrates my rib cage. Fear consumes me. Shadows grow as tall as trees. I must restrain my legs from running. Then it appears.

I am greeted first by its head, snout and fangs dripping with a blackish slime. A skinless chest exposes a brown ribcage and a purple beating heart that glows like an ember in a fire pit. Its arms reach to its feet, and its clawed fingers scratch the earth as it walks. The feet are like hoofs seen on a donkey. I look into the black holes where eyes should be, and I realize that this is the Wendigo.

"Your quest will fail, Lukas. You cannot defeat me," the Wendigo says.

"Why must I defeat you? What I want has nothing to do with you."

"If you destroy me, Lukas, you will also destroy the Great Spirit. You cannot create an imbalance in the universe," the Wendigo reasons.

I don't know what to do. Is the Wendigo the evil counterweight to the Great Spirit? This makes no sense. Is there a creator beyond the Great Spirit who made this balance?

"I sense your hesitation, Lukas. Join with me, and rule the earth," the Wendigo says and holds out its boney arms as an invitation.

I step around from the tree that shielded me. The Wendigo steps toward me, leading with its protruding snout and snapping tongue. I open my fur, and in a swift move I release my arrow into its flaming heart. The beast screams. My arrow juts out between two ribs. It falls to its knees with its claws wrapped around the turkey-feathered arrow. It falls face down onto the snow causing it to melt and creating a puddle of water encircling the creature.

Cautiously I approach with my knife in hand. The Wendigo is not moving or breathing. But is it dead? I kick its side, nothing. I exhale and sheath my knife. I take a step away and its claw grabs my wrist. I cannot pull away. Holding on, it stands and towers high above me. I am lifted like a small child. Its mouth opens and I look deep inside its jaw. Upper and lower rows of sharp fangs are juiced for its meal. The jaws snap shut on me, and there is darkness.

Chapter 2

---

oolness seeps into my mind. I try to open my eyes. A girl's face is looking back at me. She smiles and places a damp cloth on my forehead. It feels good. I try to lift my head, but the world spins. I close my eyes and clutch at the furs covering me.

She whispers, "Do not move, Lukas, lie still."

Her voice is sweet. I struggle again to open my eyes. Her brown eyes smile at me. Her skin looks soft. I want to touch it. She lifts my head and brings a cup of cool water to my lips. I sip. My mouth is as dry as a riverbed in August. I swallow. It hurts. I cry out in pain. My body convulses. I cannot stop shaking. Hands hold me. Many hands pin my arms and legs down preventing me from moving. My body is on fire.

"Let go of me," I scream.

The girl calls out to me. *Is she an angel? Am I dying?* I close my eyes and fall back into the darkness.

I am with Father but I do not know where we are. He looks at me and smiles and nods. As he does, I see a small, woven, round covering on his head. He takes my hand and places it on my head. I am wearing one too.

"You must cover your head before Hashem," he tells me.

I feel it on my head and ask, "Who is Hashem, Father?"

"He is the Great Spirit, Lukas," Father says sedately.

I look up to the sky.

"You cannot see Hashem. He is not a being. He lives beyond the restraints of the physical world," Father tells me.

"The Shaman refers to the Great Spirit as the Gitchi Manitou," I say.

"That is a name given by the natives. Our tribe refers to the Great Spirit as Hashem."

"Our tribe, Father?" I ask.

"We are one of the lost tribes of Israel, Lukas."

I am sitting cross-legged across from Father in a field of wild flowers. A slight breeze rustles the sea of colors around us.

Father begins, "Our people are of the tribe of Dan from the Kingdom of Israel. Over twenty-three hundred years ago the Assyrians drove ten of the twelve tribes of Israel from our land. These ten lost tribes roamed the earth seeking a new home for future generations. The tribe of Dan dispersed into many corners of the world. Our ancestors came to the lands of Poland where we have lived and thrived for over a thousand years."

"I am from the tribe of Dan?" I asked.

"You are, and you need to know your heritage, and where you belong in the universe," Father says.

I nod. Blooms of bright red poppies surround us as Father speaks.

Chapter 3

The darkness was gone. I felt cool, relieved and well. I lifted my head and looked around. Tall trees shaded me from the bright sun. Children ran about.

A voice spoke to me. "Lukas, how do you feel?"

A girl with lovely full lips and gentle brown eyes was talking to me. She helped me to a seated position. *Where am I? Who are these people milling about?*

"My name is Nadie. Are you all right, Lukas?" she asked.

She called me Lukas.

"Your name is Lukas," she repeated.

I shook my head. "No."

"Oh wonderful, you can speak," she said.

"Of course I can speak."

"The Shaman said that after the ceremony you might also lose your ability to speak. But I see that's not the case," she said.

"The Shaman?" I asked. "What ceremony?"

"Please be patient. I will go and get the holy man so he can explain."

Nadie stood and ran off.

This is crazy, I thought and rose to my feet. My legs gave out under me, and I collapsed.

"Lukas, please wait. I am coming."

A short man with a square shaped face and widely spaced brown eyes, and wearing a hat fashioned with owl feathers called out to me. He knelt and looked into my eyes like he was looking inside me.

"Welcome back, Lukas. You had quite a journey," said the man Nadie called the Shaman.

"Journey?" I ask.

"This is normal. First let me say it is good that you did not forget how to speak."

I did not understand what these words had to do with me.

"Your name is Lukas Pietersen. During the past full moon you have traveled to the deepest corners of your mind, and have unlocked the doors imprisoning your fears. You are renewed. But the consequences are, you have lost your memory. Everything you know has been erased from your mind. Over time, these memories may return. But that is not important."

As the Shaman spoke I tested my memory. *What is my name? Why am I here? Where do I come from?* I did not know. I felt dizzy and placed my hands over my face to steady myself.

The Shaman comforted me with an arm around my shoulder. "What is important is that the secret chambers in your mind are emptied. No longer will your fears be locked away as captives. You are now a beacon of truth and courage. You are on your path of becoming a Pequawket warrior."

I did not understand what these words meant.

The Shaman smiled. "I have brought you something that will explain who you are and what has happened to you."

The Shaman laid a bundle in front of me. He unwrapped a brown cloth to reveal many sheets of written words.

"What is this?" I asked.

"This, Lukas, is your life."

He explained to me that I wrote these words a few days before I drank a potion from the seeds of a plant known as Moon Flower. "I asked you to write all that you wanted to know about your life so that when you come back from your journey, you will have a record of who you used to be."

I gently brushed my fingertips across the surface of the top page.

"You will find what you wrote mysterious, and hard to believe, but these are your words, your life. They will serve you well as an aid to recovering your memory," the Shaman said, and stood up.

I flipped a few of the pages, scanning the words.

"I will leave you with your story, Lukas. We can discuss the next part of your training in a few days."

I thanked the Shaman, and smiled as I saw Nadie returning with drink and food. As I sipped a warm drink that she offered me, I leaned back against a sturdy tree, shaded from the bright sun, lifted the first page, and started reading.

Chapter 4

It was still early spring, but the weather was warm and pleasant. The camp of the Pequawket tribe was on a lake surrounded by tall pine trees, situated at the foothills of mountains, and fed by the late-winter runoff.

I had spent the past few days reading my story, and discovered that I had no emotional connection to my past life. Even described in my own words, I had no recollection of my widowed mother, or my murdered father. Could it be true what the Shaman said, that the doors to the chambers of my mind had been opened, and cleansed?

I stared at my reflection in the lake. Just like everything else, I had no memory of even how I looked. I had never seen this face, my face. My hair was brown, straight and long, falling beyond my shoulders. I looked dirty and probably smelled, since I hadn't bathed in a month.

I took off the loincloth wrapped around my waist and jumped into the lake. It was cold and stung my skin upon contact. I submerged underwater and opened my eyes. Looking back at me, I saw the face of an older man. I recognized this face. He smiled at me, but the image vanished as I reached to touch it.

I climbed out of the lake, and as I was putting on my loincloth, I realized that I had just experienced a memory. *I must tell the Shaman!* When I turned to make my way down to the village, I found Nadie standing before me.

"I didn't see you, Nadie."

"It is good you have bathed, Lukas." She laughed, and with two fingers pinched her nose.

"Was it that bad?"

She smiled at me, and I felt a warmth flood through me. How could this simple expression move me so emotionally? I stared at her, admiring her innocent beauty. We were probably the same age, but she seemed more youthful than me.

That evening I took my place in between the Shaman and Nadie in a circle of tribespeople around the campfire. Nadie pointed out those I should know. But as I looked around the large gathering, I knew their names from my story, but did not recognize their faces.

It was obvious who Chief Paugus was, though I did not know him either. He caught my stare and offered a greeting of a hand upon his heart, and an open palm toward me. I returned the gesture.

Nadie told me that the boy sitting across the circle was my friend, Rowtag.

I knew Rowtag was important to me. I saw his condition had not changed from the time that I wrote about him. He stared into the flames with empty eyes. It looked like his soul had left his body behind.

From his seated position at the head of the circle, the Chief raised his arms and the conversations ceased. The only sound was the crackling of the campfire. Sparks danced above us into the darkened sky. The Chief scanned every face around the giant circle before he began.

"Our strength comes from our unbroken circle," he said, gesturing to its form. "The fire burns at our center just as our heart beats within each of us. Today our circle expands, and we strengthen our tribe."

With these words all eyes in the circle turned to me. I nodded, accepting the honor. I should say that all eyes except for Rowtag's, who was still staring aimlessly into the flame.

"Lukas, you are the first man born from white parents to join our circle."

A murmur arose and mingled with the smoke from the fire.

"Just like all of our warriors before him, Lukas has taken the journey to connect with the Great Spirit, and he has returned fulfilled. There should be no one who doubts that Lukas is now on a righteous path to becoming a Pequawket warrior. We must accept him as one of us."

"How can this be permitted?" interrupted a young warrior, shaking his fist.

"Why is a white man allowed into our circle of warriors?" asked another.

The Chief looked at the two belligerent warriors. "Please excuse Kitchi and Wematin, they speak out of turn."

Nadie leaned in and whispered, "The tribe took them in as children. They were the only two survivors of a massacre, by white men. You must understand their feelings of having someone like you join the circle."

"I do understand," I said, and I placed my hand over my heart, and my palm facing down as an offering of peace to the troubled warriors.

Chapter 5

The next morning, Nadie took my hand and we ran down the path to a secret place we had discovered by the lake. We had found time to sneak away every day since I returned from my journey.

"You still have no memories?" she asked me.

"Nothing since I took the Moon Flower."

"Does reading your journal stir anything inside you, or stimulate your dreams?"

"I'm not sure. There are moments when an image flashes in my mind, but nothing I can grasp on to."

Where I struggled to recall my previous life, I felt no barriers with Nadie. After all, she was my first memory, and since I didn't write about any girls in my journal, Nadie must also be my first love. I surprised myself with this thought, but as soon as it occurred to me, I had no doubt that it was true. She was the only familiar thing in my whole life.

I was leaning on my elbows, legs crossed on the embankment of the lake, when I decided to share these thoughts. "I love you, Nadie," I blurted out.

She looked at me, and I saw the reflection of the lake sparkling in her brown eyes.

"I love you too, Lukas."

"My love for you is all consuming. You are my first memory of my new life," I said, and leaned over to kiss her. Her lips were soft, her skin delicate like the pink and blue flowers that bloomed around us.

We sat for a while, her head resting upon my chest, my arm wrapped around her.

"Nadie, why do you love me? I'm not of your tribe, and you know little about me."

Nadie lifted her head, and looked at me with wide eyes, and said, "I love you, Lukas, because of your strength."

"But are there no other warriors you could love?"

Nadie tilted her head, expressing surprise at his comment. "Do you think I love you because you're a warrior?"

"I thought so," I said my voice trailing off.

"The warriors of our tribe are good men. But you stand above them."

"What do you mean?"

"I love you, Lukas, because of your connection to the Great Spirit."

"My connection? I don't feel connected."

"Why do you think the Chief and Shaman have accepted you, a white man, into our tribe?"

I nodded and thought about what she said. But still, I did not feel such a connection.

"Lukas," she whispered into my ear. "Would you read to me the words in your journal?"

I pulled back in surprise. "Why?"

"I want to know everything there is to know about you, and your journal will tell me."

"But that is a life I do not know," I said.

"Someday you will, Lukas. Your memories will come back, and when they do I want to experience them with you."

"All right, I will read to you my journal, Nadie."

"I want you to read it to me, right here at our hideaway," she said.

My heart pounded at the idea of reading to Nadie. I asked her to wait as I ran at full speed to retrieve my journal.

As I got closer, I heard my name being called. I turned and saw Rowtag and the Shaman standing before me.

I looked at this person, who I only knew from sitting stone-face staring into a fire.

"Rowtag, you can speak."

He spread his arms and wrapped them around me. "Oh, Lukas, I have returned," he said, squeezing me tight.

"Returned from where, Rowtag?"

"From my journey to connect with the Great Spirit."

I looked at Rowtag in confusion. "How is that possible?"

The Shaman interrupted our reunion and said, "Lukas, Rowtag, we should talk."

We agreed to meet the next day at dawn.

When I returned to the longhouse, I found Nadie sitting on my bedroll.

"I am sorry Nadie, something happened on my way back," I said.

"What happened?"

"Rowtag spoke to me. He is out of his stupor."

Nadie's eyes widened and her mouth opened, but she said nothing.

"Rowtag said his journey connected him with the Great Spirit. His wolf bite wounds were treated with the Moon Flower, which had the same effect upon him as it did me, except for one thing."

"What's that?" Nadie asked.

"Rowtag has not lost his memory. He knows me. He calls me brother."

"This is wonderful, Lukas," she said.

I nodded, agreeing with her, and noticed that she had started reading my journal.

"I thought you can't read Dutch," I said, pointing at the stack of pages.

Nadie shook her head and said, "I can't, but when you forgot about me, I came back here looking for you. Your journal was sitting out, so I started looking at it without you. I hope you are not angry with me."

"No, of course not."

But as I said these words, I wondered why I was not upset. The act of flipping through my journal without me, even if she couldn't read it, should have made me feel disregarded. Was it because I had no emotional connection to the words written in my journal, and therefore did not feel violated? Or was it because my journey had flushed out the negative spaces of my mind, and such petty reactions of Nadie looking at my journal were no longer offensive?

Chapter 6

It was just before dawn as Rowtag and I waited for the Shaman. We sat across from each other, as I tended to the fire. I occasionally glanced at Rowtag who quietly broke kindling and tossed it into the flames.

"You still have no memories?" he asked, reaching for another twig.

"Nothing past the day I returned from the journey."

"Thank you for saving my life, Lukas."

"That was quite an adventure I wrote about," I said, with a smile.

"It's not just something you wrote about, it actually happened."

"I know, Rowtag. If it was someone else's story, I would have no trouble accepting it, but I just can't believe it as my own."

Rowtag stood up and sat on a stone next to me, and said, "I'll help you find your way back, my brother."

"Good day," said the Shaman, as he made his appearance.

Rowtag and I greeted the holy man.

"Come with me, it's ready," the Shaman said.

He turned and walked off. Rowtag and I shared a perplexed glance and quickly followed. The Shaman directed us into a wigwam, where at its opening was a young brave placing large stones in between burning logs of a roaring fire.

Curious, I thought, as I ducked and entered.

The Shaman gestured for us to sit alongside a circular pit dug into the earth. The wigwam was damp and cool inside and sent a chill down my nearly naked body. The brave I just saw tending the fire was now dragging a wooden sled carrying several glowing stones. He lifted the handles, and the stones rolled off the sled and tumbled into the pit. Warmth emanated from the luminous orbs that created a comfortable warmth in the wigwam. The stones looked alive, like beating hearts.

"Lukas and Rowtag, you have each taken the journey to connect with the Great Spirit," the Shaman began. "But there are the seven ways of the warrior that you still must master to complete your training."

The Shaman called out to the brave, who entered the wigwam with a container of water. He leaned over the rock pit and poured the cool water over the burning stones. A rush of hot steam rose and filled the small wigwam. I instinctively pulled back at its intensity.

The Shaman instructed us to stay close to the pit. As the heat dissipated, the brave deposited more burning stones. The temperature rose again.

"The first way of the warrior is honesty," the Shaman began softly. "A warrior is honest. There is no room for anything but the truth, regardless of the consequences to yourself."

The Shaman signaled, and the brave poured water over the newly placed stones. I was washed in a scouring heat. I closed my eyes and tried to accept the burning sensation. I dug my fingers into the earth, drawing its coolness into my body.

"The second way of the warrior is respect of life," the Shaman said, without showing duress from the unimaginable heat.

"The warrior is to hold true to the ideal that all life comes from the Great Spirit, and therefore a warrior can never be cruel, even to his enemies."

Another splash of water on the stones notched up the heat further. I touched my face to make sure my skin had not melted away. I peeked at Rowtag, whose skin seemed to be glowing like the stones.

Without pause or concern for our welfare, the Shaman continued, "The third way of the warrior is that of the hero. A warrior is never afraid to act regardless of the danger to himself. Yet the warrior is not foolish, and acts only with intelligence."

I continued to hear the words of the Shaman, but I began to fade into a dreamlike state. No longer was I sitting by the inferno. Instead, I was floating high in the sky, looking down upon the wigwam from above.

I heard the words of the Shaman. "The fourth way of the warrior is honor."

Floating further away, the Shaman said, "No one can judge your honor except yourself. Your decisions reflect who you truly are. You cannot hide from them."

White puffy clouds surrounded me. I reached out to touch them, but they eluded my grasp.

The Shaman's voice echoed like thunder. "The fifth way of the warrior is compassion. You must seek out ways to help all living things without expectations. True compassion is offered, unconditionally."

The clouds were now below me. Lightning struck, piercing the sky. Above I saw the heavens, and the stars dancing among the blackness.

The Shaman's voice was everywhere. "The sixth way of the warrior is his word. A warrior's assurances are never broken. The warrior does not disappoint."

There was darkness. The stars were gone. I was floating in empty space, yet I was not afraid.

"The seventh way of the warrior is loyalty," the Shaman's voice said from the void.

"The warrior is loyal to those in his care, to those he is responsible for. There is no greater calling for the warrior than his devotion."

I awoke with a chill. The cauldron was extinguished. Rowtag slept peacefully, curled up alongside the pit. I glanced at the cold stones and understood why the native peoples believed that all things on earth, even the stones, were alive.

Chapter 7

With moonlight illuminating our way, and fresh deer kills draped over our shoulders, Rowtag and I silently made our way back to camp. My life as a Pequawket warrior had been mostly to hunt, and to attend to the needs of the tribe, that required our youth and strength. It had been a peaceful existence.

Nadie comforted me nightly. When I expressed concern that I still had no recollection of my previous life, she reassured me by saying, "Memories are not always good, Lukas. Some are stressful. Many people are tormented by bad decisions they have made. But now your mind is free. You are not burdened by regrets or disappointments."

Our lives were in perfect alignment. Even our breaths felt harmonious. We discussed spending our lives together, and one day starting a family. I knew this was my first relationship as my journal told me, and Nadie brought this up as a concern.

"How do you know you want to be with me? I am the only girl you have known," she said.

I told her that I couldn't imagine being any happier.

"Don't you miss your mother?" she asked.

"Even if I saw my mother, I wouldn't know her."

"But she would know you, Lukas," Nadie reminded me.

"This is true, but my life is here with you, and the tribe."

My wandering thoughts of Nadie were quickly forgotten as Rowtag and I reached the wigwams, and heard yelps coming from the warriors in the camp. We dropped our kills and ran. A few heartbeats later, we reached the source of the disturbance and saw several English soldiers dismounted from their horses.

The Chief stood before them, demanding an explanation for the intrusion.

"My name is Captain Lovewell. I am looking for Lukas Pietersen," shouted the English captain.

There was confusion with the English words, but I understood. This was the same captain I wrote about in my journal. The same captain who murdered Father, and whom I betrayed, with the confrontation with the Sokokis tribe.

"Hello Captain," I said, and stepped forward.

"There you are. I've been looking for you. You are under arrest for treason against the King's army," he said, and signaled to his men.

Rifles were now pointed at me. Two soldiers grabbed me and tied my hands behind my back. If it weren't for the Moon Flower, I would have reacted foolishly. But now I did not resist, accepting my capture with dignity.

But this lack of emotion also had the effect of offering me no heartfelt animosity toward the captain. I didn't hate him. However, when the right opportunity presented itself, I knew I had to fulfill my earlier promise to make him pay for what he did to Father.

A few warriors, including Rowtag, made moves to defend me but were prevented by the Chief who ordered them to stand down.

The captain told me to share a saddle with one of his men. With my hands bound behind me, I pressed against the soldier's back, and squeezed my legs hard against the horse, preventing me from falling off. I turned to look back, and my eyes met Nadie's. She put a hand over her heart and turned her open palm toward me. I smiled and wondered if this was the last time I would ever see her.

The captain sitting tall in his saddle ordered his men to depart. We marched to the east, and toward the first light of the morning sun. A breeze blew across the tall pines in the distance.

As we rode away I heard Rowtag's voice carried by the wind. "I will come for you, my brother."

Chapter 8

We traveled a beaten dirt road leaving clouds of dust that marked our trail. Several hours later, we stopped to allow the horses to rest. I found a shady place to sit under a large oak tree, alongside a gentle stream. The march under the afternoon sun had left me parched and in need of cool water. I reached down to drink and to wash the dirt off me. As I looked at my reflection in the stream I saw my tanned face and long brown hair. I must have baffled the English who thought of me as a civilized white man living among savages. I heard footsteps coming up from behind, and turned around to see the captain approaching.

"Ah, Lukas," the captain said greeting me. "We are finally reunited."

"Captain," I said with a nod.

"Did you think you would escape your punishment for what you did to my men?"

I had no recollection of what he was referring to, except for what I read in my journal. If this truly had happened, I was indeed responsible for the deaths of dozens of English soldiers. A punishment for a crime such as this against the mighty English, was death, I assumed.

"Actually, Captain, I did think I would escape," I said plainly.

"You will be hanged, Lukas," he said, with obvious pleasure in his tone.

"Where are you taking me?"

"We are going to Castle William and Mary. It's a fort on the mouth of the Piscataqua River, which empties into the Atlantic. You will be tried and judged by the Royal Governor Benning Wentworth. Quite an honor."

"I do not recognize your authority over me, or my people," I said.

"Is that so?" The captain said, with a smirk.

"I am a Pequawket warrior. The only authority I answer to is the Great Spirit. The English are invaders, and murderers on these lands. You are the true criminals, and you will be tried, judged, and convicted by the Gitchi Manitou."

"Wow, Lukas, that is impressive. I am sure the Governor will be amused by you," the captain said and turned. "Get yourself back on that horse. We're leaving."

Several hours later, I was still tortured by the foul body odor of the soldier I was pinned up against as we rode single file along the riverbank of the Piscataqua River. But out of nowhere, a southerly breeze offered me relief from the stench. I did not know this smell, but there was a pleasant sharpness to it.

We came around the bank of the river, and I saw Castle William and Mary. It was a large wooden fort, built along the river, with high walls, and tall towers located at its corners. A large English flag was attached to a pole, towering above all else.

Its two large gate doors were swung open welcoming the captain and his men. Just as we made our last turn from the river to the fort, I saw the source of the pleasurable smell.

I was looking at the largest body of water I had ever seen. As far as my eyes could see there was water, and not still water like in a lake. These waters moved and churned and crashed where they met the land. I remembered from my journal, how Father traveled across an ocean to come to the New Netherlands. This must be that same ocean.

We entered the fort and I was grabbed by two soldiers and yanked off the horse. With my legs dragging behind me, they pulled me along by my arms to the inner yard of the fort and threw me at the feet of a fat English officer.

I scrambled to my feet and got a look at this man's round pink face. His bloodshot black eyes stared at me with contempt.

"I presume this is the fellow you told me about, Captain?" the fat officer asked.

"Yes sir, this is Lukas Pietersen. He will be tried for treason. Lukas, this is the Governor," said the captain.

The Governor strummed his fingers across his round belly where each button looked like it was about to pop off at any moment.

"How in god's name did you ever get yourself into such a mess?" the Governor asked me.

"I do not know what you mean, sir."

"All right, Captain. Get him out of here. We will conduct the trial tomorrow," the Governor ordered.

A sharp tug pulled me away from the Governor, and no more than a few steps away I was pushed through a doorway. The shoving continued and I found myself in a small, empty, windowless room, with an old soil-stained bucket sitting on a dirt floor. The door shut behind me and I was locked in.

Chapter 9

Days passed and I only saw the guard who brought me food and emptied my waste bucket. I asked if he knew anything about my trial and he shrugged and mumbled, "Don't know."

During the day, rays of light entered through the cracks between the wood logs bound together to form the outside wall of my cell. Nighttime these same openings allowed in mosquitoes who feasted on my blood. I would not swat away or kill them, as they too were creations of the Great Spirit.

I awoke from a deep sleep and saw dust particles dancing above me in the streams of sunlight crisscrossing my cell. I heard a clamor from beyond my walls. The English were shouting orders. Sounds of native war cries, and of arrows whistled through the air. The fort was under siege. *Could this be Rowtag leading a rescue?*

Battle cries continued through the night and into the next day. I was pacing my cell. Three steps, turn, three steps, turn. I felt like a trapped animal. Then the sounds ceased. A few voices spoke normally. Was the siege over? Had the Pequawkets retreated?

A sharp kick to my ribs woke me from my sleep.

"Get up, the Governor wants to see you," demanded the guard.

What has happened to Rowtag?

I stood up and tried to brush some of the dirt off me, with poor results. The guard felt it necessary to push me every few steps, as a way to keep me moving. He ushered me past soldiers guarding the doors that led into a large room. Entering, I saw the Governor and the captain seated at a wooden table. Facing them, with their backs toward me, were three warriors. *It's not Rowtag after all.*

"Lukas, come in, and take a seat. I believe you already know Chief Squandro of the Sokokis tribe," the captain said.

Cautiously, I asked the Governor, "Why am I here?"

"We need your help translating our negotiations, Lukas," he said.

I looked over to the Chief, and asked him if this was true.

The Chief greeted me with a warm smile and said, "It is good to see you my friend. You look well."

I did not recognize the man, but I knew who he was from my journal. So, to save face, I said, "It is good to see you too, Chief. I am well. The Great Spirit watches over me. Tell me, why are you here?"

"The English need to be stopped. Our people live in constant fear of them. We have no choice but to fight back."

I translated this to the Governor and the captain, who acknowledged that the Chief's accusations were true.

"The Chief is willing to end the siege, if you agree to stop your aggressions into the north," I told them.

Captain Lovewell shook his head vigorously as I spoke, but after the Governor whispered something that I could not hear, his scowl relaxed and he seemed amenable.

"Tell the Chief that we agree to his terms. We will cease our advances into the northern country," announced the Governor.

I translated the Governor's words to the Chief. But he said there was one more demand. I sat up straight in my chair trying to improve my presence, before I announced the Chief's last request.

The Governor leaned back in his chair, his fingers tapping against his protruding belly and asked, "And what would that be?"

"The Chief will withdraw immediately, with the understanding that you halt your aggressive excursions into the north, and also requests that you release me into his custody," I said.

The captain snorted, and slammed his open palms on the table. "Absolutely not."

Again, the Governor leaned over to whisper in the captain's ear. I took this moment to look at the Chief, who offered a reassuring glance.

The captain was not pleased. He shook his head continuously, while the Governor continued making his private point. The captain eventually sighed and said, "Very well."

Moments later the Chief and I were in the yard watching the large double doors open. With only three horses and four of us leaving, I would need to ride double with one of the warriors, a position I was getting used to. But this time, I was grateful for the ride.

The captain was clearly frustrated at my release. "This is not the end, Lukas. You and I will meet again."

"I hope that is true, Captain," I said, thinking that we had a score to settle. In that moment, the anger I felt toward the captain had nothing to do with the history of my forgotten life. My feelings were based more on the recent events, which were the vengeful acts against the Sokokis tribe.

The captain's face turned red as if he understood the intent of my statement, and he said, "How dare you threaten me?"

He reached and grabbed my leg, and pulled at me, while I held on to the warrior's waist. This startled the horse. It bucked, and nearly threw both of us off.

I shook my leg loose of the captain's grip, and the three horses, led by the Chief, galloped through the gates and out into the open field, where his assembled warriors were waiting.

The captain was now standing just beyond the fort's walls. He was irate and screaming, "You will pay with your life, Lukas."

I acknowledged the captain's threat with a mock salute.

The warriors mounted their horses and we left Castle William and Mary behind. I felt certain that the Governor had no intention of abiding by the agreement made with the Chief. We would see the Rangers again, I was sure of it.

I am a Pequawket warrior, and will not allow my anger to control my actions. But I must defend what is right, and not allow the Sokokis people to be persecuted by this English captain.

I told the Chief that as a repayment for my rescue I would stay with his people for a while before returning to the Pequawkets. The Chief was pleased, as we rode north along the Piscataqua River, and back to the Sokokis village.

Chapter 10

Our first sight of the Sokokis camp was of campfires burning brightly under the overcast evening sky. With Chief Squandro leading the way, the tribe greeted their returning warriors enthusiastically. It did not take long before word spread that I was the white man who saved the tribe from Captain Lovewell's ambush and likely massacre.

Women and children reached out to touch me, as a way to demonstrate their gratitude. They chanted my name—"Lukas, Lukas!"—over and over. The Chief offered a grand sweeping gesture for me to join him in his longhouse. I entered with the adoring Sokokis people still shouting, "Lukas!"

"You have proved yourself a true warrior, Lukas," the Chief said, and offered me a place to sit.

I took a seat alongside the Shaman, and two other warriors, whom I saw briefly on our journey back from Castle William and Mary.

"You are most welcome by our people," the Chief said.

"I am honored," I said, placing both hands over my heart.

"These are my sons," the Chief said, looking over to two solemn warriors.

Unlike the appreciative tribespeople, who had just given me a hero's welcome, these two seemed less enthused with my presence. But most peculiar was that they did not even look like brothers. The grumpier one was tall, lean, probably around my age, and resembled his father, the Chief. The other brother was slight in frame and looked younger. But what was most unusual, was his light skin, and blue eyes.

"I am Mingan," said the darker skin brother.

"I am Hassun," the blue-eyed brother said.

I did not want to be rude, and ask the obvious question, but the Chief took the initiative.

"These boys have different mothers. Mingan was born to the beautiful Wawetseka. You will meet her later tonight at the ceremony. My younger son, Hassun, was born to the Dutch woman, named Sofie," the Chief said.

"Will I meet Sofie tonight as well?" I asked.

The Chief looked over to Hassun, before he spoke. "I am sorry to say, Lukas, that Sofie is no longer with us."

"Is she dead?" I asked, perplexed.

"She was taken by Captain Lovewell's men, in their attempted ambush," the Chief said.

"Was that when she was killed?" I asked.

"We do not know. The last we saw of her, she was alive."

"Then we must go find her, rescue her," I said, looking at Hassun, who avoided eye contact by staring into the flames.

Before I could ask any more questions, the Chief stood up, pointed a finger at me, and said, "No, I forbid any such mission."

He turned, and walked down the center of the longhouse, leaving us behind, seated in silence. Slowly we rose and followed the Chief. Once I was outside, I felt a hand squeezing my shoulder from behind me. I turned and saw the Shaman.

"Lukas, please come with me."

I followed the Shaman past the longhouses, and into the forest. We snaked around mighty oak trees and stepped upon stones that crossed a narrow stream. Large exposed roots, and lush green moss sculpted the landscape. Streams of setting sunlight lit our pathway.

At last, we came to a pond surrounded by weeping willows. Water lilies bloomed boldly across the still surface. The song of croaking frogs filled the air. The Shaman offered me a cushy moss surface to sit upon.

When we looked upon each other, I noticed her face was free of beard stubble, and she had a softness to her that was unmistakably female. *Is the Shaman a woman?*

"Yes, I am a woman, Lukas," she said, noticing my realization.

I looked more closely at her. *Yes, of course.* She had soft brown eyes and strong pronounced cheekbones. Her black hair was braided into two strands that fell over each shoulder.

"Why are we here?" I asked.

"I brought you here because there is much I need to teach you about our tribespeople."

She reached into a pouch wrapped around her waist, and pulled out a pipe.

"We will smoke, and you will listen."

Smoke twisted and rose in a single stream into the breathless sky. The Shaman handed me the pipe, and I gently drew on it. There was a fresh sweet taste to the dried, crushed leaves. I tilted back my head, and slowly exhaled.

A soothing effect seeped into my mind. Any lingering stress from the Chief's abrupt behavior vanished. The Shaman noticed my shift, and gently nodded.

"Our people believe you are a warrior sent by the Great Spirit," the Shaman began.

"It is true that I am a Pequawket warrior, but I am a man just like all others. Certainly, I was not sent by the Great Spirit."

"Do you believe that the path you have traveled has nothing to do with the Great Spirit?" the Shaman asked.

How should I answer this? A warrior is trained in humility. I do not deserve to be treated with reverence, as the Shaman suggests.

"I am a warrior with no more importance than any other. My service is to the tribe. I do not seek the status you ascribe."

"You may not seek it, Lukas, but it is too late to deny it. You are a white man with the skills of our greatest warriors. Our people see you as different, special. I am afraid that this will burden you with unrealistic expectations."

These words weighed heavily upon me. *What was the Shaman suggesting?*

"Do you think I am unable to fulfill the duties of a warrior?" I asked.

"Not at all. There are many challenges a warrior must face. This may prove to be a difficult one. The inner struggles are always the hardest. But with self-awareness you can succeed," she assured me.

"I understand."

Later that evening as I stood by the campfire, Hassun tugged at my elbow, and said, "Follow me."

We walked away from the gathering to a place next to a large oak tree.

"Let's sit, Lukas, I want to tell you my story," Hassun said, gesturing to sit upon a fallen log.

That was when he told me his mother's story.

Sofie was born in Amsterdam. At the age of eighteen, she immigrated with her parents to New Amsterdam, the same year as my father, in 1654. Soon she met a Dutchman named

Harman Vedder. Vedder's business was like Father's, a trader of beaver pelts.

Six months after Sofie arrived in New Amsterdam, she married Vedder, and moved to Wiltwijk, a small village along the North River, with her new husband. There they sought to establish a life, and a beaver pelt trading business.

One day, Harman kissed Sofie goodbye, and ventured off to trade with a native tribe. He told her that he would return within two to three days. The morning of the fifth day of his departure, Sofie feared something had happened to him. So, on a warm summer morning, she set out into the countryside looking for her husband. It didn't take long for a Dutch woman, with no survival skills, or an ability to speak any other language, to find herself in trouble.

She stumbled upon the summer camp of the Esopus tribe. Sofie had no reason to believe the tribe to be hostile. Her husband had told stories of his dealings with the tribes he traded with, to be mostly friendly.

Sofie walked down the beaten pathway into the camp, as if she was casually strolling through a park in Amsterdam. She wore a white scarf covering her pinned up hair, and a white dress down to her ankles. Suddenly, from behind, she was hit with something hard against her back that knocked her to the ground. She turned to see her assailant. It was a brave wearing a loincloth, yelping, running and jumping.

The moment she got to her feet, she was struck again. She managed to get herself up on all fours. Her white dress was now covered in dirt, and her pale, delicate hands were scraped and bleeding.

She was kicked in her ribs, and fell over. Her lungs deflated on impact. Sofie was on her back looking at faces screaming, and spitting on her. She covered her face with her hands and curled up into a ball.

Suddenly the yelps, and hollers stopped. She felt a gentle hand upon hers. Sofie opened her eyes, and saw a young woman, who offered a reassuring smile. She took her by the hand and helped Sofie to her feet.

She was taken to a longhouse where she met the Chief. He was seated around a smoldering flame and was in the company of an English officer.

They continued to speak to one another in English. Sofie recognized enough to understand that the conversation was about her. The officer looked at Sofie, and then nodded in agreement.

Someone from behind her grabbed her wrists and bound them. The officer rose and shook the Chief's hand. It appeared that a deal had been made, and she was a part of it. A hand pushed her to follow the officer as he exited the longhouse.

Out in the open, she saw English soldiers on horseback. She was told to climb onto a wagon filled with beaver pelts. With her bound hands, she was unable to climb aboard. Someone lifted her and threw her into the wagon. She rolled and settled in between stacked piles of beaver pelts.

She heard shouts of orders, and clomping of horse's hooves. The wheels of the wagon began with a creak, and she was on her way to some unknown destination with the English army. She had been part of a bargain that she knew nothing about, and had no idea where her husband was, or if he was even alive.

Sofie didn't stay with the English army. When the company reached the foot of the mountains they were ambushed by Sokokis warriors. It was a massacre. The warriors claimed over thirty-five scalps, including that of the officer. The only survivor of the attack was Sofie. She hid herself under the beaver pelts and was not seen until after the carnage concluded.

When she was discovered by the Sokokis, the warriors wanted to burn her alive. But the Shaman intervened, because he believed that Sofie, with her uncanny ability to survive, must have been sent by the Great Spirit and should be allowed to live with the tribe.

The Chief agreed, partly because he would not want to offend the Great Spirit, and also because he found the young, white Dutch woman sexually desirable.

Hassun tried to explain why his mother would give herself to the Chief. Her Dutch upbringing would normally have prevented any physical attraction to such a man. But she knew her chances of survival were nil. If she left the tribe's protection, where would she go?

With no other viable option, she acquiesced and became one of the Chief's lovers. Shortly thereafter, she became pregnant with the Chief's son, Hassun.

That was over sixteen years ago.

Her latest predicament occurred when I warned the Chief about Captain Lovewell's pending attack. Hassun believed that she got separated from the tribe during their escape, and was found by the Rangers later on. What Hassun did not know was whether she was dead or being held captive as a possible pawn for future negotiations with the Sokokis.

I understood Hassun's pain of not knowing if his mother was dead or alive. But what I didn't understand was why the Chief refused to discuss her possible rescue. He was annoyed when I brought it up. So much so, that he dismissed us without an explanation.

When I asked Hassun the cause of the Chief's irritation, he told me that over the years, his mother had grown to become a thorn in the Chief's side.

As Hassun grew up, it became apparent to his mother that his half-brother Mingan was the favored son. With each passing year, Sofie became increasingly relentless with her comments to the Chief. She took every opportunity to make her point.

"Why don't you give Hassun the same opportunities you offer Mingan?"

"You let Mingan get away with things that you would never allow Hassun to do."

"Don't you see how you treat Hassun different than your precious Mingan?"

After years of this constant berating, the Chief looked at this as an opportunity to get rid of her. That was why Hassun told me that the Chief would not risk the lives of his warriors to rescue his mother.

As I lay my head down to sleep that night, I couldn't help but think about how Sofie's ordeal was similar to mine with my nemesis, Captain Lovewell. What if she was still alive? How could the Chief be so cold about leaving her in the hands of a man so evil?

A thought flashed an image in my mind of a creature with a dog-like head, snout and fangs dripping with blackish slime, the Wendigo. Could it be that Captain Lovewell was the Wendigo in human form?

This fear tormented all night long and gave me no relief until morning.

Chapter 11

The next day, with the morning prayers concluded, Hassun asked me to join him for a swim. With the days growing longer, and warmer as summer approached, I agreed with pleasure. It was a late afternoon as we took off for the same mystical pond where the Shaman had spoken to me.

We ran barefoot through the forest and were greeted at the pond by croaking frogs. The moss felt even softer and deeper on my bare feet than the last time I was here. The willows looked lusher and displayed deeper shades of green.

Hassun climbed the largest willow, and balanced his way along a long branch hanging over the center of the pond. With a yell, he leapt off.

"You coming?" he asked, as his head surfaced.

I laughed at the sight of his bright face among the floating water lilies.

Not to be outdone, I climbed the same tree, and made my way out onto the branch that swayed with my weight upon it, and I plunged into the chilly water. My skin tingled. I opened my eyes to blackness.

As I surfaced, I saw Hassun waiting for me on the mossy embankment. I swam over, climbed out, and stretched out next to him in the sun.

"This is a magical place," I said, as I flipped back my wet hair.

"I've been coming here since I was a child," he said.

We spent the afternoon swimming, lounging and talking. I eventually guided the conversation to Hassun's mother, Sofie.

"It is hard to believe that the Chief prevents us from rescuing your mother," I said.

"Lukas, this is something I don't want to talk about."

"Hassun, you need to know about Captain Lovewell."

"I know all about him, Lukas," he said, abruptly.

"Do you know that he murdered my father, in front of me?"

Hassun's stern demeanor melted away, and was replaced with gentle kindness. "I did not know that. I am sorry."

"Thank you, Hassun. Captain Lovewell is the Wendigo personified. Pure evil," I added.

"I understand, but I cannot disobey the Chief," he insisted.

"Hassun, when I returned from my warrior journey after taking the Moon Flower I lost all of my memories. Fortunately, the Shaman asked me to write down my life story in case my memory did not return, which so far it hasn't. I have read my words about the captain over and over. He needs to be stopped before he hurts more people. I am convinced that the Great Spirit has chosen me for this task."

"I understand, Lukas. But you must do this without me."

I paused to take in the beauty of the oasis. My life so far had been a driving force, like an arrow shot from a bow. Constantly moving forward. Its direction never in question.

"Though I am a warrior of the tribe, my ultimate allegiance is to the Great Spirit alone." I turned to face Hassun, and said, "I will find your mother, Hassun, and bring her back to you."

My desires were not motivated by ego. This, I knew, was not the way of the warrior. Yet it was easy to allow fear to seep in, and react in a way that served the ego, and not the Great Spirit.

Since I left my home I lived with the Turtle Clan, the Pequawkets, and now the Sokokis. Each one took me in and provided for me. Now I must offer something in return. It was obvious that these tribes, and I am sure others, were at risk due to this English captain, and others just like him, who were seeking to destroy a way of life that had existed for hundreds of years.

I would call upon the Great Spirit for guidance in order to find a way to stop Captain Lovewell, and rescue Sofie.

Chapter 12

It took a few days to fill my quiver with arrows, restring my bow, and sharpen my knife. I took only what I needed to move quickly, and without notice.

The journey to Castle William and Mary should take several days on foot. During my internment, I did not see any other prisoners. I assumed that Sofie was being held somewhere else in the fort, if she was there at all.

It was late at night when I was ready to take off on my quest. Hassun and Mingan were sleeping. I leaned over and squeezed Hassun's arm. His eyes opened to see my finger upon my lips signaling silence. I nodded, and offered a warm smile, which he returned. There was no need for words.

I exited the longhouse smelling the smoldering evening fires, and easily slipped past the warriors keeping watch. Quickly I found the footpath beyond the tree line that would lead me south. But blocking my way was the Shaman.

"Going somewhere, Lukas?" she asked.

"This is something I must do," I answered.

"I know, Lukas. I am not here to stop you."

She grasped my hands and looked at me. "We all share the same lineage, Lukas. Thousands of moons have passed, but there is no denying our mutual ancestry. The Great Spirit recognizes you, and will guide you on your journey."

There was something familiar to her words. It caused a tickle in my mind. *Could this be a trapped memory primed for release?*

I said goodbye to the Shaman and took off at a steady pace through the forest.

When I arrived, I was surprised to see soldiers on horseback being led out of the fort by the captain himself, through the front gates. From my position in the shadows of the surrounding tree line, I was hidden from view.

With the captain gone, I had an opportunity to get into the lightly-guarded fort, and hopefully find Sofie. I ducked further into the shadows as the procession passed close by. The captain seemed to be looking directly toward me, which was disconcerting. But he didn't see me in the shadows, and looked away moments later, to my relief.

I needed to wait a few hours until darkness before I made my attempt to breach the walls, though this might prove to be challenging, since the fort was still under guard with sentries posted on the watchtowers and patrols along the perimeter.

As the hours passed, I thought back to my time locked away as a prisoner in the fort. There had been a few moments when I first arrived, and then later, upon my departure, when I had been able to get a sense of the interior layout. If Sofie was not being held captive in the lower cells where I had been, she might be in the tall tower at the center of the fort.

Long shadows formed across the open field as the sun dipped below the tree line. I heard sounds of wagons approaching. Soon I saw that there were ten covered wagons, being pulled by twenty horses, with men holding their bridles and guiding them in to the fort, its doors wide open. I had just found my way in.

A skill, which I initially learned from Rowtag but perfected with lessons from Hassun, was the ability to move without being seen or heard. We would test each other how far we could make it through the camp without notice. Hassun was flawless.

He taught me how to move like a breath of air, gliding, rather than walking. Soon we stealthily traversed the camp together. To increase the challenge, we would take something along the way, and watch the person search madly for a lost tool or a string of beads they had just set down moments earlier. With this skill, it was not difficult to make my way onto a wagon and bury myself under sacks of potatoes.

Fortune was on my side. The potato wagon was brought in through the cellar doors, where the foods were stored in underground rooms, for access by the cooks. Dark hallways and disinterested staff allowed me to move swiftly. I found a staircase and climbed up to a landing. I peeked around an open door and saw a large kitchen. The staff was in the midst of preparing the evening meal.

There was no way in, except through the busy kitchen. I scurried back down through the cellar, and found a door that led out of the storage rooms and into a crawl space under the floorboards. There was barely enough room to lie flat, face down on the damp earth, and snake along on my belly. This forced me to leave my bow and quiver behind.

With each step of someone walking above me, the floorboards creaked, and released streams of illuminated dust that created tiny mounds of dirt that mirrored the direction of the floorboards above me. I squirmed my way along the best I could in the tight space.

Bits of light seeped through the gaps guiding my way. I came upon a section of the floor that appeared to be cut out. No one was walking or speaking in the space above, so I gently pushed against the square, and it gave way.

Like a groundhog, I poked my head through the opening and looked around. It was an office of someone important I surmised by the wooden desk that looked enormous from my vantage point. I lifted myself up, squeezed through the narrow opening, and replaced the wood floor panel.

On the desk were papers, and a large leather-bound book, with gold letters. I opened the book and saw names listed with figures next to them. What they meant, I didn't know.

Just then, I heard voices and heavy footsteps approaching the office door. I needed to hide. Being caught here would certainly mean that I would end up on the wrong side of a firing squad. I spotted a large wooden cabinet with carved doors that had just enough room for me to squeeze behind.

Just as I finished concealing myself, I heard a booming, familiar voice. *It's Governor Wentworth. This must be his office.* "Come, I'll show you," he said.

"Thank you, Governor, I would like to see this," replied the second voice.

I settled down even lower, making sure I tucked in any possible protruding body part.

"Take a look at this," the Governor said, and then paused. "Why is the journal open? I thought I closed it… Well, doesn't matter… Look here, these are the names of the soldiers under Captain Lovewell's command, and next to it is a running count of the scalps they've earned. We pay one hundred British Sterling per scalp. A tidy sum," the Governor said.

"I'd say," said the second voice.

"The captain has just left with a tracking party. They are hunting down those damn bloody Sokokis savages. A little revenge for the siege they attempted some weeks ago. The men are drooling for some scalps."

"I wish I could be here to see the bounty, but I must sail back to England tomorrow. I'm afraid my mission to establish the Lords of Trade was met with resistance by the Massachusetts government. The King will be disappointed with my inability to create a stronger administrative tie between the colonies and the Crown."

"Give me some time to see if I might be influential. I am certain they will see the error of their ways. But you should enjoy your last evening with us. Come, my Lord, let's dine," the Governor said.

I waited for the Governor and this mysterious Lord to leave before I dared make any move. When their footfalls faded away, I slipped out from behind the cabinet.

Do I dare take another glance at the journal?

Quickly I opened and scanned the first few pages. There were names such as Smith, with a number four next to his name. Four scalps earned for this soldier. I imagined that four-hundred British Sterling was a good amount of money, but I really didn't know its value.

I gathered my senses and realized that I must find Sofie quickly so that I could return to the village to warn the Sokokis about the captain's posse of scalp-hunters. I gently opened the door, slipped out into the hallway, and followed it to a staircase.

At the top of the winding staircase was a series of closed doors lining a narrow hallway. There were muffled men's voices coming from one of the rooms. This could not be where Sofie was being held. Perhaps there was another stairwell at the end of the hall that would take me up to the tower. I tried to move silently upon the loose floorboards. I took a few steps, when a door opened, and out stepped an English officer.

"What in bloody hell are you doing here?" he blurted out.

I charged at him while reaching for my knife. A heartbeat later, I landed my blade into his belly. He grabbed my hands for a moment, but I pulled the knife away hard, and he fell to the floor. My heart pounded and felt it would burst free of my chest. Sweat poured down my forehead as I stared at the dying man. I had never taken a human life before and felt my stomach churn by the horror of it.

But the moment broke, when a redhaired soldier popped out from a doorway, and was ready to challenge me. Without hesitation, I leapt over the nearly dead soldier, lying in a puddle of his blood. The redhaired soldier held out his arm, demanding I stop. I cut at his outstretched hand. He gasped in pain. I spun him around and cut his throat with one swift motion. He gurgled and collapsed next to his fellow fallen soldier.

Clipped to his belt was an iron ring with several keys. I cut the leather strap, releasing them into my hand. I heard a commotion coming from up the stairs. I dashed toward the end of the hallway, and as expected, there was another staircase leading up to the tower.

I took three steps with each leap. Standing before me was a formidable wooden door. I banged hard, and yelled out in Dutch, "Sofie, are you in here?"

I heard nothing, except footsteps moving quickly on the floor below me. I knocked again and called out.

"Yes, I am here," answered a frail voice.

I fumbled with the keys, and finally found the one that unlocked the door. I slipped in, closed the door behind me, and locked it.

"Who are you?" asked Sofie.

"My name is Lukas. I am a friend of your son, Hassun. I've come to rescue you."

She looked at me with her jaw hanging open in shock. Her eyes were sunken, complexion sallow, and her long brown hair greasy. Her once white dress was yellowed, dirty and fell loosely off her skinny frame. By the looks of her, she hadn't eaten much. But her pale blue eyes registered a sparkle when I mentioned Hassun's name.

"Is my son all right?"

"Yes, he's fine. But right now we need to find a way out of here."

There was a banging at the door, and orders were shouted for someone to find the keys. I scanned the room and ran to the only window. Looking down, I saw that without a rope such an escape was not possible. Looking up I saw exposed rafters, and thought that if I could reach them, I could pull myself onto the roof.

I jumped onto the sill, and with one arm holding on to the inside of the window, leaned out and grabbed a rafter. I released my grip on the window frame and latched on to the round wooden support with both hands, and using momentum swung myself up to the roof.

On my belly, I looked back down and saw Sofie looking at me from the window. I stretched out my arm for her, but she was out of my reach. There was panic in her eyes as the sounds of the soldiers attempting to knock the door down were becoming louder. Apparently, they couldn't find a second set of keys.

"Sofie, climb on to the sill."

"I'm scared," she said.

"I know, but you must try."

With that, she got up onto the sill and reached for me. We clasped hands and I pulled her bony frame up and onto the roof.

I took Sofie by the hand and we sprinted across the angled roof. I turned back to look and saw no one in pursuit. The view from above allowed me to see beyond the fort's tall walls. To the south was the vast ocean spreading across the vista, as far as I could see.

We reached the roof's edge, and I saw a platform that looked accessible by jumping. I instructed Sofie to wait for me, as I leapt off the roof and landed on my feet. I turned and held out my arms.

"Jump, Sofie, I will catch you."

She bent her knees and jumped like a child into my arms. She hit me hard. We fell and tumbled, with Sofie landing on top of me. Unhurt, we got to our feet and scurried down the steps.

As we turned the corner, I saw the caravan of wagons moving slowly toward the gates.

"Come, Sofie, we have our way out of here."

We positioned ourselves between the fort's wall, and the wagon procession running alongside.

"Jump on the wagon," I told her.

She quickly leapt onto a wagon in the middle of the caravan. I followed, and we slipped under the wagon's bonnet, hidden from view. Moments later the wagons were headed out of the fort and into the open countryside.

Chapter 13

____

Once we were fully beyond the fort's walls and out of the view of the sentries, we jumped off the wagon and ran. A full moon illuminated our way across the landscape. I prayed to the Great Spirit that we would make it back to the camp before the captain and his scalp-thirsty men arrived.

On foot we traversed terrain that was not possible on horseback. This was in our favor, but there were no assurances we could make up for the lost time.

I was sure Sofie had many questions for me, as I did her. But with the dangers lurking, we could not afford to waste time discussing them.

Sweaty and exhausted, we emerged from the forest surrounding the village and saw a disturbing scene. English soldiers on horseback were charging through the camp's beaten pathways. Mothers were pulling children by their hands, screaming and scattering in all directions. Musket fire exploded. Sokokis warriors scrambled to defend. Dust clouds stained with blood filled the evening air.

I told Sofie to wait, hidden from view. Since I ditched my bow and quivers at the fort, my knife was my only remaining weapon. I scoped out the battlefield.

Suddenly, I saw Captain Lovewell upon his magnificent horse swinging his silver-handled sabre in great sweeping arcs. He was slicing deep wounds into defenseless souls fleeing for their lives. Trails of blood followed the sharp blade as it followed through into the sky.

"Captain," I screamed.

Surprisingly, he heard me over the commotion. He rode his horse onto the open field to face me, and charged. His right arm was outstretched, holding the sabre up to the sky.

The captain's reach was far and wide. He swung his blade from high. I dodged the potentially deadly blow by hitting the ground and rolling out of his reach. His horse spooked on seeing my blurry image, pulled up to a dead stop and tossed the captain off.

He got to his feet with apparently only a few minor bruises to his body, but by the look on his face, a mighty one to his ego. The captain pulled a knife from its sheath, and suddenly we were equally armed.

The captain moved quickly, looking for an advantage to strike.

Even as he fought for each breath, he was still able to address me. "Ah, Lukas, the thorn in my side. You think you're clever, but today you'll pay with your scalp. You deceived me as a translator and lured me into an ambush against these savages. Now you, and the Sokokis, will pay for your betrayals."

I maneuvered out of his reach. It was apparent that I was no match for the captain's skills as a professional killer.

"I am going to cut out your heart, Lukas, and take your scalp," he said, with a frothy white substance clinging to the corners of his mouth.

He moved well, putting me quickly on the defensive, and forcing me backward. I tripped and fell over a stone. The moment I hit the ground, the Captain was on me, pinning me flat to the earth.

I watched the captain's eyes morph into the golden eyes of a wolf. His jaw opened, exposing skin piercing fangs, and a pink tongue frothed with desire. This affirmed my suspicion that indeed, the Wendigo lived within the soul of the captain.

Then I heard a crack. The captain's wolf-like head snapped forward, and he tumbled off me. Sofie was standing at my feet with a large branch in her hands, following through with a devastating swing. I stared at the frail Sofie for a brief moment, unsure where she found the strength to wield something so heavy. Then it occurred to me that perhaps it was the Great Spirit extending its hand through her, providing her with the power to strike against the evil captain. Certainly, it was possible.

I scrambled to my feet, grabbed her hand, and ran. I looked back and saw the captain mounting his horse. He looked at me. His golden wolf eyes and jaw were gone. Turning away, he rode off in the direction of his men who were retreating from the attack.

Death hung over the Sokokis camp like a black storm cloud. Sofie and I slowed to a cautious walk. We did not want to disturb the freshly-dead struggling to pass through to the spirit world. Scattered about were lifeless bodies lying in pools of blood. There were many dead, and wounded, some missing their scalps. The bounty hunters had earned their rewards.

As we traversed the decimation, I saw Hassun. He was unharmed and attending the wounded. Sofie reached down to touch his shoulder. When Hassun turned and saw his mother, he stood and embraced her. Sofie's tears ran in rivulets down her unwashed face.

"Mother, are you all right?" Hassun asked.

"I am fine, thanks to Lukas," she said.

"The Great Spirit has looked favorably upon us this day. We give thanks, and I thank you, Lukas. I am in your debt," said Hassun.

Before I had a chance to respond, I saw the Chief coming toward us. He looked at Sofie, and then at me. But he said nothing and walked by. If it wasn't for the massacre, I felt sure he would have expressed his anger with my blatant disrespect of his orders.

Later that evening as we gathered around the fire we learned the extent of the devastation: Twenty-three Sokokis were dead, thirteen were injured, and seven corpses were without their scalps.

Clearly this was an act of war, said Mingan, who was demanding immediate revenge. I watched the Chief sit solemnly, listening to the expressions of outrage among his warriors. He lifted both palms signaling silence.

Hassun comforted his brother to silence his rants about retribution. With Mingan finally quieted, the Chief looked over to the Shaman. She nodded, and began the prayers to the Great Spirit.

The survivors huddled in the Chief's longhouse, trying to offer comfort to each other. There were bursts of anger, and cries of revenge filling the air. The elders did their best to settle those in distress, and eventually the fervor settled into a subdued remorse. With the emotions shifted, the Chief addressed the tribe.

"We will not retaliate," the Chief announced.

A ripple of discontent traversed the circle.

The Chief lifted his right palm, and the whispers ceased.

"We are a tribe of great warriors," he said, looking at the astonished young men. "Sokokis warriors do not seek revenge. Instead, the Great Spirit teaches us to have the courage to respond to such an event with wisdom, not fury."

A murmur of voices circulated with mixed emotions. Young warriors like Mingan sneered, but others like Hassun nodded in approval. I too felt taken aback at the Chief's decision, but soon understood his wisdom, and admired his leadership. There would be no more killing. The dead would be buried, and a time for prayers and mourning would commence.

As the tribe disbanded from the circle, Hassun approached me.

"The Chief asked that you join him in his longhouse."

Together we entered. He was waiting for me with the Shaman and Sofie. Hassun and I sat across from them.

"I have learned of your exploits in rescuing Sofie," the Chief said, looking over to her. "You have disobeyed me, and your insubordination must be dealt with accordingly. However, I am also not blind to the possibility that your actions were motivated by your calling to the Great Spirit, and with that, you have demonstrated the courage of a warrior in bringing her back to the tribe," he said.

I looked at Sofie, who offered a slight smile and a nod.

"She has also spoken of your attempt to warn us of the attack. But as we know you arrived too late," he said, gesturing to the wounded being attended to in the longhouse.

I knew not to speak and was not sure that I could. My mouth was as dry as the rainless earth. As the Chief looked at me, I felt drawn into his soul. There, I saw hurt within him. I saw my betrayal. Words were not spoken between us, but I understood that my time with the Sokokis was over. I rose and took a moment to look at Hassun, Sofie and the Shaman before I exited the wigwam.

"Lukas, wait."

I turned and saw Hassun following me.

"Before you go, please come with me."

I followed Hassun into his longhouse. Once inside he handed me his bow and a quiver full of arrows. "Please take this."

"Thank you," I said, accepting the gift.

"Do you think we will ever see each other again?" he asked.

"Only the Great Spirit can answer that. But I do hope so, my friend."

We embraced warmly.

As I made my way from the village, waiting for me were many of the surviving tribespeople. One by one I was hugged and thanked. Even Mingan offered a genuine appreciation of my efforts. "I owe you my thanks, and my apology, Lukas. You are not the pretender I thought," he said, and embraced me.

Even though I knew Sofie for only a few days, she approached and hugged me. She touched my cheek, and asked, "Where will you go, Lukas?"

"Back to the Pequawkets, and to my love Nadie. The last time I saw her I was being taken away as the captain's prisoner," I told her.

"I hope you find her, Lukas. You deserve to be happy."

The Shaman took me by my shoulders, pulled me close to her, and whispered into my ear. "No matter the challenges you will face, do not be tempted to stray from the path. Your journey is to find your connection with the Great Spirit. I believe that you have been chosen to confront evil. May the Great Spirit give you the strength you need to fulfill your life's purpose."

"I will do my best to remain true to your words," I said.

The final farewell was from the Chief. He stood tall and stiff, exhibiting a demeanor of anger and disappointment. But as I looked into his eyes, I realized that this behavior was a public demonstration for his people watching us. My sense was that his anger was gone.

We walked together to the horse the Chief had offered to me as a parting gift. As he patted its neck, he said, "The Great Spirit will always be with you, if you are true to your heart. I think you already know that your life is to serve the many, not the few. Honor your calling. You will discover that your reward may not be in this lifetime, but it will come."

He offered a discreet squeeze on my forearm, and I slightly nodded in return. I mounted my horse and turned to the many onlookers. I placed my hand over my heart and turned my open palm toward them. In unison, the Sokokis returned the gesture of love and respect. Tears swelled up in my eyes, as I turned to face the path before me, leaving this part of my life behind.

Chapter 14

Using the tracking skills I learned from the late Matwau, I traversed the hills back to the Pequawket camp. My thoughts stayed focused on Nadie. I imagined kissing her soft lips, and gazing into her soulful brown eyes. She would be fascinated, hearing of my exploits with the Sokokis tribe, and my tribulations with my tormentor, Captain Lovewell.

I paused on my horse to look down upon the valley, and the lake. The mountains were reflected in its stillness. Streams of smoke drifted skywards. I exhaled a breath that I felt I had been holding within me for many months. A great relief washed over me. Joy filled my thoughts at the idea of returning home.

A rider approached on horseback. As he got closer, I saw it was Rowtag. We jumped off our horses simultaneously, ran toward each other, and embraced.

"My brother, is it really you? I thought you were dead," he said.

"Why would you think that?"

"It's been many moons since we have heard anything. And then, when you were taken captive by Captain Lovewell, the Chief sent out scouts to find you. They tracked you to the fort where you were being held captive. The scouts heard stories that you were killed during the siege by the Sokokis tribe."

"And you believed them?"

"When the scouts returned and told us that you were killed, I argued, asking how could this be true. I insisted that I be allowed to search for you. But the Chief denied my request."

"But why would he do that?"

"He said he would not risk the life of the son of a Chief on such a small chance of finding you."

"So you obeyed?"

Rowtag nodded, and said, "After a while, when you didn't return, I assumed you were dead too."

"Well, good news, I am just fine. You look well, too, Rowtag," I said, as we led the horses into the village.

"I am well. Everyone will be so happy to see you."

"How is Nadie?"

Rowtag stopped walking and turned to face me with a solemn look. "We need to talk, Lukas."

"What is it?" I asked, with concern.

Rowtag bowed his head, his voice barely audible. "There's more to tell you, Lukas."

"What else?"

"With you being dead. I mean gone," he stammered, before continuing, "Nadie and I became close."

"You and Nadie became what?"

"Lukas, please understand. We didn't know where you were, and it has been a long time."

For the first time since my Moon Flower journey, my heart was truly sick. Every word Rowtag spoke felt like a knife stabbing me. I put a hand on my horse to steady myself.

"She's pregnant, Lukas, with my child. We are married."

I couldn't speak. Nausea overcame me, and whatever was in my belly, rose and spewed out of my mouth.

"Are you all right?" asked Rowtag, with a hand on my back.

"Take your hands off me," I said and pushed him away, while wiping the remaining bile off my mouth with the back of my hand.

"I'm sorry, Lukas. Please understand."

"Leave me be," I said. Mounting my horse, I headed into the village.

I saw her first, before anyone else. She was looking right at me, her eyes swimming in tears. She stood there, with one hand supporting her lower back, and the other resting gently on her stomach.

I dismounted, walked tentatively over, and looked at her belly.

"Why, Nadie?"

"Rowtag said you were dead. So did everyone," she said, her voice shaking with each syllable.

"Did you think I was dead?"

"I didn't know what to think, Lukas. I am sorry. If I knew you were alive I would never have been with Rowtag."

"You betrayed me, Nadie. You and Rowtag both betrayed me. The closest people in my life."

I mounted my horse and turned away.

"Lukas, where are you going?" she asked.

"I'm going home to see Mother," I said, without looking back.

Chapter 15

The first thing I learned by asking for directions to the city of Beverwyck, was that the Dutch had surrendered the territory known as the New Netherlands to the English without firing a shot. What was once Beverwyck, was now called Albany, and the city of New Amsterdam was now known as New York.

With the loss of my memory, there was nothing I would recognize anyway, as I rode into the renamed city. It took a full moon cycle to get here, which had given me plenty of time to come to terms with my anger toward Rowtag and Nadie. At first I yelled my frustrations skyward, expecting a conversation with the Great Spirit. That proved fruitless. I hoped for some enlightenment in my dreams. But none came.

Once inside the city of Albany, I asked my way to Fort Orange. I was soon corrected that the Fort was also renamed, and was now called Fort Albany.

"Fort Albany is south of where the Mohawk River meets up with the North River," a native trapper told me.

This sounded like a familiar place to me. I pulled out my rolled-up journal from my pouch and found the part where I wrote about the Turtle Clan.

"*Cohoes Falls*," I read aloud.

This was where my life seeking the Great Spirit began. I would go to the falls, find Chief Nicholas, and tell him about Rowtag and my adventures. I was sure he would be pleased to know that his son was not only well, but married, and soon to be a father.

Finding the falls took little time. But I did not see the Turtle Clan's camp. I reread my manuscript where I described the setting by the falls. I was in the right place, but the native's village was gone. But I did see the English army. They had made camp just down from the falls. I walked my horse into their campsite and asked if anyone had knowledge of the Turtle Clan.

"The Mohawks have chased them to the east," said a scrawny soldier guarding the perimeter.

I decided to put off finding the new home of the Turtle Clan, at least until I spent some time with Mother, so I continued on to Fort Albany. The fort apparently was still an active place for the fur trade. Wagons carrying beaver pelts crisscrossed the main road.

I asked a man wearing a bearskin coat if he ever heard of the Vilna Trading & Export Company.

"I know it well, boy. In fact, I am heading that way now," he said.

I dismounted my horse and walked alongside the older man.

"Why are you wearing a fur?" I asked, since it was warm enough for only a loincloth.

"It's called fashion, my young lad," he said with a jovial, and contagious laugh.

"How do you know of the Vilna Trading & Export Company?" I asked.

"I know of it well. Why are you asking?"

"I have been away a while, and I am returning to see my mother who runs the business, with my cousin," I said.

The man stopped walking, and grabbed me by both shoulders, and said, "You must be Sara's son, Lukas."

"Do we know each other?" I asked, concerned that I should know this man.

"I am sure you don't know me. I met you once when you were a baby," he said.

"You know my mother and father?"

"I knew your father well, God rest his soul. We traveled together from our homeland in Vilna. For a while we lived together in New Amsterdam before he moved to Beverwyck and met your mother. My name is Asser Levy."

"You're Father's friend from Vilna."

"I am," Asser said.

"You know of his death? He was murdered in front of me by an English soldier."

"I heard the tragic story of Solomon's murder," he said, stopping to look at me.

"How is Mother?"

"Sara is well, Lukas. Come now, she will be happy to see you."

By the time we reached the office of the Vilna Trading & Export Company, my legs, up to my calves, were caked in mud. To keep from losing my moccasins in the mud-sucking road, I held them in one hand, and with the other, I pulled on my horse's bridle. Asser's knee-high fur boots, which complemented his magnificent fur coat, seemed more suitable for the condition of the roadway.

Asser took three steps up to the deck, turned and gestured to me.

"Wait here, Lukas. Let me go in first and prepare your mother. She is not the same woman you remember. I want to make sure you don't shock her."

I nodded approval, and Asser opened the front door and disappeared inside.

What does he mean she is not the same woman I remember? For one thing, I don't remember her at all, and even so, is he saying that she is not well.

I sat down to clean off the mud from my feet and put on my moccasins.

If I am going to see my mother, I should be presentable.

"Lukas, is that you?" I heard a voice from behind me.

I rose, and saw a frail woman, with thinning hair and a pale complexion.

"Mother?"

"Oh my," she said, pulling me close to her, and wrapping her bony arms around me. She was sobbing. I felt her raspy breath vibrate against me. She looked at me without letting go.

I offered a more obligatory embrace, which was the best I could muster, since I lacked any emotions to fuel our reunion.

"Oh, Lukas, how I have missed you. Come inside. I'll make you something to eat."

I looked over to Asser, who was standing looking at us. "I'll give you some time with your mother. But we need to talk. I'll stop later for a chat."

I assumed this was the house I was born in. But nothing looked familiar, and above all, neither did Mother. She stared at me in a way that made me feel awkward.

"Are you all right son?" she asked, while preparing a meal for me.

"I am well."

"You seem uncomfortable. I know I don't look the same. But life's challenges have been tough on me, having both my father and husband murdered. I thought I was strong, but apparently not strong enough."

"I'm sorry, Mother. It's not you. Perhaps you will understand, if I tell you my story."

Mother served me a bowl of steaming hot soup and a piece of bread. The soup filled my senses with familiar flavors. There had been only a few of these encouraging moments that felt like my memory was returning. But for now, the woman sitting across from me was a total stranger.

I told her my story from the time Rowtag and I began our journey in search of the Great Spirit, up until the betrayal of Rowtag and Nadie. Any memories before the Moon Flower episode were based on my writing, and were consequently flat in my story telling.

It took until late into the evening for me to finish my tale. Mother remained silent throughout, but nodded occasionally as a way to encourage me to continue. When I finished, she stared at me for a moment before speaking.

"The Great Spirit is not exclusive to the Algonquin speaking tribes you have crossed paths with. Many tribes and religions around the world seek guidance and community from a greater being. You have experienced what many strive their entire lives for, a connection with the Almighty. Your loss of memory is a small price to pay for what you have been given."

"But my life feels empty," I said, looking at her. "You are my mother, but I do not know you. My father was murdered before my eyes, but I feel no grief."

"That is because your journey is not yet completed. In fact, it has just begun. Have patience, Lukas. I am sure the three Shamans you have spoken of would tell you the same."

"This is true."

"There is so much more you need to learn."

I leaned across the table and kissed her on her cheek.

She then told me about her lonely life. How she and cousin Jakob continued the business after Father's death. But it was never the same. While the business provided a decent living, the joy was gone. She became a recluse, and only ventured to the office when needed for translating. All other times she sequestered herself at home.

"I'm scared to leave the house, Lukas. The outside world has not been kind to me."

Her comment was one with which I could empathize. Or perhaps I was feeling true love for my mother.

"I am sorry, Mother, for your sadness. Perhaps my presence can offer you some comfort?" I said.

"You have your own life now, Lukas, that is certainly beyond caring for me. I'll be fine. You must go out into the world and fulfill your calling."

"Are you sure, Mother, that you don't need me?"

"I would feel worse knowing that your life ended up in this place. There's a world out there for you, Lukas. That is where you belong, exploring the wonders, and seeking your connection with the Almighty."

I exhaled deeply. I did not need to fear disappointing my mother anymore; with her blessing, I could continue on my way, knowing she supported me and believed in my quest to connect with the Great Spirit.

The next morning when I arose, Mother told me that Asser was waiting for me on the front porch. She handed me two cups of hot tea and said that this was his favorite.

I opened the door, and there he was, sitting on a bench smoking a cigar, wearing his fashionable fur coat, and looking out into the busy street. He turned his head and saw me.

"Come, Lukas, we need to talk," he said, patting the spot on the bench next to him.

I handed him the cup of tea, and he lowered his nose to take in its aroma.

"Heavenly," he proclaimed, and took a sip. Then he said, "Lukas, I am interested in hearing about your adventures these past few years. Your mother said that you have quite a story to tell. You can share it with me on our trip downriver to New York."

"Trip to New York?"

"Yes, you will accompany me to the city, and you will work for me. When your father and cousin Jakob traveled with me from Amsterdam many years ago, we made a promise to each other, that in need we would watch over each other's offspring. You happen to be the only child. Cousin Jakob is unable to watch over you. As you know their business is doing barely enough to support him, and your mother. Plus, the future is in New York. I have several businesses that are doing quite well, even with the English running things now. I need someone with your set of skills who I can trust," he said, and paused for my reaction.

"I don't know. My life has been in the wilderness. How would I live in a city like New York?"

"Ah, it's easier than living in the wilderness. You will have the comforts of a gentleman. You will have your own place to live, a wagon and horses to take you places, nice clothes to wear, and who knows, you may even meet a nice young lady or two," he said, with a wink.

Leaving behind the life that betrayed me seemed like it could be a good way to move on. *Perhaps*, I thought, *I can find a new path in the new world of New York. I certainly have nowhere else to go.*

Book 3

Chapter 1

With barely a breath of wind, it took three days to sail down the North River to New York. This gave Asser and me plenty of time to talk. I asked him what brought him to Albany.

"I am getting out of the beaver trade. I've given my shares of the business to your mother and Jakob. Papers needed to be signed, so I thought I would pay them a visit."

With his fur coat, fur hat and fur boots removed, Asser sported a brownish red beard that rested upon his thick barrel chest. His curls of hair were just as unkempt as the rest of him. But he had kind blue eyes, and charm to match. He lured me into his world effortlessly, with his tales of accomplishments.

He told me of a large slaughterhouse he had just built on the southern end of the city, and how he was maintaining his business relations, even with the English taking over.

"There's a tremendous amount of money to be made trading with the Europeans. I ship them grains, flour, salt, peas and tobacco in exchange for a variety of manufactured goods like fabrics, furnishings, and common household items."

I explained to Asser that I had no knowledge of the world of commerce.

Asser smiled, patted my back, and said, "I like that your mind is not cluttered with preconceived notions on how things are done. This will give me the chance to teach you the *Asser Levy* way of doing things."

I laughed to myself about his 'uncluttered mind' comment. *If he only knew about my Moon Flower experience.*

Waiting for us dockside was a wagon, decorated with carvings along its wooden sideboards, and freshly painted in a cheerful sky-blue color. It was drawn by two well-groomed horses, and a driver who respectfully greeted Asser, and took his trunks from one of the ship's porters.

The driver looked behind me, as if to ask where the rest of my belongings were. I shrugged, and patted my bow, indicating this was all I had.

Asser sat high on the wagon, perched next to the driver, and waved like a returning hero to the pedestrians walking by, who called out his name. When their stares shifted over to me, they saw a white boy dressed like a native, which altered their jovial greetings to whispers of apparent concern to one another.

For a moment, I wondered if I would be accepted in the city, or shunned as an outsider who fraternized with savages.

It didn't take long to traverse the hardened dirt roads. Along the way we passed dilapidated wood homes that looked like they had withstood many tough winters. Surrounding the homes were small plots of land, where families farmed their crops.

I tapped Asser on his shoulder, and asked him, "What do the people grow here in the city?"

"Same things the natives grow, like wheat, corn, peas, pumpkins and potatoes," he said, pointing to a few Negro men working in their gardens.

We passed by a building painted red with a sign over the front door that read SCHOOLHOUSE. Its shutters were swung open, and I saw heads of students sitting inside, their voices filtering out into the street.

We turned down William Street, as the sign read, posted to a pole. Suddenly, the beaten down wood plank homes were gone, and I now saw large, brick buildings.

I had never seen structures so tall and massive. In comparison, the buildings of the white folks up river were all small and constructed of wood. The effort to build something so grand obviously required great skill. I tried to imagine what it took to place one brick next to another and stack them to the sky.

We pulled up alongside one building, and stopped. Asser jumped off.

"Let's go, Lukas. This is home," he said, sweeping his arm across the expanse of bricks, and decorative stonework adorning the windows.

"How many people live here?" I asked, looking up at the seemingly endless rows of windows.

"Just me, and my wife Miriam. Come now, she will be excited to see you."

I couldn't believe that Asser and his wife lived in this home alone. I followed him up the stone steps to the grand entrance.

The doors opened to a large room with walls covered in dark wood panels. I had been in white men's homes before, like my parents, but I had never seen anything like this. Lit candles in tall stands illuminated the space.

"Who do we have here?" a voice shrieked.

"Darling, this is Solomon and Sara's son Lukas," Asser said.

She stared at me with her mouth open—presumably at the sight of a stranger wearing nothing but a loincloth and moccasins, in her elegant home.

"Miriam, say something to the boy," Asser insisted, as he removed his fur coat and hat.

"Oh my, I am so happy to meet you, Lukas," she finally said, a little choked up.

"It's nice to meet you too, Mrs. Levy."

"Come, now. Let's show Lukas his room, get him some proper clothes, and something to eat," said Asser.

"Oh my, oh my," Miriam continued to murmur.

Chapter 2

A young Negro boy showed me to my room. He told me his name was Abraham, and said there were clothes for me on the chair.

"They were David's clothes. He was about six years younger than you," he said.

"Was David their son?" I asked.

Abraham shook his head, and said, "Very tragic. He was caught in the middle of musket fire between an English and Dutch soldier. Probably the only shots fired in the English takeover of New Amsterdam."

I thanked Abraham and said I would try on the clothes. Before he left, he suggested that I wash myself.

"Over there is a basin with warm water, and that there," he said, pointing to a square grayish formed block, "that's soap. You wash yourself with it."

I smiled, and told Abraham that I was familiar with the washing procedures, even though my body odor gave the impression to the contrary. Just as Abraham was about to leave, he stepped back into my room, and closed the door behind him.

"You look exactly like David. Like you were brothers," he whispered.

I looked at Abraham, not knowing what to say. He sensed my awkwardness, and politely told me that dinner would be served shortly.

"I'll come and fetch you when it is time," he said, and left.

With Abraham gone, I took a moment to observe my room. A grand stone fireplace, dormant now as it was summer, sat opposite a large window. I stepped across floorboards to look out the window. With its shutters open, I saw out from the third floor upon the street below, and from this height could see the dock where the sloop ship we sailed upon was still tied up.

Fabric panels, which I supposed could be pulled closed at night, were draped between the four corner posts of my bed. I lay down upon the mattress and sank into its feathers, thinking, *These new comforts won't be hard to get used to.*

I did my best to scrub the stink off me. The soap had a familiar odor, like animal fat burned in a fire, but I suppose it pleased Asser and Miriam, so I washed.

I had no memory of wearing anything but my seasonal native clothing, but I knew that during my life with mother and father, I must have worn traditional white man's attire.

Neatly folded on a chair, standing against a wall, were the clothes. I picked them up and separated the various items. There were a pair of black leather shoes, polished to such a shine that I could see my reflection in them. Stuffed into the shoes were white stockings. I put them on, along with the brown breeches that reached below my knees, just enough for the stockings to be tucked up into.

A crisp white shirt was only visible at its collar, due to the brown waistcoat that buttoned up to my neck. Lastly, I slipped on the red coat, whose large bright gold buttons matched their smaller versions on the waistcoat.

A large mirror hung on the wall across from the bed. The last time I looked at my reflection had been in the still lake at the Pequawkets summer camp. *Is this going to be my new life?* I asked myself, looking into the mirror. I had gone from running free in the wilderness to this new world of living in rigid civilized society. *Have I made the right decision?* I could not answer that question just yet.

Abraham knocked at my door and entered.

"You look very nice, Mr. Lukas."

"Just call me Lukas," I pleaded.

He smiled awkwardly, but nodded.

"Dinner is being served. Please follow me, Lukas."

The clothing was stiff, and itchy. But the most troublesome were the shoes. They felt like blocks of wood tied to my feet. Abraham noticed my clumsiness and told me, as he waited for me to catch up, that I would get used to them.

"What if I don't want to?" I asked.

Abraham shrugged and offered his hand to help me, which I, of course, refused.

I heard Asser and Miriam speaking as I reached the main floor, and followed Abraham into the dining room. That was when Miriam screamed.

"Oh my. I cannot stand it," she bawled, and ran into the kitchen.

I looked at Asser who shrugged and told me to sit.

"Did I do something to upset her?" I asked.

"No, Lukas. It's just that you have an uncanny resemblance to our late son, David. Especially now, wearing his clothes."

"I'm sorry, but Abraham asked me to put these on," I said, running my fingers along the lapel of my jacket.

"Don't worry, Lukas. She'll be fine. Miriam is happy having a young man back in the house again. She will just need time to get used to it," Asser said, patting me on my back.

I remained silent. Perhaps my uncanny resemblance to her deceased son made her wish I could simply replace him, but we all knew that was not possible.

Miriam returned, carrying a tray of sliced meat. "Please excuse me for my outburst, Lukas. I am better now."

"I'm sorry if I upset you, Miriam," I said.

"Oh, that's all right, Lukas. I'm fine," she replied.

Following behind her was Abraham and a young Negro girl, both carrying trays of food.

"Lukas, this is Alice. She and Abraham live with us, and help us around the house," Miriam told me.

I looked at Alice who seemed painfully shy, as she was barely able to make eye contact.

"Hello, Alice, it is good to meet you," I said.

"Now," Miriam interrupted, and walked over to the window. She looked out, and announced, "It is time."

Miriam placed a white shawl over her head and approached the table where five tall candles were lit in a candelabrum. She placed both palms over her eyes and recited a prayer in a language I was unfamiliar with.

As she finished the prayer she said, "Good Shabbos."

After dinner, Asser escorted me into another room, with a fire already tended to by Abraham.

"Is there a fireplace in every room?" I asked.

Asser shook his head. "Yes, nearly every one. Now come sit with me, and talk."

I was anxious to get out of the clothes, but out of respect for Asser, I sat down on the wood floor next to the fire.

"Lukas, let's discuss your future," he began.

"My future?"

"Don't you have plans for your life?"

"I haven't thought about it," I said.

"Well, you leave that to me. My business interests have not only continued since the English now run things, they have prospered. I've become a *denizen*. This elevated status permits me to do business like a citizen of the English Crown. This, my boy, is the best calling card across Europe."

I offered a clumsy smile, then asked, "How would I fit into these plans?"

Asser stood up and walked over to the fire. He looked down at me sitting cross-legged on the floor. "On our voyage down the river, you told me of your exploits with the natives. This is impressive, and potentially useful. You have proved yourself a warrior. Was this not your goal?"

"It still is. I have a long way to go before I can call myself a warrior. It's a lifelong journey," I shared with him.

"Perhaps the path you have journeyed was to prepare you for your new life here, with me."

I leaned back to see Asser's face towering above me. He was looking into the fire.

"What do you mean?" I asked.

"I want you to be my assistant, my confidant. I need someone who is smart, resourceful, and above all, trustworthy."

He returned to his wooden rocking chair, waiting for my acknowledgment. I offered a subtle smile, enough for him to continue.

"You will be my shadow. I want you to observe where I go, what I do, whom I speak with. If someone speaks to you directly, be polite, and smile, but say nothing. This will be your education into the world of commerce, and you will be learning from one of the best."

It was hard to imagine how my skills of survival in the wilderness would be of much use in the city. Life here would have a new assortment of challenges, and difficulties, that I would need to learn and master.

"I'm willing to give it a try," I said.

"Marvelous," Asser exclaimed. "But Jews do not do business on Shabbat. Tomorrow we will go to Shul, and pray."

I knew from my journal that Father was Jewish. There was also a lingering thought that tickled my mind about some deeper connection to the Jewish faith, but I couldn't bring it to the surface.

Asser noticed me reflecting, and said, "Your father Solomon and I grew up together in Vilna. We lived in a village called a shtetl. This was a community of close-knit Jewish families. We were forced to leave because of people's hatred of us. It's time you learn who you really are, Lukas."

Later that night, I moved off the too-soft feather bed, to the solid wood-plank floor by the open window. With a more comfortable surface to rest upon, I thought of Asser's words. The plight of the Jews was much like that of the native peoples I lived with. They had also been forced from their generational lands, and sought ways to live their lives on terms they determined.

Chapter 3

W hen morning arrived, I headed downstairs. The front door was locked with some elaborate device that I fumbled with.

"Lukas, do you need to go outside?" Abraham said, appearing out of nowhere.

"I need to go," I said, assuming he understood the reference.

"Outside?" he said, surprised.

"Well, you don't do it inside?" I asked.

"You use the pot in your room. I was about to come up and empty it when I saw you at the door."

"A pot in my room?" I said, and then remembered the hideous bucket I used in the prison cell at the fort.

"Come, I'll show you," he said, and I followed him back upstairs to my room.

I told Abraham that I didn't need instructions on how to use the pot. After I relieved myself, Abraham took the pot away.

When Abraham returned, he helped me dress for my visit with Asser, to the synagogue. The clothing continued to make me itch incessantly. I asked Abraham how long synagogue lasted. He told me that he had no idea, since he was never invited to attend.

While I waited for Asser in front of his grand home, I appeared to cause the people passing by to give me a double take. Perhaps they thought that I was the Levy's late son David, who had risen from the dead.

"There you are my boy," said Asser, as he emerged from the front door.

"Where is the synagogue?"

"We don't have our own building yet. The English are less fond of the Jews than the Dutch. So we meet at a friend's home, and we have a Rabbi. Come, I'll introduce you."

There was an uncanny feeling of familiarity to the morning ceremony I attended with Asser. Perhaps it was Rabbi Wolf, a curious name, who led the prayers similarly as a Shaman would. Asser told me that the words he spoke were called Hebrew.

"It's the ancient language of our people," he said.

While the words were foreign, I felt a connection, or should I say a fondness to the sounds, and lyrics of the prayers. The synagogue was in the home of a man named Henry Mendes. Asser said he was one of the twenty Jews who were forced to leave Brazil after the Portuguese conquered it.

"We are a people in need of a homeland. In our little congregation, we have both Sephardim and Ashkenazim Jews," Asser whispered to me during the ceremony.

On the walk home, I asked Asser about these different kinds of Jews. He told me that they were no more different than the various tribes of the natives I lived with.

"Do all native peoples worship the same Great Spirit?" Asser asked.

"They do," I replied.

After we arrived back home, I asked Asser if it was all right for me to explore the city.

"Of course, Lukas. Just make sure you return soon. Miriam is preparing a wonderful lunch for us."

"I will, Asser," I said, and headed up the staircase to my room to change my clothes.

"Just one more thing, Lukas," Asser called out.

I stopped, and turned my head.

"Please don't wear that loincloth anymore. Abraham will show you proper play clothes," he said.

The clothes Abraham gave me were certainly less suffocating than the outfit I just removed, but still way too much to wear on a beautiful summer day. But I did my best as I dressed in sturdy woolen pants, and a cloth shirt. I figured that I would eventually get used to these city costumes.

I soon found my way to the waterfront on the North River, only a few minutes' walk from the Levy's home. There was a shady place to linger under a large tree, where the water lapped upon small stones. To the south was the harbor, where the sailing ships docked. Upriver was the direction of my former life, Mother and the native peoples I left behind.

The stones along the shore were smooth, flat, and small enough for skipping across the still river. I leaned sideways into my throw, so the flat part of the stone skimmed the surface. My best attempt skipped five times before sinking into the murky river.

"Nice toss," a voice said from behind me.

I turned around and saw a boy about my age with a skinny dog.

"Hello. What kind of dog do you have?" I asked.

"He is a greyhound. His name is Hank," said the boy.

"Are you English?" I asked, bending down to pet Hank.

"I guess my accent gave me away," he said, with a warm chuckle.

"It's kind of obvious," I agreed.

"My name is Alan. My dad is an officer in the Army. He leads a Ranger Brigade."

"I am Lukas," I said, extending my hand.

We shook hands as Hank took off barking, chasing after a gaggle of geese.

"Hank," Alan yelled, and ran after his dog.

Chapter 4

On the Sunday morning after Shabbos, I couldn't stop looking at myself in the mirror. My outfit for my first day of work was elaborate, and took a while for me to absorb. I hated to admit it, but I looked good. The white shirt was as smooth as the surface of a still pond. Abraham told me it was because he did something he called *pressing* it.

I especially liked the burgundy coat. It started wide at the shoulders and tapered in at the waist, before flaring out with its tails, almost like a turkey. Tucked into the shirt at the collar was a matching burgundy-colored cravat. That's what Abraham called it. I never heard this word before, in any language.

Asser was waiting for me as I stepped through the front door. He greeted me with a tip of his beaver pelt hat, and I returned the greeting with mine.

Just before I stepped off onto the street, and into the waiting wagon, Miriam appeared and called out, "One second, Lukas, let me take a look at you."

I turned for her assessment, and she said, "You look perfect," and gave me a kiss on my cheek.

"Come now, Miriam, leave the boy alone. We have work to do," insisted Asser.

On the short ride to the office, Asser asked me where I had walked to the day before. "You were gone for hours. I want you to know that I was not worried about you, but Miriam was."

I laughed to myself, wondering what Miriam would think about the last few years of my life crisscrossing the wilderness, and living among natives.

"There's no need to worry, Asser. I spent the day with a new friend I made down by the waterfront. His name is Alan. His father is an English army officer in charge of a Ranger Brigade."

"That must be Captain Lovewell's son. Excellent choice for a friend."

"Captain John Lovewell?" I stammered.

"Yes, the same. Well done, Lukas, you must encourage this friendship with his son. This could lead to many lucrative opportunities," he said, patting me on my back.

My first day certainly didn't need this distraction. What would happen if the captain and I casually ran into each other? Asser knew nothing about my volatile relationship with Captain Lovewell, and I'm sure he wouldn't be pleased if I caused a disruption to his business relationship with the English.

But avoiding the captain would be challenging, since Asser was introducing me about town. He seemed to know everyone in the city.

What I learned about Asser was that besides the slaughterhouse, and a butcher shop he owned, he was also an Attorney at Law, which meant he dealt with many of the legal issues himself that his enterprises encountered.

While he had no official place of business, like an office, he shuttled about from meeting to meeting, with me trying to keep up.

Asser told me that he liked to finish his workday early on Fridays, so he had time to enjoy the summer weather before sundown, and the beginning of Shabbat. I asked Asser and

Miriam if I could spend the afternoon exploring. Asser agreed, but said I should not go north of the wall on Wall Street.

"The English are discussing taking the wall down that separates the city from the wilderness. There are plans to expand the city north. But right now, I cannot say if it is safe."

"It is undoubtedly not safe, Asser. There are savages living up there," Miriam said, expressing fear in her eyes.

Asser nodded, and said, "She's right. Best to stay within the city limits. There are many places you can explore south of the wall, Lukas."

I felt my face grow hot as my blood boiled at their ignorance. I knew this would not be the only time I heard the natives referred to as savages, but I also knew I would never get used to it.

After my first week with Asser, I had seen the entire city. We visited the docks, and I saw the small sailboats that transported people up and down the North River, as well as the enormous sailing ships that traversed the great ocean to Europe and back.

The English controlled the city, but their presence was not obvious, except for one of their warships docked in the harbor, and the sailors milling about. With Asser offering his loyalty to the Crown since the takeover, we had no issues or restrictions coming or going anywhere in the city.

But the wall was something that interested me. It looked similar to one that would surround an English fort, except this one ran straight across the island, from shore to shore. A series of watchtowers were spaced across the expanse, with English army sentries standing post.

I walked along the wall and came to the main gate, which was open. To my surprise there was quite a lot of activity coming and going. The impression I had gotten from

Asser was that the hazards lurking beyond the wall were so dangerous that no one should dare go beyond it.

Through the open gates I saw two natives guiding in their wagons. I expected them to be stopped and questioned, but they continued on their way through the gates without anyone checking or verifying. So I casually did the same, and walked out through the open gates and beyond the wall.

I followed the narrow road as it wound its way through a hilly terrain. The world beyond the wall was mostly untouched, and probably untamed, but I would hardly call it dangerous.

I walked for a while, but with sunset only a few hours away, I couldn't spend much time exploring. But instead of returning on the same pathway, I cut into the brush, and made my way through the forest. I came across a stream that meandered in the same direction I was heading, so I followed it.

It was wise to be cautious. No doubt there were natives on the island, and I was curious to find them. I wondered if my months away from life in the wilderness had left me out of practice in moving without detection. I looked down at my stiff woolen pants, and clumsy shoes, and shook my head. My clothing was not at all suitable for the task.

I stayed low in the stream and moved swiftly. I balanced upon the stones scattered across its surface. To my surprise, I heard voices. There was a gathering up ahead. The smells of smoke, sage and sweetgrass were stimulating. As I approached, the voices came into focus. This was an Algonquin speaking tribe. There was talk of the crops in the fields, and laughter of children playing. My heart beat loudly. Suddenly I was worried about being discovered. I dared not move forward.

I stepped away from the stream, and toward an outcropping of rocks. I scaled to its peak, so I could see the assembly. It was indeed a native camp. Longhouses were scattered between the stream and the tree line. My pulse quickened. But not from fear, it was from a yearning.

With the sun approaching the horizon, I realized I had little time. Shabbat would begin soon, and I needed to be back before sunset. I scurried down the rocks and found the pathway leading south back to the front gates.

Time was running short, but the gates were in sight. Getting closer I saw they were already shut tight. There were no guards on this side of the wall. I looked up to the sentries but I couldn't see from this close of an angle, and I did not want to bring attention to myself, and get caught on the wrong side of the wall.

I ran toward the setting sun over the North River. It was an unobstructed path alongside the wall. Upon reaching the shore, I saw that the wall continued beyond and into the river. With the sun dipping into the horizon I dove in and swam a few body lengths around the wall.

Upon the shoreline, on the south side of the wall, I stumbled upon the sandy beach. I tore off my waterlogged shoes and ran barefoot back home. I felt the warmth of the sun on my back, giving me hope that I still could make it home in time.

I jumped onto the front portico, gripped the wrought iron doorknob, and pushed my way in. Asser, Miriam, Abraham and Alice were standing in the foyer side-by-side staring at me, with looks of bewilderment upon their faces.

"I made it," I announced with a smile, as I pushed a strand of wet clinging hair off my eyes, with a growing puddle of the North River forming beneath me.

Chapter 5

fter the morning prayers were completed, Asser took me for a walk down to the docks. The activity was greater than usual. A sailing ship was docked, unloading its cargo. As we got closer, I saw dozens of Negro men in chains, being led down the gangplank.

"Who are those men?" I asked Asser.

"New arrivals from Charles Towne. They will be taken to the slave market, and sold to the highest bidder," Asser said.

"Slave market?"

"Lukas, those men are slaves. Just like Abraham and Alice. Nearly half of the homes in the city have slaves."

"Abraham and Alice are slaves?" I asked, shocked.

"Of course. I bought them at the slave market a year ago. They're brother and sister. I took both of them, so they would have each other," Asser said, trying to sound benevolent.

"This is wrong, Asser. How can you own another person?"

"I provide a good life for Abraham and Alice. They live in a beautiful home, never go hungry, and I have a tutor who comes to teach them how to read and write, and do basic mathematics," Asser said.

"But that is not the point. Are not all people created as free beings by the Great Spirit?"

"Perhaps that is true. But this is the world we live in. Only the strong survive." Then he cleverly shifted the conversation away from what he found uncomfortable. "Which brings me to your excursion yesterday. "You took a risk going past the wall, as well as disobeying me," Asser said, reclaiming his moral authority.

"I've taken greater risks," I said, challenging him.

"Have you?" he asked, raising an eyebrow.

"There is much you do not know about me."

"Lukas, let's not argue. You're young, passionate, and I appreciate your idealism. But the world we live in is not perfect. We make do with what we have. How do you think I have built my businesses? When the English took control, I pledged allegiance to the Crown. I have no loyalty to the Dutch, English or anyone, except our family, and of course Hashem."

While we walked back in silence, I focused my eyes straight ahead, refusing to look at Asser. Eventually, my temper cooled enough to ask, "Can you tell me which tribe is living north of the wall?"

"They call themselves Lenape. Before the Dutch came, they lived on the island in great numbers. They named the island Mannahatta, meaning *the land of many hills*."

"I know what it means," I said.

Asser ignored my smugness and continued, "Now with the English making plans to expand the city North, it is only a matter of time before they will be forced off the island completely."

"I suppose you're all right with this?"

"I have no opinion. It falls under the laws of nature. Some species thrive, and some wither," he said with a smirk.

"Are we all not the same species?"

"Now you're asking the right question, Lukas," he said, pausing for its effect to linger.

"Let me answer that by asking you a question first. Do you think that the Almighty created the Native, or even the Negro in his image?"

"I believe that the Great Spirit created all of his creatures in his image."

"That is where you are wrong, Lukas. We are not created equal. This you will learn in time."

I just stood there with my mouth open.

Asser took a step closer until we were only inches apart, and stared into my eyes. He put his hands on my shoulders and gripped me tightly.

"I admire your integrity, and I can't fault you for your beliefs. But in my experiences, I have witnessed all types of men, and what I've concluded is that we are not all equal. Some are strong, and some weak. Why is that?"

Asser looked away for a moment, then bore his eyes deep into mine, and said, "It comes down to the basics of learning what it takes to survive. How do you think I, being a Jew, was able to achieve what I have accomplished in my life?"

He paused, waiting for a response that I was unwilling to give.

"It is because we are not all equal. I am not equal to that man begging for a morsel of food, living under the docks with the rats, and neither are you, Lukas," Asser said, releasing my shoulders.

Asser turned away from me and walked down the cobblestone street toward home, leaving me standing there, speechless.

Chapter 6

After dinner, I excused myself and headed to the river. I needed to figure my life out after hearing Asser's perspective about the hierarchy of man. My first impulse was to run away. *But if I did flee, where would I go?* The Sokokis Chief had banished me for betraying his order not to rescue Sofie, and I refused to go back to the Pequawkets, and live with the humiliation of seeing Rowtag and Nadie together. I was sure she had given birth by now.

I picked up a handful of stones and skimmed them across the river.

I've never avoided challenging situations before, why would I consider it now? Perhaps the Great Spirit has put me here to fight for the oppressed. My skills are with weapons for the hunt. But what if I can learn from Asser how to battle his way? Perhaps he can teach me how to change the opinions of those in power. He has had some success defending the rights of Jews in the city. Why can't I do the same for the natives? Can I learn to resolve conflicts by changing minds through non-violent, effective persuasion?

Skipping stone after stone into the North River and deep in thought, I didn't see Alan walking toward me.

"Lukas, I thought I would find you here," he shouted.

I looked up, and saw Alan approaching with a warm smile. This was the first time I had seen him since I learned that Captain Lovewell was his father. I felt my face flush in anger, but I decided, for now, not to express it to Alan. *Perhaps I can learn something useful from him*, I thought.

"Hi, Alan. I like coming here. It gives me time to think."

"What are you thinking about?" he asked.

"Alan, how do you feel about the native people? Do you think it's right that they are being forced from their homes where they have lived for generations?"

"I don't know if I ever thought about it," he said.

"Do you think the white man sailed across the ocean, and just found this uninhabited island, and decided to make a city?"

Alan looked at me and shrugged.

Shaking my head, I continued.

"You see that wall?" I asked, pointing to the section running past the shoreline and into the river.

He nodded.

"Have you ever considered why there was a wall separating the city from what's beyond that?"

"My father says it's where the city ends," he said with excitement for finally having an answer.

"That's where the city ends for now. There are natives living not far from the wall."

"How do you know?"

"I've been beyond the wall," I said, proudly.

"You have not. You're lying."

"Would you like to see for yourself?"

Alan looked around, and whispered, "Is it safe?"

"What are you afraid of?"

"My father tells me the natives are savages. If you're captured, first they carve the skin off your body with a knife, then they chop off your scalp with an ax, and burn you alive, while the entire tribe watches, and cheers," he said, wide eyed.

I was tempted to share my knowledge of who the real savage was—his father Captain Lovewell, but decided to hold my tongue. Perhaps I could recruit Alan in my efforts to change opinions. Imagining the son of Captain Lovewell arguing in favor of the natives, I smiled to myself.

"It seems you need an education. How about it?" I asked gesturing to the wall.

Alan stared at the tall barrier with a combination of fear and curiosity swirling within his blue eyes.

"Meet me here tomorrow morning before sunrise," I said patting him on his back, before I walked away.

Chapter 7

Alan was waiting for me at the appointed time. The still-moonlit sky reflected off the gentle laps of the river upon the shoreline.

We stepped into the river and swam around the wall. Emerging on the north side, I turned to Alan and placed a finger to my lips, indicating silence. The sun would soon illuminate the sky so we needed to move quickly from the wall and into the forest.

Alan clumsily followed. I figured he would not have my skills of undetectable movement, and his *heavy feet* could be a problem.

I whispered, "Step where I step, and stop touching every branch we pass."

I found the stream and crouched low, moving from stone to stone. Allan did well at keeping up and staying silent.

The smell of the smoldering morning flame was the first clue that we were approaching the camp. The cornfield provided cover for us when we emerged from the stream. The corn was still not tall enough to cover us, so we continued to crouch and move. Alan stayed close behind me, as we reached the clearing.

Pushing a few stalks aside, we saw the village. There were several longhouses laid out haphazardly on the open field. The tribe was active with its daily morning rituals. I glanced over to Alan, whose eyes were as wide as round river stones.

"Let's go," I whispered in his ear.

"Not quite yet," he insisted.

Several more minutes of gawking later, he was ready. But as we turned to make our retreat, we found ourselves looking up the shafts of six long spears, each held by a warrior gesturing for us to stand.

To my surprise, as well as the warriors, Alan took off in a full run through the cornfield. I shook my head at his stupidity.

A single warrior chased after him, and without breaking stride, loaded a sling and flung a stone that connected with Alan's skull. He stumbled to the ground, and the warrior was on him instantly. His hands were bound behind his back, and he was escorted to where I was being held. Blood from his wound trickled down his neck and back.

Alan looked at me, frightened, as we were ushered through the village, and into a longhouse.

"What are they going to do with us?" he asked.

"Calm down, and don't say anything," I told him.

This longhouse looked like the one where a Chief would reside. A ceremonial fire was burning at its center, and a raised platform sat just beyond it. But there was no Chief. We were instructed to sit.

Alan leaned in, and whispered, "Are they going to torture us?"

"I told you—don't say a word."

A commotion at the entrance alerted me to the arrival of the Chief. Leading the entourage was a young warrior who could have been the Chief's son, followed by the Shaman, and then the Chief.

They sat on blankets laid out on the platform and looked down upon Alan and me. The Chief wore a blue cloth sash wrapped across his chest, with a beaded necklace hanging from his neck. His forehead was marked with symbols.

"Who are you?" the Chief asked in English.

The Chief's use of English caused me to hesitate for a moment before answering him. He surprised me by not speaking his native language. I had been considering addressing him in Algonquin, as a way of showing our friendship. In that pause, however, I thought of my warrior training, weighed the risks, and decided to hold my tongue.

"My name is Lukas, and this is my friend Alan," I said calmly.

"Why are you spying on us?"

"I wanted to show Alan a native village. We live below the wall, and he was curious. We meant no harm," I said.

Suddenly Alan jumped to his feet, and shouted, "You need to release us. Do you have any idea who my father is?"

"Alan, sit down, and shut up!"

"My father is Captain Lovewell, and you don't want him coming after you."

The Chief looked at Alan, and said, "Captain Lovewell? Yes, we know the captain."

I shook my head, and smacked Alan on the back of his leg. "What have you done?"

The Chief, Shaman and his warrior son were whispering among themselves.

Alan looked at me. "You see, Lukas, they're afraid. Soon we will be let go," he said.

The Chief's son sneered at him, and shouted, "Take them to detention."

They bound our hands and dragged us out of the longhouse. Alan was screaming threats about what his father was going to do to them. Once outside the longhouse we were pushed along a series of pathways, crisscrossing in a multitude of directions. Finally we saw a small wigwam standing aside from the longhouses. We were shoved inside, and all I could see through the open flap were the legs of the warriors guarding us.

Shortly thereafter, a warrior poked his head in and instructed us to get up and come outside. Alan continued to fuss about his mistreatment, even after I warned him that they could shut him up, in an unpleasant way.

As predicted, we were gagged and blindfolded. My hands were bound tight behind my back. I was pushed and stumbled, but regained my footing. Fingers dug into my shoulders and steered me down a slope.

I heard Alan mumble, as he struggled to speak through his gag. My feet splashed into water. We were in the river. Hands guided me onto a seat in what I imagined to be a canoe. Moments later we were gliding across water.

The sounds of the oars slicing the water were audible alongside our captors' conversation.

"Where are we taking them?" a voice asked.

They didn't know that I understood their words.

"The Chief wants them removed from the island in case the Ranger captain comes looking for his son," another voice answered.

"So what do we do with them?"

"We paddle across the river to the other side. Once on shore, we crush their heads with a rock, and dump the bodies in the marshlands."

Careful not to bring attention to my awareness of our pending demise, I sat still. I needed to free my hands, but the ropes were tight around my wrists. But if I didn't escape, I was dead, and so was Alan.

If I could jump into the water, I might have a chance of dropping my arms low enough to lift my legs through my bound hands, so they would be in front of me. Then I could pull off the gag and blindfold.

"Alan, we need to jump. They are going to kill us. Jump now," I managed to say through the loosened gag, and then lifted myself and fell out of the swiftly moving canoe.

I briefly heard voices yelling before submerging into the North River. I spun my body and shot my legs through my bound arms. I ripped off the gag and blindfold, and with surprisingly little effort, I was able to loosen the knots with my teeth, and emerge for air. The warriors immediately spotted me, turned the canoe downstream, and began paddling hard in pursuit.

As the current pulled me along, I spotted Alan. He had also removed his bindings, but unlike me, he had reached the shoreline and was now moving into the tall grasses of the marshland. I needed to get myself to shore before I found myself in the middle of the harbor. But the warriors were able to paddle much more rapidly than I could swim, and within moments, they pulled me out of the river.

With enough distance between the warriors to ensure that they could not catch up to him on foot, Alan called after me, "We will come for you, Lukas. Don't worry. Father will rescue you." Then he turned and was gone.

Chapter 8

With Alan's escape, the only option the warriors had was to return me to the Lenape village, where to my disdain, I was thrown back into the prison. At least the ravenous mosquitoes were pleased with my return.

I was left until morning, when a sharp kick to my ribs woke me. Still without sharing my knowledge of their language, I was instructed with hand signals to follow the same two inhospitable warriors.

The Chief's longhouse was active with anxious faces of warriors scurrying about. Orders were barked out, and I understood that they were preparing for a confrontation, which I assumed could only mean a visit from the English Rangers.

Firm hands pushed me down to a seated position before the Chief's unoccupied ceremonial platform. Moments later the Chief appeared and asked where the captain's son was. The warriors answered that they did not know.

The Chief looked at me, clearly upset, and said, "You have become a problem."

"My humble apologies," I replied in Algonquin.

His worried expression shifted to bewilderment. "You speak our language?"

"I do, Chief, and I regret the anguish I have caused," I said, placing my hands over my heart.

"How do you know the language?"

"My mother taught me as a child, and I have lived with tribes in the North," I answered.

"I would like to learn more about your life, but we have a problem, thanks to you and your friend."

"No," I said, "this is a problem *you* caused. Please, for your own sake, release me before the Rangers advance. I am sure Alan has found his way back across the river by now, and is telling his father the tale of how you planned on murdering us and dumping our bodies in the marshlands. I can stop the Rangers from taking revenge on you."

"How can you stop them?" the Chief asked.

"By giving them something more valuable."

"And what would that be?" he asked, with a tilted head and a hint of sarcasm.

"The English will send Captain Lovewell with his Rangers to negotiate for your surrender. You can offer me in exchange."

"Why would they want you?"

"All you need to know is that the captain would give up his own mother to get his hands on me."

The Chief needed no more convincing. He barked out orders, and I was ushered to stand alongside the leadership on the open field, in front of the longhouses.

As I stood there, waiting for the confrontation, I thought about the consequences of surrendering to the captain. I expected no mercy from the man. But I was not afraid.

I looked at the Lenape tribe standing alongside me and felt proud that I could spare the lives of many of these fine people.

The village dogs barked wildly as the English appeared, marching on horseback across the cornfield. It was indeed Captain Lovewell leading over twenty Rangers. The warriors spread out in an attack position, surrounding them. It was precarious for both sides.

The Chief stood proudly alongside the Shaman and his son. I was concealed behind a line of warriors, but I could see the captain, and his officers, and I also saw Alan. He had led them here. *That little swine is just like his father*, I seethed.

Captain Lovewell approached alone on horseback. He showed no fear.

"I am John Lovewell, captain of Ranger Company," he said, gesturing to the snorting horses and anxious men behind him.

The Chief took a small step forward to announce, "My name is Chief Mehocksett of the Lenape nation. Why are you threatening us, when we offer you no harm?"

"You say you offer no harm. My son…" he twisted in his saddle to point at Alan seated on a horse behind him, "has told me about your abduction, and who knows what else would have happened to him if he hadn't escaped."

"Your son was caught spying on us," the Chief said.

"He tells me he was forcibly taken off the beach south of the wall, while walking his dog."

Why would Alan lie like that? Hank wasn't even with him when I brought him around the wall. I couldn't be still any longer, and stepped through the line of warriors concealing me.

"Hello, Captain," I announced, loud enough for all to hear.

He squinted his eyes at me.

"Ah, Lukas. I should have figured you would be behind this mess," he said.

"Alan and I are friends. He wasn't abducted as he says. We came past the wall together. He wanted to see the tribe up close. This is entirely my fault. Take me, and leave these people alone."

The captain didn't hesitate. He ordered two soldiers to grab me. I was bound at my wrists and leashed to a horse that jolted me forward. The entire tribe watched me as I ran to keep up with the trotting horse. It took all my energy to keep from tripping and being dragged along the rocky ground back through the city gates. What would Asser and Miriam think if they could see me now?

Chapter 9

T he English army had no choice but to use the Dutch prison facilities they inherited when they took over control of the city, until they could build their own. I was not complaining, because the Dutch treated prisoners more humanely than the English did. The window allowed fresh air, and a straw bed provided me some comfort.

Unfortunately, the English guards seemed compelled to compensate for my accommodations with physical brutality. They took pleasure in pummeling me with bare fists, and sharp boots. So the soft bed and gentle breeze did little to relieve the pain from dozens of bruises they inflicted upon me.

A jangle of keys drew my attention to the cell door. It took a moment to clear my foggy head and focus on who my visitor was. I saw one of the guards, whose fists I came to know intimately, fumble with the keys. Waiting behind him was a man dressed in the black gown of a barrister.

"Get to your feet," the guard ordered.

Sharp pain washed over me as I sat up, and then slowly stood.

"Lukas, my boy, are you all right?"

I recognized the voice before I saw his face. It was Asser.

"Hello, sir. It looks like I got myself in a bit of trouble," I said.

Asser ordered the guard to leave us alone. He gave Asser a disrespectful shrug and locked us both in the cell.

Asser and I sat down on my bed. I told him the story, and how sorry I was that he was now involved.

"Lucky for you, Lukas, the fact that I am an Attorney at Law means I can represent you. I have already spoken with the captain. He is adamant about prosecuting you for illegally crossing the wall."

"That is a crime?" I asked.

"It's a minor offense, Lukas, but apparently he has some unfinished business with you. He mentioned something about leading his Rangers into an ambush with the Sokokis tribe," he said with raised eyebrows.

"I actually prevented an ambush."

"That may be, but the captain has convinced the Governor to try you for murder."

"Murder?"

"For fifteen of the King's soldiers killed by the Sokokis," he said.

"I stopped a massacre."

"That will be for the Governor to decide," Asser said.

"What do I need to do?"

"Listen to me, and do everything I say. I'll do my best to defend you. But I'm afraid that only a miracle will keep you from hanging. You have been a thorn in the captain's ass," Asser said.

"I suppose I have. But deservedly so," I said. "Asser, Captain Lovewell is the one who murdered Father."

Asser ran his hands through his hair. "Are you sure?"

"Of course I'm sure. I was there," I answered.

"You told me you have no memory of what happened, except for what you wrote in your journal."

I nodded that this was true. "But why would I write it if it didn't happen?"

"I don't know, but you cannot convict someone of murder without proof."

"But you can see why the captain and I have a troubled past."

"Indeed I do," Asser said.

I stood up and went over to the barred window. Gazing out, I asked, "What will happen to me now?"

From behind me Asser said, "The captain has used his influence to get the Honorable Mattias Nicoll to preside over the trial. Judge Nicoll is a former Mayor and is now one of the two judges of the highest court in the city. He will not be sympathetic to a boy with a Dutch mother and a Jewish father, who has sided with the natives."

"So what's the point of a trial?"

"Exactly what I was thinking," he answered, coming to stand beside me.

"What do we do then?"

"I've made other arrangements."

"What does that mean?" I asked, turning to look into his eyes.

"I have paid off the captain to drop all charges," he said with a smirk.

"How much is a Dutch-Jew worth?" I asked.

"Five-hundred Pounds Sterling."

My mouth hung open for a moment before I said, "You have that much money?"

"It's a stretch. But if we don't come up with the money, you will be hanged."

"But why would you do this for me?" I asked, holding up my hands.

"I have my reasons, and I will tell you. But in order to get you released the captain is insisting on a condition to the arrangement."

"Which is?"

"You must travel with me to Amsterdam on the next ship, and you are never allowed to return. If you do, you will be arrested, and no doubt executed."

I shrugged and said, "I suppose I don't have much of a choice."

Asser nodded and placed his hand on my shoulder to comfort me.

"I accept the offer," I said, and stood up and walked over to the barred window. Looking out upon the busy street, I said, "It's time to see the world."

Miriam was waiting for me when Asser and I arrived home. She wrapped her arms around me and hugged me tight against her soft body. When she finally released me, I saw tears flowing down her pink cheeks.

"Thank God you're safe," she managed to say, between the sobs.

Asser stepped in between us, and said, "Come, Lukas, let's go sit in the parlor. We need to talk."

I followed Asser and Miriam into the parlor. Abraham and Alice were already in the luxurious room, standing by the carved wood-framed sofas. Abraham offered me the tall chair that Asser usually claimed. I glanced over to Asser to make sure he was all right with me taking his seat, and he nodded his approval.

Miriam and Asser sat side-by-side on the sofa. Asser took hold of Miriam's hand and offered a slight smile before he began.

"You asked me why we paid a ransom to have you freed. We have good reason. When we met in Albany I told you that your father and I were friends, and that was why I asked you to come live with us. This is true. We were best friends since childhood. What I didn't tell you was that Solomon and Sara Pietersen are not your parents. We are."

The words hung there for a moment, sending my mind into a whirlwind of confusion. My journal made no mention of Asser being anything more than a friend of Father's.

"I don't understand. How can this be?"

"Around the time you were born, I was arrested for exporting beaver pelts to Amsterdam without a proper license from the Dutch West India Company. My sentence was for five years in prison, back in the Netherlands. We couldn't afford to keep a home here while I was imprisoned, so Miriam needed to come with me. But we didn't think it was safe for a newborn to sail across the ocean, so we asked Solomon and Sara to take care of you while we were gone.

"After I served my sentence, we returned to New Amsterdam, and I traveled to Beverwyck to retrieve you. You were such a happy boy. You called Solomon and Sara Papa and Mama. I couldn't take you from them. They loved you so much they didn't want to give you up. So I left you there." He paused, and looked at Miriam who was now standing by the window.

"When Asser returned without you, I was so upset that I didn't speak with him for weeks. But in time he convinced me that what was most important was your happiness," Miriam said.

"The next year your brother David was born, and Miriam's heart was full again," Asser said.

"Until he was shot by an English soldier," Miriam added and leaned in to whisper, "And the man who killed him was never even punished. My poor boy."

Asser walked over to Miriam, put his arm around her, gave her a squeeze, and said, "That was a long time ago, darling."

"So, you are my parents," I said aloud for the first time, trying to make sense of what I was being told.

Miriam and Asser both nodded.

I suppose if I had any memory of my life before taking the Moon Flower I would have had more of an emotional response. But as it was, all I could say was, "Thank you for telling me."

Book 4

Chapter 1

My farewell with Miriam, or perhaps I should say Mother, felt emotionally one-sided. I had never seen someone so affected and physically distraught. Her sobs evolved into total-body heaving so violent, I was afraid that she could hurt herself by the sudden jerks her histrionic breathing caused.

Asser explained to Miriam, as well as to Abraham and Alice who both had tears running down their cheeks, "One should never say never. Lukas may return one day. Stranger things have happened."

I stood woodenly, looking on but feeling nothing. While Asser and Miriam had quickly settled into the role of loving parents, I had nothing to draw upon that allowed me to reciprocate. Even if my memory did return, what use would it be, since I had been given to Solomon and Sara as an infant?

Waiting for us in front of the house were two English rangers on horseback who were there to make sure that I boarded the sailing ship, bound for Amsterdam. Our wagon was loaded with our trunks and supplies. Asser, Abraham, and I squeezed onto a bench meant for two people. With Abraham at the bridle, and the Rangers leading the way, we headed off for the docks.

Asser had arranged transport on the Dutch warship called the *Golden Lion*. When I asked why a warship, and not a passenger ship for our voyage, he explained that the seas had become dangerous because the English Navy was challenging the Dutch Navy for dominance.

"There is also the possibility of being robbed by pirates. Some ships don't even make it far off the coast before being attacked by an assortment of thieves," he told me with a bit of excitement in his tone. "That is why we are sailing to Amsterdam on the largest warship ever built."

"Why would the English allow a Dutch warship in the harbor?" I asked.

"It's part of the treaty they signed when the Dutch relinquished control of the city. They have docking privileges for trading purposes."

I had seen many sailing ships dock at the harbor, but I had never seen a warship. As we turned the last corner, a section of it was visible in between the dwarfed buildings. Moments later with the city behind us, I saw all of the mighty vessel, and nothing could have prepared me for such a grand vision.

The rising sun cast a soft orange light upon the oil rubbed wood planks making up its port side. A multitude of ropes, as thick as a man's wrist, swept across from mast to mast, towering far into the blue sky. Small boats were busy moving supplies to the ship from the dock, which now did not look so vast with the *Golden Lion* taking up much of the harbor.

A command was shouted from somewhere on the ship, and its hatch doors swung open. There were row upon row, three stories high, of cannon muzzles pushed forward and projecting from its formally hidden chambers. Each cannon reflected the morning sun and sparkled brilliantly. I counted over forty cannons and imagined there were another forty on the starboard side.

"Are they going to fire at us?" I asked Asser.

Asser laughed, and said, "No, son, they are just going through their drills before we cast off."

"Oh that's good," I said, flushed with my embarrassing question.

"Are you ready for an adventure?" he asked.

"I am," I answered.

Chapter 2

After a chilly farewell to the English soldiers, and a heartfelt one from Abraham, I saw the rowboat we would be taking from the docks, to cross the harbor in order to board the *Golden Lion*. With our trunks lowered into the belly of our tiny vessel, Asser and I boarded. A man with tattooed arms gripped the oars and pulled hard, allowing us to float away from the docks.

With every stroke we glided closer. The scale of the ship silhouetted against the buildings had been impressive enough, but the view from the water accentuated how small and relatively insignificant we were. The cannons had now been withdrawn and the hatch doors closed. It was unfathomable to imagine that this sailing ship was made by the hands of men.

"We board starboard," informed our rower.

"That's the other side of the ship. We will go around the ship's stern, which is its back," Asser said.

I told Asser that I wanted to learn everything about the ship while we sailed to Amsterdam.

"There will be plenty of time," he said, and reminded me that it could take three months, depending on the weather and other factors.

In order to observe the complete splendor of the stern of the Golden Lion I needed to tilt my head back, as if I were looking up into the sky. Starting at the bottom there were seven carved figures of women spaced evenly apart at the widest part of the bow. One of the women had a face with chiseled cheekbones that reminded me of the Shaman from the Sokokis tribe. Perhaps she and her finely carved sisters represented the ship's wisdom, just as the Shaman represented the tribe's.

The next level up, and nearly twice as tall, were wood sculptures of five armed Dutch soldiers, warning enemies of the ship's brave warriors.

The crowning glory was the Golden Lion himself. The figure was as large as the two sections below. A thick mane flowed, as if it was a royal crown. The Golden Lion was standing on its hind legs with its tremendous paws and claws extended out, fighting off a devilish-looking creature.

I imagined there was much to learn about the significance of these Dutch symbols. Perhaps someone onboard this grand vessel would be able to enlighten me.

With the stern now out of view we docked along the starboard side. A large hatch was propped open just above water level, allowing us to easily board.

A sailor instructed us in Dutch to follow him through the bowels of the ship. It took us a while to climb the narrow ladders, as we ascended its many levels. Eventually, wide staircases that looked like they belonged in a home like Asser's took over while we ascended all the way up to the poop deck, the highest deck of the ship, which towered far higher than any building on the island. As we paused to take in the view, I saw the wall at Wall Street, and the forest and rolling hills beyond it. There was a thin plume of white smoke twisting and rising into the sky, marking the site of the Lenape Nation, that got me into this trouble.

This reminded me that I needed to show Asser some gratitude. After all, he paid a fortune to get me released or I would have surely found my neck in the hangman's noose. I imagined that the voyage ahead would afford me ample opportunities to voice my appreciation.

As I looked down to the tiny figures of people scurrying around the docks, I wondered if I would ever step foot on this land again. My sentence clearly stated that I was never to return to New York. But I wondered who would pay any attention to someone of little importance like me, except, of course, Captain Lovewell.

A crack of an unfamiliar sound overtook the calling of the birds circling around the towering wood masts. The canvas sails were being raised into place. Sailors pulled the thick ropes so fast their arms appeared to be a blur of motion. Up above, there were more sailors clinging to the ropes like spiders to webs, guiding the giant sails into place. There was another crack of sound and the sweeping winds engaged the sails. We were moving.

Chapter 3

With the benefit of a rising tide and favorable winds, we left New York Harbor on time, and sailed eastward.

Asser had worked out an arrangement with the Dutch West India Company to provide us with a stateroom usually reserved for high-ranking naval officers. As we unpacked our trunks and sorted our clothes in the spacious wood cabinets, Asser told me that we had been invited to dine with the captain tonight. It was a good thing Asser had insisted he buy me an outfit suitable for such an occasion.

A short distance from our stateroom was the Officer's Dining Hall. A well-appointed officer in a crisp white uniform greeted us as we entered. "Welcome, gentlemen, I am Lieutenant Marc Overmars. We are pleased to have you as our guests this evening. Allow me to introduce you to our captain."

"I already know the captain. We have been friends for years. But my son Lukas has never had the pleasure," Asser said.

The first thing I noticed about Captain Thomas Tobijas was his sculpted red mustache, and crop of bushy hair on his chin. His hair, also red, was long and fell softly upon his shoulders.

"Asser, it is so good to see you again. I hear your son got into a bit of trouble with Captain Lovewell. This must be your boy," the captain said, taking a good look at me.

"Hello, sir," I said, unsure whether to shake hands or salute.

The captain ended my confusion by reaching out his right hand. "Only officers and enlisted men salute, Lukas. It's nice to meet you."

"It's an honor to meet the captain of this magnificent ship," I said.

"I understand from the report I read about your case that you have had some interesting experiences living with the natives."

"I have indeed, Captain."

"Perhaps you can share your stories once we are out to sea and I have some time to spend away from the bridge."

"I would be honored, sir."

Dinner was followed by discussion in an adjacent room called the Smoking Lounge. The captain took a puff of his cigar and exhaled a long stream of smoke that danced and bounced about. He said the tobacco was called Sweet-scented and was grown in a place called Virginia.

He offered me a cigar as well and instructed me to "puff on it gently."

The smoke had a pleasurable effect on my lungs. The captain smiled as I partook, then added, "You must try French wine as well," and filled several glasses from a carafe of deep red liquid, that he told us came from grapes in a region of France called Bordeaux.

I had never tasted wine, though I had seen it served at Asser's home. Its taste reminded me of the root teas brewed in the Pequawkets longhouse, except with a more delightful flavor. The effect of the cigar, along with the wine, made me want to climb the tallest mast and gaze out upon the vast ocean.

"This is the joy of living," announced the captain, with his Virginia Sweet-scented cigar in one hand, and a goblet of French Bordeaux wine in the other.

"Indeed it is, Captain," Asser replied.

"You are an interesting boy, Lukas. Please tell me about your life before you reunited with Asser," said the captain.

The Captain seemed to have forgotten his earlier request that I tell him my story once we were well out to sea. Maybe the wine was having an effect upon him as well?

I shared my tale, well into the night, to a riveted audience, and probably could have finished sooner, but the Captain felt inclined to ask many questions. He was especially fascinated learning about Ranger Captain Lovewell.

"It's a remarkable thread that this English Ranger has sewn through your life," the captain said.

"That's true. I hope this is the end of it," I said.

"I don't know, Lukas. I have a feeling you have not seen the last of him," the captain said, blowing a ring of cigar smoke across the room.

Once back in our cabin Asser was sleeping within minutes. I lay for a while but couldn't sleep, so I stepped outside onto the deck, to observe the evening sky.

The twinkling stars surrounded and covered me as if I was floating among them. The brightest ones felt within my reach, while the distant stars were barely a flicker. *I have been on mountaintops, and experienced the vast openness of the heavens, but nothing has been like what I am witnessing now.*

Solomon, Jakob, and Asser had no doubt experienced the same sense of wonderment on their voyage across this same vast ocean many years earlier, dreaming of their new lives, just as I was dreaming now.

Chapter 4

Officers barking orders stirred me from my sleep. Asser just moaned and turned his body and continued his raspy snore. I quickly dressed and made my way from our quarters down to the main deck, where the men assembled for pre-dawn exercises.

The captain allowed me to observe, as long as I didn't get into anyone's way. Sunlight slowly brightened the eastern sky. Large sea birds were attracted to the briskly moving vessel and acted as escorts while we sliced through the black waters.

Today's drill would include test firing all eighty-two cannons. I hurried to wake Asser, who was already dressed and eating breakfast. "We are not to go any further this morning than the poop deck," he told me, sipping a cup of tea.

I quickly ate a sticky bowl of porridge, and guzzled a lukewarm pot of tea, then rushed out to the deck above our stateroom. Men were already perched as lookouts high above on small landings called crow's nests, that were attached to the masts. Sailors armed with sabers and muskets staged themselves strategically on the maindeck and quarterdeck. They did drills on how to defend the *Golden Lion*, and how to board an enemy vessel.

The sound of the gun port hatches clapped hard against the ship's hull as they swung open. I ran to the railing on the poop deck and looked over the side. I saw three rows of the cannon muzzles poking out past the ship's hull.

Commands were shouted, and the first row of cannons fired. The *Golden Lion* shook so hard I was surprised it didn't shatter into splinters from the vibrations. The men on the crow's nests wrapped their arms around the masts and held on for dear life. Then the second round fired, and finally the third. Far off into the distance, cannon balls soared great distances before splashing harmlessly into the sea.

Not all days were as exciting as the training exercises with the cannons. Typically, Asser and I had nothing to do except entertain each other. One day with calm seas and a pleasant breeze moving the *Golden Lion* along at a nice pace, we had a conversation about the history of the Jews in Poland.

"You know, Lukas, our family can trace its history back over one hundred and seventy years. That's seven generations."

What an unusual coincidence, I thought. In my journal, I had written that Chief Nicholas of the Turtle Clan once told me that the journey of seeking the truth was not limited to this lifetime, but encompassed learning from the seven generations from our past, and in turn leaving a legacy for the seven generations yet to come.

Asser told me that in the early to mid-sixteenth century, Poland was considered the hub of the Jewish world. It began in 1492 when the Jews were expelled from Spain. Even though he spoke of a time long ago, his voice trembled, and he paused several times to compose himself.

"Our country became the cultural and spiritual center for our people. Some scholars say that at its peak nearly three quarters of all Jews in the world lived in Poland. But sadly, it is not this way any longer," he said, wiping away a single tear that ran down his cheek.

Most days it was just Asser and me finding things to occupy ourselves with. We teamed up to play a fun and competitive game of sliding a round, flat stone along the deck, and have it stop within designated boxes, that earned various points. We played against other members of the crew and won a few matches.

Other times we played a new English card game called All Fours. The name referred to the goal of the game, which was to win four games by accumulating the most points.

One afternoon as we were taking a walk along the deck, Asser asked me, "Would you consider calling me Father?"

I stopped walking and leaned against the railing, and thought for a moment before answering, "I suppose this is possible. But please give me some time. After all, you just told me about this a few weeks ago."

He said he understood, and that I shouldn't feel pressured.

"Whenever you're ready," he said.

Asser advised me that we should dress in our business attire upon our arrival at the Port of Amsterdam. I asked if the dinner clothes I wore the other evening were suitable.

"Not to worry, son. I have another surprise for you."

Asser opened the cabinet doors and pulled out a package wrapped neatly and secured with twine. He cut the binding with a pocketknife, and carefully laid out a black jacket, white shirt, and black breeches.

"This is for you, Lukas," he said, sweeping his hand across the bed, where the elegant clothes were set out.

Quickly I removed the clothes I had worn for the entire three months at sea, and dressed in my new elegant costume. Standing before the mirror with Asser looking on, I couldn't resist the urge to smile.

"You look excellent, son," Asser said.

I had to admit that I did. The coat was magnificent. Large wood buttons slipped into embroidered slits, allowing the coat to taper to my narrow torso. Then it flared out below my waist as the tails traveled all the way down to my calves. At my wrists were contrasting white ruffles that matched the cravat neckpiece.

I laughed to myself, thinking not too long ago I was wearing a loincloth in the summer, and hunting for bison furs to warm me for winter. Now I was dressed as a gentleman, and I had to admit to myself, that I didn't mind it a bit.

"Thank you, Asser," I said warmly. "You have shown me things I never imagined existed. I owe you my gratitude," I said placing my hand on my heart.

"Hold on, there's one more thing," he said turning back to the cabinet. "A Dutch gentleman would not be seen without this."

Asser handed me a black felt hat made from beaver pelts. It was soft to the touch and as I ran my fingers across it, a strange emotion overtook me. A brief image of beaver pelts piled high on a wagon flashed into my mind. It disappeared just as quickly.

"Are you all right? You look pale," Asser asked, seeing my momentary discomfort.

"I'm fine," I said, regaining my composure.

"What are you waiting for? Try it on."

I carefully placed the hat on my head. It fit perfectly. Looking at my reflection, I barely recognized myself.

"Come now, I have something else you need to see."

I followed Asser from our cabin and climbed the stairs onto the poop deck. As I reached the top step, I saw hundreds of sailboats and ships in a harbor that nearly wrapped all around the anchored *Golden Lion*. The docks were full of people, wagons and horses moving in all directions. There were all sorts of buildings of various heights, all of them side by side, without a bit of space in between. What was most striking was the array of brilliant colors each home displayed, as they encircled the harbor.

"Welcome to Amsterdam, son," announced Asser.

Chapter 5

Asser and I said our farewells to Captain Tobijas and his officers. I thanked them for their warm hospitality. I thought this would be the last time I would ever see them, but apparently Asser had business relations with the captain, and a few of his officers.

"How long before you sail again?" Asser asked.

"Not for a month," the captain answered.

"That's plenty of time. Come by my office when you get settled. We can discuss the details of that home you're interested in on the Amstel," Asser offered.

"Thank you, Asser. I'll try to see you in a few days," the captain said, and turned to me. "It was very nice meeting you, Lukas. I see great things in your future, which doesn't surprise me with Asser as your father."

I thanked the captain, and for the first time thought about what Asser could actually teach me. After all, I had learned from wise Chiefs and sacred Shamans, why couldn't I also learn valuable lessons from my own father? He had proven himself successful on two continents, in a world that put him at a disadvantage because of his religion.

Small rowboats shuttled officers, sailors and Asser and me from the *Golden Lion* to the docks. Sitting facing the shoreline, I twisted to take a farewell glance at the ship that had delivered us safely across the vast ocean.

Waiting on the dock were scruffy looking boys who gave me looks as if they wanted to accuse me of some sort of undeserving privilege. A craggy old man barked orders to his unruly bunch. "Let's get the trunks, boys, and load them onto Mr. Levy's wagon."

Amsterdam was nothing like New York. First thing I noticed, was it was not new at all. The buildings not only looked as if they had been there for generations, they were also tucked tightly next to each other, taking up every available piece of valuable land. But the most significant difference was that each street crisscrossing through the city was also adjoined with a waterway they called a canal. Traversing these canals were small rowboats, each carrying items to be delivered somewhere. I could make out such things as fruits, vegetables, flowers, furs, and an assortment of household wares.

"It's a beautiful city, do you not agree Lukas?" Asser asked, as we maneuvered the tight streets teeming with pedestrians, wagons and pushcarts, all filled with products for sale.

I nodded vigorously and said, "Do you still have a home here?"

"Indeed I do. It is right on the Herengracht Canal."

When we finally arrived in front of Asser's home, the canal was wider and the homes lining the streets were at least double the size of those we saw closer to the docks. Asser's home was built with red bricks with three stories of tall windows that I imagined offered magnificent views of the canal.

Waiting for us as we pulled up to the curb were two older Negro men. Asser introduced Cesar and George as the house staff. They shook my hand and called me Master Lukas. While they unloaded our trunks, Asser and I entered the house. Out of earshot, I asked Asser if these men were slaves like Abraham and Alice.

"They are," Asser said sternly, anticipating my disapproval.

I said nothing but thought, *If and when I have my way, this mistreatment of human beings as chattel will not continue.*

Chapter 6

On the voyage Asser and I had spoken about my future plans.

"You will attend the *Athenaeum Illustre* to study international trade. There you will learn from the best. I will then get you a position with the Dutch West India Company."

The thought of a career in international trade sounded like a good idea.

Asser offered me encouragement by telling me, "You already have a head start in business. After all, you learned the beaver pelt trading business as a child."

I smiled, and hoped that one day, if my memory did return, I would remember such lessons from my youth.

When I asked Asser if I could visit the university, he told me that classes were held at the homes of faculty instead of at a formal university.

"Isn't that unusual?" I asked.

"There's no need for a building. After all, frugality is the road to riches," said Asser with a smile.

I nodded, not sure he was being totally serious with me.

Classes began a few days after our arrival. We met each morning at the home of Professor de la Vega. Asser already told me that the professor was a Jew from a small Spanish city called Cordoba. His family immigrated to Amsterdam when he was a child. He became a successful merchant and wrote a popular new book, called *Confusion of Confusions,* about the history of stock market speculation.

He used his book to teach us the subject of finance. On the first day of class he taught us these four basic rules:

1)   *Do not offer advice for the purchase or sale of shares.*

2)   Predicting the future is a fool's game.

3)   *Do not hesitate to take profits or cut losses.*

4)   Good fortune never lasts, and bad luck usually gets worse.

5)   *Do not get caught up in the fad of the day.*

6)   Remember the tulips!

7)   *Do not expect quick riches.*

This is a game not just of money, but also of patience.

Knowledge of the stock market and economics in general were dull in comparison to Professor de la Court's course on international trade. In his class we learned the true source of the wealth being earned in Amsterdam: the transatlantic slave trade.

Professor de la Court presented this abomination in a way that made light of this crime against humanity. But it was obvious that the most valuable commodity among the various goods crisscrossing the ocean were Negro slaves from Africa.

A large map of the Atlantic Ocean was mounted on the wall in front of the classroom. Professor de la Court pointed his chubby finger to the channel dividing England from the continent.

"It begins here. Commodities such as guns, cloth, iron and beer are shipped to the Gold Coast," he said, sliding his finger down the map to the underside of the hump on the west coast of Africa.

"These goods provide the currency to trade for gold, ivory, spices and hardwoods that are shipped back to Europe. But the trade routes also include the transportation of Negros to islands across the ocean to a region of many islands called the Caribbean. From there they are sold, with a portion shipped to cities along the Atlantic Coast," he said, and paused to light the pipe resting on his desk.

"The Caribbean Islands trade their abundance of sugar, molasses and wood. Desirable commodities of rice, tobacco and indigo are shipped from Charles Towne, and whale oil, lumber and furs are transported from New York," the professor said.

Each time he mentioned New York, he expressed a visible snarl, which I assumed had to do with his poor opinion about the Dutch giving up New Amsterdam to the English, without a fight.

I spent six days each week going to classes with subjects covering finance, international trade, and accounting and real estate law. There was no time for anything else. My day off was Sunday, when I caught up on schoolwork from the previous week and studied for upcoming exams.

There were only twelve students in the Athenaeum Illustre. All were Dutch born except for me. A fact that didn't go unnoticed. The boys were also sons of rich men being groomed to step into their family businesses.

I could tell that my fellow students were wary of me. Besides the snickers I would hear behind my back, there were also overt insulting questions.

"Hey Lukas, are you really a savage?"

"Have you ever scalped any English soldiers?"

One of their favorites was, "What do you get when you mix a Jew with an Indian? You get Lukas the Redskin Jew."

Ultimately, they thought of me as a stranger from a strange land, too foreign for them to comprehend, which was ironic since they were studying international trade. So I kept to myself, and went home each evening as soon as classes concluded.

Chapter 7

Except for the occasional insults from my fellow students, the first few weeks of classes were mostly uneventful. This, however, was about to change.

One late afternoon, after a long day of classes, I found Cesar waiting for me at the front door. He said Asser and Professor de la Vega wanted to see me in the library. With no idea what this could be about, I thanked Cesar, and knocked on the heavy wood door.

"Come in, Lukas," shouted Asser.

I entered and saw Asser and the professor sitting in two chairs by an open window.

"Lukas, please join us," Asser said, pointing to an empty chair. "Of course, you know Professor de la Vega," Asser added, as I sat down.

"It's nice to see you sir," I said.

"Lukas, how are you enjoying your classes at the Athenaeum Illustre?" asked the professor.

I nodded and said, "I like them a great deal."

"Your father and I have been discussing an interesting opportunity that involves your participation. If you agree to it, we believe it can be a terrific start to your career in international trade."

I looked over to Asser who nodded approvingly.

"What is this opportunity?" I asked.

"There is a trade vessel traveling to the Gold Coast at the end of classes next month. I will be heading this voyage, and I need an assistant. Your father and I think this would offer you a chance for real world experience," he said, and waited for my response.

"You want me to sail with you to the African coast on a trade mission?"

"That's correct, Lukas. Are you interested? This is something that is not typically offered to my students."

"Why me?" I asked.

"Well, Lukas, I am impressed with your intellect and the poise you show in class. Plus with your diverse background that your father shared with me, you should make a fine assistant."

"May I ask why you are heading up a trade mission? I thought you were a professor."

"Excellent question, Lukas. Teaching bright and promising students like you is what I do part-time. I also provide my expertise to the Dutch West India Company. Occasionally, they send me on trade missions to negotiate deals."

"How long will we be gone?"

"No more than a month."

Before I could ask anything else, Asser cut in. "Oh, come on now, Lukas. Stop being difficult. Of course he wants to go. Isn't that right, Lukas?"

Although I still had questions, I had to admit that I was intrigued enough to consent. "When did you say we leave?" I asked.

"That's my boy," Asser said, leaning over to thump me on the back.

Chapter 8

The day after classes ended for the semester, Asser and I headed down to the docks. As we approached, we saw the professor waiting for us.

"This is very exciting," he said, as I reached for my trunk off the back of the wagon.

"Is this it?" I asked, looking at the ship, anchored out in the harbor. While I had no great expectations for the *Fluyt*, it did look well built, sleek and efficient.

I looked over and saw the professor assessing my reaction. "She may not be the most beautiful lady of the seas, like the magnificent *Golden Lion*, which I understand you and Asser had the pleasure to sail upon. The *Fluyt* is basically a cargo vessel, designed to transport twice as much goods and material as a warship. We construct these ships at half the cost of our rivals, which gives us major competitive advantages."

I nodded, and turned to say my farewell to Asser.

He placed two hands on my cheeks, and said, "This is quite an opportunity, Lukas."

"Thank you, Father," I said. The word slipped out, perhaps encouraged by the emotions of the moment.

Asser embraced me, squeezed me tight, and said, "Make me proud."

"I will," I said, seeing tears well up in Asser's eyes.

When we reached the quarterdeck, I looked out and spotted Asser climbing onto his wagon. I waited for him to turn his head for a last look, and waved to catch his attention. He spotted me and returned my farewell.

The waters of the Port of Amsterdam were as hectic as usual. Small rowboats were still loading the items we planned to trade with. The professor said that the trinkets, beads and fabrics we offered amused the Africans. But what provided the most value in trade were the guns and ammunition.

In return, we traded for spices like pepper, some unusual hardwoods, ivory from elephant tusks, and the most valuable commodity, and the main reason for our trade missions, the gold. The professor explained that the market for these goods throughout Europe was strong, and he expected the venture to be very profitable.

He did not bring up the topic of the slave trade, but I shared my disdain about slavery with him anyway, and he assured me that we may encounter some slave business upon our arrival at the Gold Coast, but he promised me that we would have nothing to do with it.

The second day at sea brought us into stormy weather off the coast of France. This was unlike the voyage on the *Golden Lion*, where we enjoyed perfect weather and pleasant sea breezes, from New York to Amsterdam.

"You were lucky," the professor said.

The crew of the *Fluyt* showed remarkable abilities in maneuvering and manipulating the massive sails in the violent seas. I watched in awe from the deck. It took tremendous effort not to lose my grip and be thrown overboard into the black, churning seas. The professor decided to stay dry in the cabin, while I witnessed the massive cargo ship rise to the peak of mountainous waves, and then drop precipitously into the gullies forming between them.

After the storm passed and the seas calmed, we had a pleasant journey over the remaining five days it took to reach the African Gold Coast. The professor pointed out that there were English, French, Portuguese, Danish and Dutch ports that ran up the many miles of the African coastline.

"There you can see the English port," the professor said, pointing to a ship anchored in the distance, the English flag fluttering from its mast.. "I believe that's the *Isabella*. That ship cruises up the Gold Coast, accumulating slaves from the villages. Then they sail to the port of Charles Towne in America. The English like to get their slaves cheap without merchants acting as middlemen."

"You make it sound easy," I said.

He shook his head. "It's not easy at all. Cheaper costs come with greater risks. First, it takes at least five months traveling up the coast, making trade deals along the way until they are full. Then they need to transport the slaves without them dying from disease. After all, there is no profit in a dead slave."

This was a sordid business, and I did not want to be a part of it in any way. I had my doubts that the professor was innocent of involvement in the slave business. He had remarkable knowledge about the details, and most likely shared in the profits of the Dutch slave syndicates we were taught about in class.

We dropped anchor at Fort Amsterdam. It was located on the coast near a small fishing village, called Kormantin. As we climbed down to a rowboat to take us ashore, the professor told me that the fort was built by the English in 1645, and was captured by Admiral Engel de Ruyter of the Dutch West India Company twenty years later.

The gates to the fort were open, allowing people to come and go as they pleased. There were no sentries at the guard towers, giving the sense that security was not a concern as it was back at Castle William and Mary, where I was held prisoner in the fort's dungeon.

I followed the professor through the gates, where waiting for us was a man with long black hair and eyebrows, and a mustache that appeared as if it was sculpted in place. He greeted us with the kind of pageantry I would have expected to be reserved for royalty.

"My old friend Joseph de la Vega," he said, allowing each syllable to roll off his tongue as if he was singing a song.

"It is nice to see you, Governor. This is Master Lukas Levy, the son of Asser Levy."

"What a handsome young man you are, Lukas. I am eager to get to know you better," he said.

"Thank you, Governor," I said, offering a feeble smile.

"Nonsense with the formality, Lukas. My name is Jan Valckenburgh. Just call me Jan."

"It is an honor to meet you Jan," I said, obliging the flamboyant man.

"Come inside. You must be hungry. Joseph, did you bring me the rum you promised?"

Of course I did, Jan. I know how much you love your rum," the professor said, and he pulled out a bottle from a satchel he had slung around his shoulder. "They're unloading a crate now. I thought you would want a head start," he added, with a smirk.

"How marvelous. Come, let's celebrate your arrival."

Chapter 9

I spent all day, every day for the next week, following the professor and taking meticulous notes. We started each day in a large office with the window shutters open, providing a cross breeze, that did little to relieve the sultry humidity. After less than half an hour, I was soaked in sweat completely through my shirt.

The professor, the Governor, and I sat on one side of a wide table. Across from us were matching chairs, where rotating merchants entered and sat to negotiate a deal with us, the representatives of the Dutch West India Company.

My task was to transcribe the conversations. The first day was a disaster, because I could not write fast enough to capture the words of Governor Jan. But with time, I eventually understood his speech. I was able to capture nearly every word spoken and write them legibly into the daily journal.

Trade was done with eight basic commodities, four of which came from Europe in exchange for four from Western Africa.

Each side in the negotiation tended to exaggerate the value of the particular goods they offered. For example, a pepper merchant was amusing, as he attempted to mesmerize us with his *unique pepper*. This was a pepper that not only spiced food, but also promoted healing of many diseases and injuries. He gave us anecdotal proof of a man wounded in his leg by an arrow.

"The pepper was applied on the wound, and it healed within days. He walks without a limp, and only a small scar marks the spot where the injury occurred," said the merchant.

With our work finished for the day, we looked forward to dining with the Governor. Fresh supplies were unloaded off the *Fluyt*. The dinner table was a bounty of Dutch favorites of fruits, meat, nuts, wine, and, of course, rum.

I watched in amazement as they guzzled the rum as if it was water. The rum had the effect of transforming these two intelligent and well-mannered men into drunken fools.

"So, Lukas, I understand from the professor that you were born and raised in the New World," said the Governor, pouring himself some more rum.

"That is true. I spent many years growing up in the Dutch city of Beverwyck, which is now called Albany, since the English took it over."

"Damn English bastards," the Governor said, and toasted a glass to it.

The more they drank, the more the conversation deteriorated into slurs and derogatory statements. At that point, I excused myself with the reason of being tired and in need of sleep. Barely noticed, I headed back to my room. With the shutters open, the windows offered not only a view of the moon reflecting off the ocean, but also a pleasant sea breeze. The sounds of the soft lapping of the waves upon the shore called to me. I decided to go for a swim.

I heard boisterous drunken voices as I passed by the Governor's dining hall. The large gates to the fort were still in the open position. If someone wanted to attack, now would certainly be a good time. But I had to assume that the risk of such aggression was not considered likely.

Hanging in the western sky sat a full moon, reflecting its light like a pathway from the serene ocean to the shore. There were a few people still walking along the beach.

When I dove in to the gentle laps of waves, the warmth was like nothing I had ever experienced in the chilling lakes and ponds of northern climates. I floated on my back and observed the thousands of stars populating the evening sky.

I emerged from the water and saw a figure standing on the beach looking at me. I turned to make sure that it was me he was watching, and not someone else swimming nearby. But there was no one else.

As I approached, I saw the person waiting for me was a man of an unusual stature. He seemed to be only the height of a young boy, with a barrel shaped chest, and a large hump protruding over his right shoulder. He had a groomed gray beard and a felt hat dyed in the same shade. He wore a long black coat, not suitable for the hot and humid weather of the Gold Coast.

I nodded a greeting, and the man extended his right hand. "My name is Benjamin Lay," he said in English.

"Good evening sir. I am Lukas Levy," I said, offering my hand.

We shook hands. He gripped mine firmly, which I returned in kind.

"You arrived on the *Fluyt* yesterday?"

"I did. We are meeting with the Governor," I answered pointing to the fort. "May I ask the reason for your introduction, sir?"

"Call me Benjamin. May I address you as Lukas?" he asked.

"Of course," I said.

"Thank you, Lukas. Let's go sit on the rocks so we can talk. It is not easy for me to stand for too long."

I gestured for him to lead the way. The hunch on his back rocked from side to side, as he made his way across the unsteady sand. When we reached the small outcropping of rocks, he swung his hump like someone swinging a pack strapped to one's back and sat down.

"You don't know me, but I know who you are," he said.

I shook my head and said, "How can that be?"

"Before I answer that, let me explain a little about myself. I have made it my life's mission to fight for the rights of the oppressed. For the past five years I have been focused on defending the rights of the native peoples. But most recently I have been fighting against the slave trade." He paused to run his fingers through his white beard.

"That's honorable, Benjamin, but what does that have to do with me?" I asked.

Benjamin patted my hand, and said, "Not too long ago, I was in New York visiting an old friend. As it happens, this friend is familiar with your father, Asser Levy. He was representing him regarding some real estate issue between his church, and the English Governor."

"You were in New York?" I asked.

Benjamin nodded, and continued, "We were taking a walk along the docks, when you and your father came along. My friend pointed you out and told me about your run-in with the English captain, and that was why you were about to board the warship, the *Golden Lion,* anchored in the harbor."

As Benjamin spoke to me, I looked out across the great ocean. I couldn't believe that I could travel such a great distance and run into a man who knew of me from my homeland.

"I also learned how Asser found you after you spent years living with the natives and brought you to the city. But you were restless and got yourself in trouble with the natives again."

I nodded.

"Your story is inspiring, Lukas. When I saw you disembark off the Fluyt I recognized you immediately."

I stared at this unusual looking man, with this incredible story.

"This is hard to believe," I said.

Benjamin smiled at me. He tried his best to straighten his spine, as he said, "I have spent my life serving God, and I've come to understand that the Almighty provides guidance in the most unusual ways. Why else would you and I meet?"

For the first time in months, I thought about my quest to connect with the Great Spirit. Perhaps meeting Benjamin was indeed divine providence. With that, I decided to trust him.

We spoke for hours about my life with the natives, my spirit journey with the Moon Flower, and how I learned that Asser and Miriam were my real parents.

He knew all about how I was forced to leave New York, and never allowed to return. I concluded my story with how I reached the Gold Coast.

"You have lived a full life for someone so young," Benjamin said, and leaned in close to me, and whispered, "Lukas, I have a proposition for you."

"A proposition?" I asked, startled.

"There is an English slave ship called the *Isabella*. I came here on this ship a month ago. Since then the crew have been running up and down the coast for the past month buying slaves. Tomorrow it sails with over two-hundred men, women and children for Charles Towne where they will be sold at the slave market."

"We saw the *Isabella* when we approached on the *Fluyt*. Why did you sail here on a slave ship?" I asked.

"Good question, Lukas. I am a Quaker. Do you know what that is?"

I shook my head, since I never heard the word.

"We are Christians, with a belief that there is God in every human being. Even slaves and native peoples."

"So why would you travel on a slave ship?" I asked again.

Benjamin looked around to make sure he was not overheard. "Quakers are against slavery. I came here representing the church, as an observer. But the ship owners and the slave merchants couldn't care less about the church's objections."

"I am against slavery too," I said.

"Of course you are. That is why I am speaking with you now. When I saw you disembarking off the ship, I couldn't believe my luck. Lukas, my true intention is not just to observe, but to bring the attention of the world to the brutality in the sale and transport of human beings as if they are cargo. You can help me do this," he said, looking wild-eyed at me.

"What can I do?"

"I am writing a pamphlet called *The Abolition of Slavery*. It will be based on my observations. When we get to Charles Towne, I plan to have the pamphlet printed into many copies. I would like you to distribute them for me to places like Philadelphia, New York and Boston."

"But, as you already know, I am not allowed back in New York," I reminded him.

"I don't think you will be stopped in New York. After you and your father sailed for Amsterdam, Captain Lovewell's son, Alan, disappeared. There were some rumors that he headed north and is living among the natives. The captain has been preoccupied with searching for him."

"Alan has run away to live with natives? That is hard to imagine."

"That's what I heard. It may not be true. But what's important is that there is no one in New York to bother you."

"So, let me understand what you are proposing. You want me to get on a slave ship with you, cross the Atlantic Ocean, help you write an anti-slavery pamphlet, get it printed in a place called Charles Towne, and spread your story to the cities along the American coast?"

Benjamin nodded his agreement with a smile.

"What about the professor? Do I just sneak away without telling him?"

Benjamin grabbed my hand with his stubby fingers and looked at me.

"You told me your story, Lukas, on how you left your mother to live with the natives. Can you tell me why you did that?"

"To seek out the Great Spirit."

"Well then, Lukas, you know the question you should be asking yourself." He paused, waiting for me to ask.

"Which path will further my quest in seeking out the Great Spirit?"

Benjamin smiled, and said, "That is the question, Lukas, and I think you know the answer."

Book 5

Chapter 1

I spent two months on the slave ship, the *Isabella*, sailing from the African Gold Coast to Charles Towne in the province called Carolina. I spent most of my time hiding during the day and sleeping at night on the floor in Benjamin's cramped cabin.

This night, shortly after disembarking from the Isabella, I slept on a straw mattress in the back room of the Quaker Meeting House on Queen Street, which seemed luxurious in comparison to my previous accommodations aboard the slave ship.

I imagined that the professor had returned to Amsterdam and told Asser about my sudden disappearance. At first, I regretted slipping away onto the *Isabella* without telling the professor. But he would have never allowed it, and certainly the Governor would have forcibly prevented me from boarding.

After my decision was made, I still needed to participate in the next day's negotiations and activities without raising any suspicions of my plan to abscond.

Benjamin thought it best that I sneak on board well before sunrise and hide inside his cabin. I buried in the sand my international business man's clothes that Asser provided for me. A stained white linen shirt and brown breeches would be my new wardrobe.

I was onboard and safely stowed away for several hours in Benjamin's cabin, when I was stirred from my sleep by the jangle of chains and footfalls of slaves being boarded and held in the cargo hold of the *Isabella*. I heard disturbing sounds of men, women and children crying and moaning in agony that pierced through the noise of the metal chains dragging along the ship's wooden floorboards.

It was that first day, even before we set sail, that I knew I had made the correct decision to leave behind my privileged life and renew my journey in search of the Great Spirit. While the life of international business was exciting, and financially rewarding, much of it was driven by taking advantage of the poor and powerless.

The *Isabella* was built as a cargo ship, similar to the *Fluyt*. But to accommodate hundreds of slaves, the ship owners divided the hulls into holds with little headroom. This created unhealthy conditions, allowing the spread of disease. Benjamin said it made no sense to treat the slaves so poorly, especially since the slave business was very profitable. A slave purchased in Africa for twenty-five Sterling could be resold in Charles Towne for one hundred and fifty Sterling.

One major problem was the lack of drinking water. Being held in the sweltering hold below deck caused severe dehydration. By the time we arrived in Charles Towne, over fifty slaves had perished, and were casually tossed overboard.

About halfway through the sea journey, I took the risk of sneaking out of my hiding place in Benjamin's cabin to witness the slave-hold with my own eyes. I was only able to catch a glimpse, but the image was so seared into my mind that not even another dose of Moon Flower could ever erase it.

Shackled to the floorboards were men, women, and children with no room to move. The most they could do was to prop themselves up on their elbows, which some did, when

I poked my head into the hold. Staring back at me were glowing yellowed eyes of desperate men, women and children. The stench of human waste and sweat choked me to gag.

That moment confirmed my determination to make sure that Benjamin Lay's quest to spread the word about these atrocities succeeded.

Chapter 2

———————

It took Benjamin a few weeks to finish writing his pamphlet, *The Abolition of Slavery.* He generously included some of my observations, and opinions on the white man's ongoing despicable behavior to exploit less developed cultures. I shared my experiences of the brutality of English officers placing bounties for scalps of innocent natives, as if it were sport.

Then on a sunny day in late August, after spending the past month in Charles Towne, Benjamin showed me a bundle of papers and announced, "It's ready."

"You should leave tomorrow," he said, as we entered a tavern on Chalmers Street.

"Is Philadelphia the closest city that has a printing press?" I asked as we took a table next to a window overlooking the horses and wagons making their way over the round cobblestones.

"I'm afraid so. You can make it in about two weeks. I've already made arrangements for a fine horse. When you get there you'll see a fellow Quaker named William Bradford. He has opened Philadelphia's first printing press establishment. Apparently, he helped a German immigrant named William Rittenhouse to construct the first paper mill in English colonies. After all, what's the use of a printing press without paper?"

The next morning, with the pamphlet's written draft safely stored onto a pack on the horse, I said my farewells to Benjamin.

"It's been an honor knowing you," I said, bending down to shake his hand.

"Likewise, Lukas. I wish you safe travels."

Benjamin might have been small in stature, but he was a giant of a man when measured by character and integrity.

"Just stay on The King's Highway. It will take you directly to Philadelphia," he reminded me.

"I will," I said, and gave him a hug.

As we released each other, tears welled up in his eyes. "I will miss you. You are a good boy," he said.

"I will miss you too." I mounted my horse, and waved goodbye, probably for the last time.

Chapter 3

U nlike the cobblestone streets of Charles Towne, or the elegant canals of Amsterdam, The King's Highway, despite its grand name, was just a dirt road meandering through forests, leading north.

Packed securely to my saddle was Benjamin's draft of *The Abolition of Slavery*. My instructions were to follow the highway to Philadelphia and find the printer William Bradford.

"Do not worry about payment. Arrangements have been made with the Quaker Church in Philadelphia to cover the expense," Benjamin told me.

Benjamin had given me a few coins in case I was in need of a roof over my head, or to buy a meal. But I planned to hunt for my food with the bow and arrows Benjamin traded for with a Cherokee native. It was a simple but suitable bow. The buckskin quiver, however, was beautifully adorned with hawk feathers, and held ten well-made arrows.

We also traded with the same Cherokee for a horse, a beautiful red stallion in prime condition. He told us that it was his own horse, and even showed us his markings seared into its coat on its rump. Benjamin warned me that I should be careful because many of the Cherokees stole horses and claimed them as their own.

"Just in case you meet its true owner on your journey," he told me.

"I call him Wili," the Cherokee told me.

"I will honor Wili, and call him the same," I said, bringing a smile to the native.

It was a while since I had been on horseback, and I hoped to find mutual respect with my new friend. Most of the morning Wili and I traveled under a canopy of branches sporting delicate white flowers. Its sweet fragrance delighted my senses. A gentle breeze released its buds into a shower of white flakes upon the trail. Wili sensed the white carpet of petals beneath his hooves and snorted his approval.

With sunset only a few hours away, I decided to find a place to make camp for the night. I remembered from my journal of my days with Rowtag, looking for shelter in the winter months. But with the balmy weather of the south, I could sleep under the stars. Benjamin had advised me to take cover, regardless of the climate. "There are robbers on the highway. You must sleep with one eye open," he had warned.

I found a secluded spot not far from a brook running high from the recent rains. Wili was pleased, lapping up the cool water. After he was satisfied, I tied him up behind an overgrown patch of blueberry bushes, which were still weeks away from ripening.

My thoughts returned to Rowtag and Nadie. Their child would be almost two years old by now. I imagined the three of them living together as a loving family. I clenched my fists, hoping to push away the fire inside me and instead wish them happiness and the blessings of the Great Spirit. But as much as I tried, all I could see was Nadie's face and her look of surprise when I saw her last.

Even the pool of water that Wili was drinking at reminded me of the lake where we first fell in love. Her long straight black hair and lovely brown eyes invaded my mind, mixing with a flood of memories of our time together.

Before I headed out to hunt, I set up a few deadfall traps in hopes of capturing a rabbit or squirrel. Perhaps I would be surprised upon my return.

Dusk was a good time to track deer. But these woods were foreign to me, and if I did stumble upon a herd, I would have good fortune to thank, rather than my skills as a hunter.

There would be no such luck tonight. But I did find some grasses growing in an open field that Wili would enjoy. I pulled them up by the roots and headed back to the campsite. Finding food for Wili was easy. Maybe my dinner would be waiting for me in one of the traps.

Wili was pleased with the grasses I laid before him. Unfortunately, I went without a meal that night.

Shortly before daybreak a soaking thunderstorm rolled in from the west. This meant that the animals would hunker down, and any hopes for a kill would need to wait for the skies to clear. In addition, Wili became restless, bucking and stomping his hoofs in protest. There would be no traveling or hunting until the storm passed.

Nearly half a day went by before the storm subsided and moved off to the east. The time to hunt was now. The deer would be hungry, and on the move in search for food.

I ran back and pulled some wet grasses for Wili to munch on while I hunted. I took off uphill to a clearing and found a spot hidden from view and upwind, so my scent would not frighten the deer away.

It didn't take long to spot a family grazing on some green leafy plants. I spotted a female and took aim for her. I preferred female meat to the male, since their meat was more tender.

I focused on her lungs for a quick kill. If I struck her elsewhere, she would take off and might run as far as a mile before bleeding out. I waited for the doe to show me her broadside before I struck.

Just as I was about to release the arrow, I realized that I had never fired this bow before. But it was too late to take a practice shot, so I simply held my breath and released the bow. The arrow whistled across the distance and struck true and deep.

I awoke with a full moon illuminating my campsite and decided that Wili and I would travel at night to make up for the lost time it took to hunt the day before. As I secured the bow to the saddle, I gave thanks to the Cherokee who provided me with a reliable weapon.

I reached into the saddlebag and pulled out a map of The Kings Highway that Benjamin drew for me. The moon provided enough light to see a line segmented at points with an X. Next to each X was a name of a city. At the bottom was Charles Towne. Above that was a place called Norfolk, my next destination. Then came Philadelphia where I was to get the pamphlets printed. After that, with the pamphlets to distribute, I would visit Trent Towne, New York, and finally Boston.

I gave Wili a gentle kick. He paused for a moment before moving forward. I hoped it wouldn't take long for him to figure me out. By the time we reached Norfolk, in about seven days, I intended for him to respond to the slightest squeeze of my legs or the gentlest of tugs upon his bridle.

Chapter 4

Plumes filled the sky. At first I thought they were dark storm clouds, but the sharp smell accompanying them told me this was not bad weather rolling through, but something of significance was burning. Wili and I left The Kings Highway to find the source. Moments later, as we crossed a large open grass field, the air seemed to have an oppressive weight to it.

The forest was on fire. I saw flames and sparks dancing and leaping across tremendous evergreen trees, rapidly spreading the inferno. I had never witnessed a wildfire before, and the sounds and spectacle sent a chill through me.

Sensing my fear, as well as his own, Wili reared back. I pulled hard on the bridle to keep him steady. We still had a safe passage of retreat if the flames came any closer.

Then I saw deer escaping the flames onto the open field where Wili and I stood. Following in close pursuit was a native tribe of warriors on horseback, with bows drawn and arrows being released into the fleeing herd.

The deer were in full panic and charged across the field right before us. Many fell, but some regained their footing and continued to run wildly into the unaffected woods behind us. The warriors pounced on the wounded and ended their suffering with a knife thrust to the throat.

It was a scene of efficient devastation. In a matter of minutes the warriors had slain over thirty deer. *Could the natives have something to do with the burning of the forest to ashes?* I wondered. The slaughter seemed hardly coincidental.

A warrior approached on horseback and spoke to me in Algonquin demanding that I identify myself. His dialect and accent were unusual, but I understood.

"I saw the fire from The Kings Highway," I said, pointing the way to the road.

The warrior jerked back his head in surprise at my ability to speak a version of his language. But he was determined to dismiss me. "Go back to the road, and let us be," he ordered.

"Please forgive my curiosity. But I have never seen the hunting of deer this way," I said, looking in the direction of the burning woods.

"The purpose of setting the fire is to fell the trees for the growing of our maize. It's also a good way to hunt," he said, gesturing to his fellow warriors carrying off the slain deer, to what I assumed was their longhouses.

I nodded and offered my admiration by placing my palm over my heart.

"Where are you going?" the warrior asked.

"I am headed to the city called Philadelphia."

"What is your name?"

"My name is Lukas. What is your name?"

"I am called Nootau," he said, and looked at the branding seared onto Wili's rump.

"That's a Cherokee sign," he said, shifting my attention away from the flames.

I turned to look at the crosshatch symbol. "Indeed it is. I traded for Wili, as well as my bow and arrows, from a Cherokee in Charles Towne," I said, patting Wili on his neck.

Nootau paused, and looked deeply into my eyes, and then said, "Come join us, Lukas. Tonight there will be a celebration for the hunt, and the clearing of the forest. You can spend the night and resume your journey in the morning."

"I would be honored," I said.

As I prepared to leave the next morning, I thought of the previous evening Nootau and I had conversing with each other. Before we found a secluded place to speak, I offered my respect to the Chief and the Shaman, as well as the rest of the leading members of the Powhatan tribe.

But the time I had with Nootau was most enlightening. I shared with him my journey, beginning with the Moon Flower to order find the Great Spirit. He was especially interested in my experiences.

"What was it like? What did you see?"

"I faced my greatest fears, and was forced to battle them," I said.

Nootau nodded and leaned forward to ask, "Has it opened your eyes to the truth?"

"This is indeed the challenge, Nootau. Up until a few weeks ago, it seemed that I became sidetracked for a while, but hopefully I am back on the path," I said.

"Please explain, Lukas."

"The allure of privilege can easily blur the purpose of the journey," I said.

"I do not know this word, *privilege*."

"It's a word that seems to describe the journey of the white man," I said.

"You are a white man, Lukas. Is this *privilege* what you seek?"

"I am more like you, my brother, than my outward appearance may suggest. I have shunned the white man's world and have returned to my journey," I said.

"What is your journey, Lukas? You say it is to find the Great Spirit. What does that mean?"

"It's about becoming a warrior. Demonstrating courage when faced with fear."

Nootau nodded in agreement, and added, "That is the way of the warrior, Lukas. To be truthful no matter the consequence."

"That is right Nootau, regardless of the consequence."

I looked at Nootau and wondered if I was seeing him for the last time. Regardless, I was certain that our brief friendship would last a lifetime.

"Safe travels, my friend," said Nootau.

"Always seek the truth," I said, bidding him farewell.

Chapter 5

The Friends Meetinghouse in Philadelphia did not look like any house of worship I had seen. It was a handsome stone building with chunky wood shutters painted a bright white. As Benjamin had explained to me, "You do not need a special building to pray in. Worship may take place anywhere men assemble."

When Wili and I arrived, my lack of a shave and proper clothing caused the three men working on the hinges for the front door to stop their work and stare at me, as if I were an intruder.

But my words cleared things up. "Good afternoon, gentlemen, Benjamin Lay sent me."

"Ah," came the chorus of understanding.

I was nearly pulled off Wili and felt each man's hands warmly pat my back. But just as quickly, they ushered me inside the meetinghouse, safely hidden from curious passersby. They were anxious to hear about Benjamin's health, the journey aboard the slave ship, and if I had the pamphlet.

When I told them it was still strapped to my saddle, they looked at each other in horror.

"Go and get it, Samuel," said one of the men.

When Samuel returned, he held the package out for all of us to see. They let out a collective sigh of relief. After the men quickly perused the pamphlet, they finally introduced themselves. The three Quakers were John Armstrong, Samuel Bownas, and Stephen Crisp.

"We will bring this to Bradford's print shop tomorrow," said Stephen.

John put a hand around my shoulder, and said, "You must be in need of rest. We have arranged a room for you here in the meetinghouse. Tonight, we have a speaker coming, so you will need to shave and dress like a proper Quaker." With that, he handed me a razor, placed on top of neatly folded clothes. "And don't forget this," he added, handing me a round black felt hat with a ribbon and a buckle strapped to it.

Lying upon a writing desk in the room provided for me by the Quakers, was a printed advertisement for tonight's event. I had never seen something produced by a printing press. The letters varied in size, which I assumed was to add emphasis to certain words. For example, the largest words were at the top of the page announcing the speaker's subject for tonight's presentation.

JEWS IN AMERICA

ARE THE NATIVE AMERICANS A LOST TRIBE OF ISRAEL?

A READING BY THE QUAKER AUTHOR THOMAS THOROWGOOD

I reread the words several times, making sure my excitement was justified. Did this man, Thomas Thorowgood, have proof of such a connection? I thought back to what Asser told me about my Jewish heritage. Could there be such a connection between these two ancient peoples?

Perhaps this meeting with the author Thomas Thorowgood would get me one step closer to the Great Spirit. I paced the small room. Our meeting could not come soon enough.

Chapter 6

Many arrived at The Friends Meeting House moments before Mr. Thorowgood's talk was to begin. I had been sitting in a front-row seat for over an hour, awaiting my opportunity to meet the author.

I did my best getting into the Quaker clothes. They fit me fine, although they were very itchy against my skin. As the men and women of the congregation filed in, I was introduced. Most had heard about Benjamin's manuscript, as well as my journey with him aboard the slave ship. Men shook my hands vigorously, while the women offered a respectful curtsy.

The large room held over one hundred men, women and children anxious to hear from the author. Voices called out that caused me to turn and look down the center aisle. I saw walking and greeting those already seated John Armstrong, Samuel Bownas and Stephen Crisp. They sat next to me, in the only three empty chairs in the meetinghouse.

A soft murmur of conversations ceased at the sound of three loud knocks. All eyes looked down the aisle to see a tall thin man with a gaunt face, walking with a cane.

"Who is that?" I whispered to John sitting next to me.

"That's our Pastor, Elias Hicks," he whispered.

Behind him was another, older man, at least a head taller than the pastor, with two crops of white hair above his ears. I assumed this to be the speaker, Thomas Thorowgood. Both men walked to the front of the hall. The pastor turned and faced the congregation.

"Welcome all," he began, and looked out to the many people now crammed into the large room. Those without seats were standing along the walls and children were sitting cross-legged on the floor in the aisle, and up front where the pastor and the author were standing.

"Before I introduce our speaker, the honorable author, and Quaker Thomas Thorowgood, let me acknowledge a special guest who is among us tonight," the pastor said looking directly at me, and crooked a finger to signal me to join him at the podium.

I could feel the eyes of the curious congregants upon me. I looked over at Stephen, John and Samuel, who were flipping their hands as encouragement for me to get up.

When I reached the pastor, he wrapped his bony arm around my shoulder, and pulled me in close. I felt his fingers digging into my arm.

"My friends, this is Lukas Levy," he announced. A buzz of conversation spread with the recognition of my name.

"He has traveled aboard the *Isabella*, the cursed slave ship, with our good friend and Quaker, Benjamin Lay."

The buzz rose to a full-throated acknowledgment at the mention of Benjamin's name.

"Lukas has delivered Benjamin's pamphlet, *The Abolition of Slavery*, which is now being printed into many copies for distribution to the north."

The announcement broke the congregants into applause.

"Thank you, Lukas. We look forward to getting to know you before you travel to the north spreading Benjamin's words," the pastor said.

I nodded to the pastor and smiled, and he released his grip, which I assumed was my cue to return to my seat.

As I settled back into my seat, the pastor continued, "Now let's get to tonight's special program. Our speaker earned his Master of Arts from the prestigious University of Cambridge. Since then Thomas Thorowgood has devoted his life to serving the Quaker Church in England, and then throughout America for many years. He is here tonight to speak of his fascinating studies from his book titled *Jews in America*," he concluded to a polite, subdued applause.

Thorowgood stepped forward to shake the pastor's hand. He wore the traditional Quaker black coat, with a white cravat around his neck.

"Thank you, Pastor Elias," Thomas said with a baritone voice that carried throughout the cavernous hall. "You may find my conclusions bizarre and strange," he began to a collective nodding of heads in the audience, which brought a smile to the speaker.

"And I must agree with you. When I first considered the idea I also thought it farfetched. But the more I studied the thesis, the more it made sense," he said, and reached into his pocket to pull out his notes.

"The premise is that the native peoples of America are descendants of one of the lost tribes of Israel."

This remark caused a stir among those I assumed had not heard details of tonight's topic.

"As Quakers, we know the story of the ten lost tribes of Israel. My theory contends that the Tribe of Dan traveled to these lands many years ago. You may ask what proof I have to make such a claim."

Despite his conviction, Mr. Thorowgood didn't seem to convince anyone in the congregation about his theories. There were audible chuckles of laughter, and vigorous shaking of heads at his comparisons of beliefs between the natives and the Jews.

I thought his arguments were sound, such as both prayed to only one God, and men and women do not worship together, and then there was the intriguing observation of how both the Jews and the Natives divided themselves into tribes.

On the other hand, and of particular disfavor that bordered on insult, was his statement that both cultures believed they were the chosen ones, or God's favorite.

While some arguments seemed worthy, others fell flat; such as having similar marriage customs, or in the treatment of the dead. The members of the congregation constantly interrupted his presentation with ridiculous questions such as, "Are you saying that Jews hunt for their food like Indians?" Another one was, "I've seen Jews, they look nothing like the Natives, why is that?"

They seemed to think it their right to question every assertion he made. He was doomed to fail from the start.

After nearly everyone had left, Mr. Thorowgood spoke with the only supportive voice in the audience, me. When the pastor inquired if he was ready to return to his home, where he would be spending the evening, he told him that he would join him shortly.

Mr. Thorowgood sat next to me on the pew, crossed one leg over the other, placed an elbow on his knee, and looked at me.

"Lukas, do you believe what I said tonight has merit?"

I nodded, and said, "I do."

He tilted his head, hesitated and added, "I sense you also have a story to tell."

We spoke late into the evening. I shared my life's adventures with him. He asked me many questions.

"You have lived the life I have been writing about, Lukas. It's obvious that our paths were meant to cross."

I had never met anyone with such curiosity. It spurred me on to be equally inquisitive.

"Your book has brought my dreams to life. But how do you know these things?" I asked.

"It is not something I know. I came to my conclusions based on certain assumptions. You can say my assertions are based on my observations."

"And tonight, my dreams and your observations seem to have confirmed one another," I said.

"Indeed, they may have, Lukas."

A few days later I was ready to travel north on The Kings Highway to New York. Mr. Thorowgood told me that I could always reach out to him through the church.

"Just walk into any Quaker Church or meetinghouse and leave a message. Somehow it will make its way to me."

Regrettably, I could not reciprocate with such a convenience.

"I cannot say where my life will lead me at this point. My immediate plan is to distribute Benjamin's pamphlets in New York and Boston."

"Perhaps your future lies in God's hands, Lukas."

"Perhaps it does," I answered.

Chapter 7

All sorts of scenarios played out in my mind during the three days it took to journey from Philadelphia to New York. I imagined being recognized by some English officer and arrested for violating the order not to enter the city. Or perhaps Asser had returned from Amsterdam thinking I was dead, and saw me riding into town wearing the Quaker clothes I had been given during my visit to Philadelphia. Wouldn't that be a surprise?

But I had made a promise to Benjamin that I would distribute the pamphlets to "persons of influence" in New York, and then onto the city of Boston.

No one paid Wili or me much mind as I paid the fare and boarded the ferry to New York. With Wili tied up, I grabbed a view along the railing with the other passengers. The last time I looked out onto the vast harbor was when I was boarding the warship the *Golden Lion*. There was nothing as grand to look at today, but it was still active with sailboats, canoes and rowboats, traversing in a hodgepodge of directions.

Standing next to me was an elderly man who greeted me.

"Good day to you, sir," I replied.

"I see you are a Quaker," he said, looking at my clothes.

"Actually, no sir. But I am on Quaker business," I told the man.

He removed his spectacles and pulled a cloth from his pocket to give the lenses a polish. "And what kind of business would that be?" he asked.

"Distributing a pamphlet written by the Quaker Benjamin Lay called *The Abolition of Slavery*."

"I would be interested in reading this pamphlet," he said, slipping his spectacles back on.

"They are packed away on my horse. When we reach the dock I would be happy to get one for you."

"That would be very generous of you. May I ask your name?"

"My name is Lukas Levy," I told him, and immediately regretted my naïveté.

He looked at me with a curious expression and asked, "Are you the son of Asser Levy?"

"I am. Do you know my father?"

"You haven't heard the news?" he asked quietly.

I shook my head.

"Your father boarded the ship the *Gilded Beaver* at its port in Amsterdam, with its destination to New York," he said, gesturing to the harbor. "From what I read, they sailed into a violent storm in the North Atlantic that sank the ship. I'm afraid to say that there were no survivors."

"Are you sure?" I asked, feeling the blood rush from my face, and firmly gripping the handrail.

"I am," he said, clutching my arm to steady me.

I shook my head. "No, this can't be. This can't be."

"Come, Lukas, let's sit down," the man said, bringing me over to the bench bolted to the deck.

I leaned my head into my hands. "What about Miriam?" I asked a few moments later, lifting my face and looking at the gentleman.

"Miriam, your mother, has been overwrought thinking she lost her husband, and you as well. But I see you are not dead."

"No, but I've disappeared for a while," I said, now regretting my selfishness.

"I am sorry to give you the bad news, Lukas."

"Asser is dead," I mumbled aloud.

The man put his arm around my shoulder to comfort me.

"What is your name, sir?" I asked.

"My name is David Gans. I met your father when I lived in Amsterdam. He was a good man, Lukas. My deepest condolences."

As the ferry approached the dock I wished Mr. Gans farewell.

Wili snorted when he saw me coming for him. "Come on now, we must hurry and find Miriam."

Chapter 8

I saw Alice sweeping the front porch as Wili and I turned the corner. She stared, seeming not to recognize me, until I realized the Quaker clothing must be confusing her.

"Hello Alice, it's me, Lukas," I said dismounting Wili.

She dropped the broom and held out her arms. "Oh my, we thought you was dead," she said.

I stepped onto the porch and walked into Alice's embrace. She buried her face against my chest and said, "Thanks God you alive Master Lukas. Mrs. Miriam will be much happy to know it."

We entered the house. Nothing had changed since I had been here last, about a year earlier.

"She in the courtyard," Alice told me as I followed her.

We passed Abraham, watering the house plants. He did a double take when our eyes met. He put down the watering can and wrapped his arms around me tightly.

"Master Lukas! You're alive!"

"I am, Abraham. Is it true what I heard about Mr. Levy?"

Abraham looked at me, his eyes releasing streams of tears down both cheeks. "It is, I'm afraid. Poor Missus, she is not doing well."

"Come now, Lukas, she's out here," Alice said, pointing to the doors leading to the courtyard.

Miriam was tending to her flowers when I stepped out onto the brick pavers lining the courtyard floor. She looked thinner since I had last seen her, and her skin was pale, without its normal pinkish color.

"Hello, Mother," I said.

Miriam turned around, holding a garden trowel, and stared at me. Her mouth opened without a sound. I took a step closer to her.

"It's Lukas," said Alice.

"Oh, my heavens." She stood up straight and approached me cautiously. "Is it really you?"

"It's really me," I said.

With that, she quickly closed the distance between us, and enfolded me in an embrace, shuddering with silent sobs.

I pulled back and looked into her tear-filled eyes. "I heard about Father. I'm so sorry," I said.

She grabbed my hand and led me to the stone bench built into the rock wall surrounding the courtyard.

"The last letter I received from your father said that you disappeared on a trade mission to the Gold Coast of Africa. He blamed himself for your loss. He said there was no point in staying on in Amsterdam any longer with you gone." She paused to gather herself.

"Several weeks later I received the news that the ship he was aboard from Amsterdam had perished in a storm. There were no survivors."

Hearing the words from Miriam finalized the fact that there was no mistake. Asser Levy, my father, was dead.

"He was a good man," I managed to say.

"He was. And he cared for you very much. Now, tell me what happened to you. Why did you vanish? Asser wrote to me from Amsterdam that they searched for weeks looking for you. They thought you were taken hostage by Negro savages."

"No, I snuck on board a slave ship headed for Charles Towne in Carolina."

Miriam's jaw released like a trap door in the floor, and asked, "Why, Lukas? Why would you do such a thing and not tell anyone?"

I looked over to where Alice and Abraham stood, and answered, "Because of them."

Miriam frowned. "What do you mean, Lukas?"

I told her about how I snuck onboard the slave ship without telling the professor.

"Why would you do such a thing? This makes no sense," she said, placing her cold hands on top of mine.

Her inability to understand my reasoning forced me to give up trying. I told her of my plans to distribute Benjamin's pamphlets in the city, and then move on to Boston.

Her eyes widened fearfully. She shook a finger at me and said, "Oh no, Lukas, you cannot stay here, you will be arrested."

"Not necessarily. I heard that Captain Lovewell has left the city with his Rangers in search for his son, Alan, who apparently ran away to the north to live with the natives."

"Oh Lukas," she moaned. "What did you fill that boy's head with?"

I made some inquiries at the Quaker Church about the captain the next day. Indeed, he and his Rangers had traveled north in search of Alan. They had been gone for months. The news that filtered back was that the Rangers were on a rampage, slaughtering native tribes and using Alan's disappearance as justification.

The pastor at the church was pleased with the pamphlets and assured me that he would make sure they would be distributed as Benjamin requested.

"But Benjamin asked me to see to this personally," I told him.

"That's honorable of you, Lukas, but I'm afraid it's too dangerous, even with the captain gone. You have become renowned in the city since the loss of your father at sea. If the authorities find out that you are alive and distributing anti-government propaganda, they will execute you on the spot and Asser won't be here to rescue you."

"But what about Boston?" I asked.

"I'll send a courier to Boston. You must leave the city right away before someone spots you," he warned me.

That night I said goodbye to Miriam. She had lost a son, a husband, and now was losing me for a second time.

"Where will you go?" she asked. I could barely understand those simple words between her sobs.

"I will find my friend Rowtag, and the Pequawkets. They need to be warned about the captain if it's not too late."

After I packed a few things on my saddle, I mounted Wili.

I turned and saw Miriam standing at the doorway, clutching the arms of Abraham and Alice.

"Please don't forget me, Lukas," Miriam called out.

"I won't, Mother. I'm sorry it has to be this way. Farewell," I said, and rode off upon Wili toward the wall, and into the moonless night.

Damage to the wall at the shoreline allowed Wili and me to easily get to the north side. We traveled along the road in darkness, passing the Lenape tribe undetected, and reached the northern end of Mannahatta by morning.

As the sun rose to a warm start to the day, Wili and I took a ferry across the North River to the western shore. "Let's go find Mother and Jakob," I said to Wili.

He snorted and shook his head in approval. As we reached the shore, I mounted him and we headed north along the river bank.

As we rode, on a pleasant, cloudless day, I wondered what I would say upon arriving at the house that I thought was the place of my birth, and stood facing the woman I mistakenly called Mother.

Chapter 9

Fort Albany was active with many English soldiers milling about. With good fortune I would go unnoticed. I rode Wili through the gates and headed to the Vilna Trading & Export Company.

Paver stones of brick had eliminated the muddy roadways I remembered the last time I had been here and met Asser, for the first time. Many of the buildings had been replaced with new wooden structures.

But the same, weather worn Vilna Trading & Export Company sign was still swinging in the gentle breeze blowing off the river. I dismounted Wili, and told him to wait for me, as I tied his bridle to the post.

I stepped up to the porch and opened the door. As I entered, I saw Jakob sitting at a desk.

"Hello, Jakob."

He looked up and rose from his chair. "Lukas, what are you doing here?"

"I've come to see Mother," I said, then wondered if I should now be calling her by her first name, Sara.

"Oh, Lukas, you haven't heard," he said walking over to me.

"Heard what?"

"Your mother passed away last winter," Jakob said, gripping my shoulder.

I pulled out the chair from the desk where Mother used to work, and sat down. My eyes became blurry as they filled with tears.

"What happened? Was she sick?" I choked out.

"She was weak and got the winter fever and couldn't fight it."

"This is all too much," I said, wiping tears away.

"I'm sorry, Lukas. You know she loved you very much."

"I mean all this death, it's too much to bear."

"What do you mean?" Jakob asked, pulling up a chair and sitting across from me.

"I gather you didn't hear about Asser?" I said.

Jakob shook his head. I told him the story of my life since that day, a year earlier, when I met my true father, Asser Levy. He listened while I shared the tale that brought me to Amsterdam, then to the coast of Africa where I met Benjamin. I described how I stole aboard the slave ship, *Isabella*, and my subsequent journey that led me back to New York City, where I learned of Asser's fate.

"I'm so sorry to hear of Asser's death," Jakob said, then his eyes widened as he asked, "But hold on, Lukas. Did you say that your true father was Asser?"

"Yes, he and Miriam told me the story of how Sara and Solomon took me in as a child while Asser and Miriam needed to tend to a legal matter in Amsterdam."

Jakob's brow furrowed, and he said, "Asser and Miriam are not your parents, Lukas."

"What are you saying?"

"Sara and Solomon are your parents," he insisted.

I closed my eyes and shook my head. *How could this be happening?* I looked at Jakob and asked, "Are you sure?"

"Of course I'm sure, Lukas. I was here for your birth. I saw Sara holding you the day you were born."

"Why would Asser tell me such a lie?"

"Knowing Asser, he did it for his own benefit. Having you think he was your father would cement your loyalty to him. His business enterprises needed new blood and I'm sure someone like you was perfect."

"But the way Miriam acted seemed so real. I think she truly believed I was her son."

"Miriam has suffered severely from melancholy since losing David. Asser tried bringing in doctors to try to treat her. He told me she had hallucinations of seeing her son walking throughout the house at night."

"She did look at me strangely," I offered.

"I can assure you that Solomon and Sara Pietersen were your parents, Lukas," he said, placing an arm around my shoulder as comfort.

I thought about what a fool I was falling for Asser's phony sincerity. *Another example of a white man exploiting the weak and powerless.* I slammed my palm upon Mother's desk top and rose from the chair. "This is outrageous," I shouted.

Jakob opened his palms, and said, "Well, Lukas, it appears Asser's plans didn't turn out like he intended."

"Apparently not," I said.

"Come, Lukas, let me take you to see your mother," Jakob said, wrapping his arm around me, and leading me to the front door.

The graveyard was a few hours' walk. I asked Jakob why Mother was buried so far away, and not in a nearby cemetery. Jakob stopped walking for a moment to look at me and said, "She thought you would visit her there more often."

At that, I smiled, remembering my journal. We were not far from the Turtle Clan's former campsite. Mother must have known that when she specified her wishes for her burial site. She wanted her final resting place to be where my journey began. This thought melted away the anger I felt from Asser's betrayal.

The cemetery had a low white picket fence surrounding the perimeter, beyond which were rolling hills of grass and brush.

Jakob and I walked among the headstones, until he stopped. "Here she is, Lukas," he said pointing to a grave standing among overgrown weeds.

I walked over and saw carved into the stone:

SARA PIETERSEN BORN 1630 – DIED 1689

"Did she suffer much?" I asked.

"Once the winter fever took her, she didn't last long," Jakob said.

I stood quietly for a moment looking down upon the grave. I got to my knees and removed a few old dried leaves, scattered across where she lay.

"I am sorry I wasn't here for you and Mother when you needed me. It seems I have disappointed many people lately," I said, picking up a few pebbles.

"It's all right, Lukas. You had your own life to live. She was well taken care of during her last days."

I nodded.

"What will you do now?" he asked.

"I'm not sure. What you told me both relieves me and confuses me."

"Perhaps that is because your journey is not yet finished, Lukas," he suggested.

I looked away from the grave, and into Jakob's eyes. "I believe you're right."

Book 6

Chapter 1

I rubbed Wili's neck as we looked upon the glorious Cohoes Falls. "This is where it all began, my friend. At least that's what my journal says."

Wili snorted and took a step closer toward the cool mist.

"No, boy—we'll go east," I said, and pulled gently on the bridle.

Wili immediately responded, and turned away from the thunderous cascade, which was no surprise, since I'd been riding him for hundreds of miles, from Charles Towne to Albany. At this point, he felt my thoughts and anticipated my needs.

"Wili, we will head east and follow the most traveled pathway through the Green Mountains, until we find the campsite of the Turtle Clan, and the great Chief Nicholas."

The pass through the mountains was well-defined and not difficult to maneuver with a strong horse like Wili. Within two days, we were heading down to the valley below. As we emerged from the forest into a clearing, I saw a young crop of maize growing in open fields. Sitting atop Wili, I had an unobstructed view of longhouses beyond the crops. "What do we have here?"

I approached carefully, untied my bow and maneuvered my quill in place as a precaution. Two warriors on horseback rode out to greet me. Wili wanted to move to meet them, but I pulled on Wili's bridle and said, "Let's wait for them here boy." *I'm the one at the strategic disadvantage; better to let them come to me.*

I dismounted Wili and waited cautiously. Both warriors leapt off their horses before they even came to a full stop, and came running toward me. I quickly moved closer to Wili and put my bow down. They would be too close for it to be of any use. But I placed my hand on my knife. If they were to attack, at least I would be ready for the fight.

As the warriors got closer, I saw their faces were not those of men ready to engage in a battle. Instead, they were smiling.

"Lukas, what a surprise! Is it really you?" asked one.

I wiped the sweat pouring down my forehead with the back of my hand and took a deep breath to calm my racing heart. There would be no fight. These men knew me.

One of them held me by my shoulders, and said, "You were just a scared little boy the last time we saw you."

Then it all came together. According to my journal, I knew these men must be Chogan and Askook, warriors of the Turtle Clan.

"Please excuse my strange behavior," I said. "But after I left the Clan, I consumed the Moon Flower in a ceremony to connect with the Great Spirit. That experience caused me to lose all memories of my life up until that day. Luckily, the Shaman had me record my memories in a journal," I said and pointed to my pack. "I know that your names are Askook and Chogan, but I cannot say who is who."

"That's funny, Lukas. I'm Askook, and this is Chogan. Or is it the other way around?"

The warriors laughed at the joke.

The other warrior looked at me, and said, "What was it like, doing the Moon Flower? We have heard of warriors who have consumed the powerful plant."

I nodded, and said, "It elevates you, in a way that opens your mind and allows you to see the world in a clearer way."

They listened for a few minutes, showing genuine interest, until one of them said, "All right, Lukas, let's take you to see the Chief and the Shaman. Save your story for them. In the meantime, I am Chogan, and this is Askook. We are happy to see you."

As we rode across the maize field toward the longhouses, Chogan and Askook explained how the Mohawks finally forced the clan to relocate their campsite to the east.

"There were too many clashes, too many deaths," Askook said.

I imagined the difficulty of abandoning the site where the people of the Turtle Clan had lived and prospered for generations.

"It was a matter of our survival," Chogan said.

It started small, with a few of the clan recognizing me. But the news spread quickly about the visitor. Within moments, men and women who must not have seen me in years were calling out my name. The young naïve boy who had left years before with the son of the Chief, in a quest to seek out the Great Spirit, was being greeted as a returning hero.

A pathway cleared, and I saw what must have been the Chief approaching. He was dressed exactly as I wrote about him in my journal, wearing a white robe tied with the brown and orange belt, and draped across his shoulders was a long orange cape.

"Lukas, is that you," he bellowed with a smile.

"Hello, Chief," I said, knowing my uncertainty of who he was must have been evident in my eyes.

"It is good to see you, my son. You look well," he said. The sight of me seemed to bring a youthful vigor to his aging face.

I offered at best an awkward smile but was unable to return the joy that the Chief exuded. Fearing my strange behavior might seem disrespectful, I said, "Please excuse my unease, Chief. It's good to see you, too."

Chogan, sensing my embarrassment, said, "He consumed the Moon Flower, and lost his memories."

I nodded and looked at the Chief.

"Ah, I understand. Relax Lukas, you are among friends. Come, there is much you need to tell me," he said, and led me into his longhouse.

As I walked down the center of the longhouse, a woman ran toward me, wrapped her arms around me, and said, "Lukas, I never thought I would ever see you again. Tell me about Rowtag. Is he alive?"

"Anna?" I asked, thinking this must be the Chief's wife and Rowtag's mother.

"Don't you remember me, Lukas?"

The Chief leaned over and whispered into her ear. She looked at me, nodded and smiled.

I answered her first question. "The last I saw him he was alive. He has married and has a young child."

Anna placed her hands over her heart. "Where is he, Lukas?"

"Anna, let us sit. Lukas will tell us everything," the Chief said, patiently.

As I sat by the fire with the Chief, Anna, and several warriors, including Askook and Chogan, I shared the story of all that happened to me since I left the Clan four years earlier.

Suddenly, the Shaman appeared and greeted me with a question. "Have you encountered the Wendigo on your journey?"

I sat silent for a moment, staring at the Shaman, trying to process the question.

"I did indeed encounter the Wendigo in many forms throughout my travels. But I imagine that the greatest challenges are still to come."

"Captain Lovewell?" the Chief asked, referring to my telling of the story about the Rangers searching for the captain's son.

"Indeed. The captain is the living Wendigo. I must warn the Pequawkets and you must be on alert as well. It is best I do not linger here too long."

It was well into the evening before I concluded. The Chief and Anna were both relieved to know that their son Rowtag had survived a wolf attack, and was doing well living with the Pequawkets. I asked if someone would now go and retrieve Rowtag from the Pequawkets. "He is your future Chief," I said.

Chief Nicholas shook his head, and told me, "He has decided not to return. I cannot force him, nor do we want him as Chief if it is not his will."

"Why don't you stay with us, Lukas?" Anna kindly asked.

"I would love to make a life here. But my journey is not done. The Wendigo must be stopped," I said.

The next morning, Wili and I were ready to head toward the White Mountains. I said my farewells to Askook, Chogan,

Anna and the Chief. Before I mounted my horse, the Shaman pulled me aside and said, "You have come far, Lukas. You are indeed a warrior, but you should know that as a warrior, you will be constantly challenged."

"I am aware," I assured the Shaman.

"The only chance you have of defeating the Wendigo is by first resolving your inner conflicts. Find a way, Lukas, to connect with the Great Spirit for guidance. Only through the Gitchi Manitou will you find the happiness you seek."

Chapter 2

As evening approached, I spotted a group of caves that looked similar to what I had written about in my journal. I figured this must be where Rowtag and I first encountered the ravens, and where he had explained to me how these remarkable birds scouted for the wolves. But with the cover of the summer foliage, Wili and I were well hidden from view of the ravens, and consequently from any danger of wolf attack.

I set up a few deadfall traps, and the next morning I was gifted with a squirrel. The breakfast of roasted meat filled my belly. With Wili rested, watered and fed we headed down the mountainside, and out into the open plains.

"I am sure we will cause quite a fuss when we ride into the Pequawket camp tomorrow," I told Wili.

He paid my words no attention, but kept a steady trot over the grassy plains. He seemed at ease with no more mountainous terrain to climb or descend.

The Pequawket longhouses were tucked nicely against the foothills of the mountains. Running alongside the village was a mighty river that roared in the springtime but moved gently this late in the season.

I imagined Rowtag and Nadie teaching their child how to swim in the nearby pond. The baby must be two years old by now. I shook my head, thinking about the last time I had seen them and how I had stormed off in anger.

"That's not the way of the warrior," I lamented to Wili.

Wili jerked his head up and down, agreeing with me.

The Pequawket village came into view under the midday sun. It was a hot day and only a few plumes of smoke drifted into the sky. I gripped the bridle and let out a long exhalation. Sensing my anxiety, Wili came to a stop.

"It's all right, Wili, let's go in slowly," I reassured him.

The village gave an appearance from afar that all was normal. I saw people moving about as expected. However, as Wili and I approached, there were no warriors to greet the stranger. This was unusual, and could be dangerous if I was planning to do harm.

Once in the village, I dismounted and led Wili through the meandering paths to Chief Squandro's longhouse. I tied Wili to the post and walked inside. A flurry of people moving about and speaking among themselves made it apparent that something significant had occurred, which was probably the reason for the lack of security.

I pushed my way through the onlookers to the center of the longhouse, where I saw the Shaman presiding over a body lying upon a blood-stained platform built upon logs. Standing next to the Shaman was the Chief, who was observing the Shaman as he provided medical care to the injured person. The Shaman was giving instructions to an older woman who was attending the fire, where it looked like a remedy was being prepared.

As I approached, I saw someone step up alongside the Chief—it was Nadie. I jerked my head slightly forward, and my eyes opened wide at the sight of her. This was the first time I had seen her since that day over two years ago when I left the Pequawket's camp in anger.

I had a moment to look at her before we made eye contact. Her skin was as smooth as a river stone, and her almond-shaped brown eyes sparkled from the reflection of the flame burning below her. My heart and breath ceased at once, and it wasn't until our eyes met that they resumed. I exhaled, and said, "Hello, Nadie."

She gave me the briefest of smiles, then pointed to the body. I took a step closer and at last I could make out the injured person—it was Rowtag.

"What happened to Rowtag," I called out.

With his back facing me, the Chief turned his head and summoned me over. I came close and the Chief put his arm around my shoulder and said, "Your friend is dying."

I looked at Rowtag, who now saw me and called out, "Lukas, is that you?" He held out his hand for me to grasp.

"Yes, it's me, Rowtag. What happened?"

"I was ambushed," he said.

"The musket shot went in too deep. There's nothing I can do," said the Shaman, holding up his hands covered in Rowtag's blood.

I leaned in to Rowtag. "I'm sorry for leaving the way I did."

"I do not begrudge you your anger, my friend. I understand. Stay with me now. It's finally my time to be with the Great Spirit," he said coughing up blood.

Within minutes his eyes closed, his grip released from my hand, his last breath passed through his lips, and he was gone. Silence encompassed the longhouse.

I stood by Rowtag's body, listening to the Shaman offer his prayers and watched as his body was wrapped in sheets of birch bark in preparation for burial. A hand squeezed my shoulder and I turned and saw the Chief.

"Let's take a walk, Lukas," he said.

We walked for a few minutes without speaking until we reached the edge of the stream running along the outskirts of the camp. The Chief gestured to a few large boulders for a place where we could sit. He moaned a bit as he settled his aged body.

"It seems that I arrived just in time to say goodbye to Rowtag," I said.

"Times like these bring us closer to the Great Spirit."

"Can you tell me what happened?" I asked.

"A foolish mistake got Rowtag killed. Scouts warned us that Captain Lovewell and his Rangers were seen in the south. Rowtag decided to go see for himself. He told no one he was going," the Chief said.

"Was that when he was shot by a Ranger?"

"I don't think so. He never made it that far south. Something else happened. I don't know. But I doubt it was the Rangers. I'm sending Kitchi and Wematin in the morning to find out."

"I'll go with them," I said.

"No, Lukas, I want you to stay here. Kitchi and Wematin can handle this."

I remembered these warriors. These two were the fiercest men I had ever came across. As a white man, they were never particularly fond of me, but always respectful.

"Let me go too, I can help."

"We need you here with the tribe," he said.

But staying here with the tribe will mean seeing and speaking with Nadie, I thought. *What words can I possibly say to her on the day she lost her husband and I lost my closest friend, Rowtag?*

Chapter 3

The first day after the death of Rowtag, I woke up early to attend to Wili. He was still tied to the same post. I should have brought him to the stables with the other horses.

"I'm sorry, Wili, for neglecting you," I said petting his favorite spot under his neck.

"Talking to your horse?" said Nadie, appearing on the pathway to the stream and holding the hand of a small boy.

Her sudden appearance caused my heart to race. I took a breath to compose myself and then said, "Wili and I speak often. He is a great listener."

I leaned over, and asked, "And who is this fine little man?"

"This is my son, Huritt," Nadie answered.

"Hello, Huritt. My name is Lukas. Would you like to meet my horse?"

Huritt's large brown eyes sparkled with delight as he nodded. I held my hands out to him and he raised his arms, allowing me to lift him. With one hand squeezing my neck, he reached his other to touch Wili.

"His name is Wili. Wili, this is my new friend Huritt."

Wili nodded, acknowledging the introduction.

"That's how he says hello, Huritt."

"After I get some water," Nadie said, lifting the bucket to show me, "I'll bring Huritt back to the longhouse, and come back to see you. We should talk."

"I would like that," I said to Nadie.

I placed Huritt back down, and said to him, "I'll see you soon, my new friend."

"Huritt is a beautiful boy," I said to Nadie when she returned.

"Thank you, Lukas. He has been a blessing to Rowtag and me," she said, while we walked along the pathway leading to the pond.

"Does he know what happened?"

"I told him that his father has gone to live with the Great Spirit," she said as tears ran down her cheeks.

"I'm sorry about Rowtag, Nadie," I said, putting an arm around her as we walked. She lay her head upon my shoulders, and I felt her sobs overtaking her body.

"I can't believe you showed up moments before his death," she said when she was finally able to speak.

"Do you know how he got shot?"

"I don't. He left at night without telling me where he was going. When I woke up he was gone. The next time I saw him was yesterday when he rode in slumped over his horse."

I nodded and pursed my lips, acknowledging her sadness.

"We have much to talk about," Nadie said, as we came to the pond.

We sat next to each other at the water's edge and talked for hours while I threw pebbles into the pond. There was much to tell. When I finally caught her up with my life's story since my abrupt departure over two years ago, she asked me, "Has there been anyone in your life, Lukas?"

"You mean since you?" I asked.

She nodded.

"No, Nadie, there has been no one since you."

Nadie looked at me with her bloodshot eyes, and smiled.

Chapter 4

The Pequawket burial site was located in a pleasant setting between the village longhouses and the foothills of the mountains. Rowtag's grave was easy to find, since it was the only one with a fresh mound of dirt still free of weeds and grasses.

There was so much to say, as I sat cross-legged and spoke to my friend.

"We met when we were two young boys looking for adventure that evolved into purpose. We believed in each other's dreams of becoming warriors. Since then, our lives have become entangled, like vines wrapping around a tree. Your journey is now over and you are with the Great Spirit. Yet here I am, still seeking a reason for my journey. I will miss you, my friend."

I returned from the burial site in a melancholy mood. Just at the depth of my self-reflection, I heard a commotion and ran to its source. It was Kitchi and Wematin returning to the village.

Sharing a ride with Kitchi was a man with his hands bound behind his back. As they approached, I saw the prisoner's unmistakable blond hair.

"Alan! What are you doing here?" I asked.

"Lukas, why am I not surprised to see you?" he said, scowling and shaking his head.

I looked over to Wematin and asked, "Why is he here?"

"You know him?"

"Yes, he is Captain Lovewell's son. We met in New York."

"He is the one who shot and killed Rowtag," Wematin said.

"Is this true that you shot Rowtag?" I asked translating for Alan.

Alan nodded, and said, "Yes, I shot the savage."

"You're just as pitiful as I remember you. Now you have killed my friend. I don't know who is worse, you or your evil father."

Alan was escorted to the Chief's longhouse. I followed close behind, anxious to hear the details. Whatever the truth was, the consequences would be significant, considering the status of the prisoner.

The Chief was speaking with the Shaman as we entered. He gestured that we should approach. The warrior gave Alan a push that caused him to stumble and fall. I reached down and grabbed onto his arm to help him to his feet.

"Don't help the rodent," barked Kitchi.

I shouldn't have helped, but I felt sorry for him for having a father like the captain. If he had been born into a different family, he might actually have stood a chance to become a good person.

As we sat the Chief asked me, "Who is this?"

"His name is Alan Lovewell," I said.

The Chief looked at me, surprised to hear the name.

"He is the son of the captain," I acknowledged.

"Lukas, why do you always attract trouble?" the Chief asked.

I opened my palms to the sky and shrugged.

Chapter 5

After hours of interrogation we learned Alan's story of why and how he shot and killed Rowtag. It apparently began after overhearing his father discussing a plan of relocating the Algonquin speaking natives off the lands throughout New England.

Alan had shared with me a few times his desire of becoming a Ranger just like his father. So with desire in his heart to slaughter natives, he decided to sneak away, and create a name for himself.

What he didn't think about was how to survive the wilderness. His life of comfort and ease in the city had equipped him with no survival skills, and eventually he found himself in trouble.

He made it past the wall and up to the northern tip of Mannahatta. The ferryboat took him and his horse to the eastern shores of the North River. From there he rode along The Kings Highway.

He had no problems on the well-traveled road. But one evening, during a heavy downpour, he veered off the roadway looking for shelter. He rode upon his horse for hours and eventually found a hollowed-out tree, where he tucked himself within its protection, while his horse withstood the storm, and he waited for morning.

When daylight came, and the rains finally stopped, Alan tried to find his way back to the main road. The city-boy wandered for hours. If it wasn't for two beaver traders passing by, who knows what would have happened to him. They provided directions that brought him to the nearest town.

With some coins in his pocket, he found a meal and a comfortable bed at a respectable establishment, called the Dutchman Inn.

That evening, after a few too many ales, he got himself into a conversation with a large man with a pockmarked face. Though he spoke perfect English, Alan said he thought his accent was French.

Alan lied, saying that the English Rangers had sent him on a secret mission. He told the Frenchman that his instructions were to scout for locations of native villages for the Rangers, who would then follow up and *drive the savages from their land.*

The Frenchman offered, for a small fee, to be Alan's guide, since he knew where every tribe lived. Alan seized the opportunity and agreed with the stranger, who insisted on getting paid half up front, and the rest in portions as he located each tribal village.

Off they went, traveling due north on horseback, not following the more easterly direction of The Kings Highway. The Frenchman located several tribes and marked them on a map. Little did Alan know, the Frenchman was just as clueless as he was. The map was a ruse to convince Alan of the Frenchman's tracking abilities.

After a few weeks of travel they accidentally stumbled upon Rowtag. They found him alone tending his horse. Alan believed that coming home with a scalp would be the ultimate proof that he was worthy to be a Ranger. How could his father refuse after Alan provided a real native scalp?

The Frenchman told Alan to shoot him from behind an embankment of trees. "Then once he's dead, you just scalp him with your knife."

As Rowtag tended to his horse, Alan shot him in the belly. Alan saw blood run down his loincloth and onto the ground. Rowtag managed to mount his horse and get away before Alan could reload and fire again.

Alan was found alone and lost. The Frenchman took off, flush with Alan's coins. Alan was so distraught that when the warriors gave him a description of Rowtag, he confessed.

Now Alan was locked away as a prisoner, awaiting his punishment.

Chapter 6

I had to admit that it was difficult seeing Alan caged like an animal, even if he did murder my closest friend. He sat on packed earth in the corner of a cage made of sturdy tree branches. His arms were wrapped around his bent legs and his forehead rested upon his knees.

"Hello, Alan," I said walking into the longhouse segregated for the horses and the occasional prisoner.

Allan lifted his head and looked at me. I could see he had been crying. "You need to get me out of here, Lukas. If my father finds me like this, you know what he will do."

I did know, but the Chief would not permit me to take Alan back to the city.

"It is out of my hands," I informed him.

There was not much more to say. When I asked Alan about his actions, his reasoning was a disjointed ramble of nonsense. So I left him to think about what he had done, and await his punishment.

As I left the well-guarded longhouse, I saw Kitchi walking toward me.

"I've been looking for you," he said.

"What will happen to him?" I asked.

Kitchi put a finger to his lips to silence me. He whispered, "Let's find a place to talk."

We took the path that wound around the longhouses and out into the burial ground. I glanced over at him as we walked. Why had Kitchi approached me? We had never spoken much when I lived with the tribe. But perhaps his dislike of me was something that I imagined.

We stopped in front of Rowtag's grave where a dandelion had sprouted.

"He felt distraught, betraying you with Nadie," he said, gesturing to the grave.

"I understand," I said.

"There was no way of knowing what happened to you. Time had passed, and he and Nadie grew close."

"I know what they did wasn't meant to hurt me," I said.

"After Nadie gave birth to Huritt, things were good between them for a while. But soon they drifted apart. I noticed that any time your name came up in conversation, she seemed to spark to attention. I think she still loves you, Lukas."

These words caused memories to explode like cannon fire in my mind. I thought of all the happy times we'd had together when we'd first fallen in love. *Could it be possible that she never stopped loving me?* I had to see her again, and soon.

As we walked back, I asked, "What's going to happen to Alan?"

Kitchi inhaled and let out a slow deliberate breath. "It has been a long time since we have punished someone for murder. I have been told stories about how our tribe burned prisoners alive, and not in a roaring fire. It's more like a roasting, placing one hot coal after another, eating away at the body. During this slow agonizing torture, the prisoner's fingers are broken then yanked and twisted by the children. There are also stories of skin being sliced off and forcing the prisoner to eat his own flesh. I could go on, but I think you get the idea."

I felt sick thinking that Alan could face this ordeal.

"We can't let that happen to him," I said.

"Don't get any ideas of trying to rescue Alan. He did kill Rowtag, plus you will never get him out of there."

"What if he dies before the ceremony? Can we poison him?" I asked.

"It is true what is said about you, Lukas. You are always looking for trouble," Kitchi said, shaking his head.

Chapter 7

There was still no decision about when Alan's punishment ritual would take place. I hoped the Chief would decide to at least wait and see if I was right about the possibility of the captain coming to rescue his son. Alan could be a useful asset in a trade, and in return, sparing the tribe from a bloody and brutal fight.

In the meantime, my days were filled helping Nadie take care of Huritt. When she was busy with her responsibilities to the tribe, I took him for swims to the pond, or walks up into the mountains. He was curious, stopping to look at things that I imagined I would have also paid attention to as a small boy. I wondered how long it would take Huritt to forget his father. I could never replace Rowtag, but the boy would need a father figure, someone who could teach him about hunting, and if he desired, provide the guidance in seeking out the Great Spirit as a path to becoming a warrior. *Perhaps I could be that man*, I thought.

In the evenings while Huritt slept, Nadie and I took walks and shared our stories. She spoke warmly about Rowtag, but I could tell from her words and mannerisms that she and Rowtag didn't have the same connection she had with me. This thought gave me hope that we could rekindle our romance.

"Rowtag was caring and loving during the pregnancy. Even after Huritt was born, our relationship was good, for a while. But eventually, we grew apart," she sighed, and then continued. "But it was no one's fault. The only connection we had was Huritt, and I suppose that wasn't enough to base a happy marriage upon."

I nodded and said, "I'm sorry about how things turned out, Nadie."

She smiled, and said, "I am, too. But enough about me, tell me your story."

I told her of Asser and Miriam, and how I lived with them in New York City. She was fascinated with the stories of my travels that took me across the great Atlantic Ocean to Amsterdam, where I learned the intricacies of international trade, and how I sailed on the *Fluyt* to the African Gold Coast, and first learned of the atrocities of the slave trade.

The story about meeting the dwarf-size Quaker man Benjamin Lay intrigued her, and how he recruited me to sneak on board the slave ship, the *Isabella*.

"Men, women and children were chained together in the hull of the ship, Nadie. I have never seen humans treated so poorly."

Nadie put her hand to her head, her jaw slacked open. "I cannot imagine the horror," she said.

"I will never forget the looks of despair on their faces. This made me determined to help Benjamin distribute his pamphlet, *The Abolition of Slavery*."

I recounted my meeting with the author of the book *Jews in America* during my time in Philadelphia.

"It was a remarkable presentation, Nadie."

"What was it about?"

"The Quaker Thomas Thorowgood believes that the native tribes occupying our lands originally came from a far away place, known as Israel, many moons ago. These people were like us in our ways and customs. They even lived, as we live, in separate tribes. At some point in their ancient history, a fierce oppressor invaded and forced the tribes to disperse across the earth."

"That's sounds remarkable. Do you believe this is possible?"

"I do, Nadie. There are profound similarities that cannot be easily dismissed. Plus I have this sense of a deeper connection that I can't bring to the surface. It feels as if it is locked away somewhere in the deepest recesses of my mind."

Nadie let out a sigh and grabbed my hand. We were sitting under the willow tree as the pond's surface reflected the full moon.

"Maybe you haven't completed your Moon Flower journey. Perhaps you need to return and find the answers you are seeking."

"Are you saying I should consume the Moon Flower again?"

She nodded, and said, "Perhaps. You should speak with the Shaman. He will advise you."

"But what if I lose my memory again, and don't remember you?"

Nadie smiled, leaned over, and kissed my lips. She pulled away, and said, "I am not worried. You will not forget me, Lukas."

The softness of her lips upon mine sent a rush of warmth coursing through my body. I'd fantasized about this moment of kissing Nadie for the first time, after my long absence. But my imagination underestimated my reaction, because my heart was pounding like war drums. This assured me that indeed, she could not be forgotten.

Later that evening, I found the Shaman in his longhouse.

"Are you ready?" he asked, and gestured for me to sit.

The layers of blankets provided a soft bed I would rest upon during my journey. As I sat down, the Shaman handed me a small clay cup filled with the brownish liquid. I gazed into the greenish spiral design forming upon its surface.

I looked up to the Shaman. "Will I lose my memory again?"

The Shaman's eyes were still powerful, even if his face was showing his advanced age. His wisdom had always comforted me. He stroked his chin with his aged hands and said, "It is true that taking the Moon Flower a second time is tempting fate, Lukas."

The Shaman asked if I wanted to write down my memories of the last three years. I shook my head, and said, "The first time I consumed the Moon Flower, I had no expectations of the journey I was about to undertake, and consequently I closed off many chambers in my mind. Today, I have a purpose, which is to open those doors, all the doors, and expose whatever it is I am hiding. I am no longer afraid. I will not forget."

I lifted the cup to my lips and drank.

Book 7

Chapter 1

A light, so faint it is nearly swallowed by the darkness,
illuminates Mother who is holding my hand.
"Is it the truth you seek?"
I nod and follow her.
"Why do you question me, Lukas?"
I don't know what she means. I shake my head.
"What do you feel when you are with me?"
"I feel love."
"Then why do you not know your mother?"
"I do know her. It is you."
"Why are you here, Lukas?" Mother asks.
"To connect with the Great Spirit."
"You are connected, Lukas."
The light flickers out. I am in darkness.

Alan is perched ten feet high on a platform, lying tied down on his back. He stares into the gray sky where black as coal ravens scout the scene. The wolves will be here soon for their bounty, the ravens will settle for the scraps.

Alan screams out in pain. The ritual has begun. I hold a knife out and carve into his skin, slicing a small piece of flesh from his leg, and hold the bloody tissue in the air before guiding it into Alan's mouth.

I hear his voice. He shouts my name. I look out from the platform and I see Captain Lovewell.

"Put down the knife," the captain commands, riding high in the saddle of his mighty horse. He lifts a gleaming sword skyward. His poise is stunning.

I look at the bloody knife in my hand. Alan screams. His body is a seething skinless form of a man. I toss the knife away.

"What have you done to my son?" the Captain pleads and leaps from his horse to the platform supporting Alan and me. He lifts his sword and swings down into the darkness.

Father is with me under the willow. Its green branches flutter in the breeze.

"Why do you struggle, my son?" Father asks.

"I need to know the truth," I say.

"Why do you need to know the truth?"

"How else will I know who I am? What is my purpose? How do I connect with the Great Spirit?"

"Ah, you mean Hashem?"

I nod.

"The truth is already known, Lukas. It is locked away within rooms in your mind. Open the doors to defeat the demons. The truth is waiting for you. Your freedom and connection with Hashem are within your reach."

It is nighttime. I hear people snoring, interrupted with an occasional cough. All else is quiet. I feel weak, but manage to prop myself up on my elbows.

Where am I? I do not recognize this place. I get to my feet, but just as quickly I am consumed by dizziness and collapse. A cool cloth swipes across my forehead. Sparkling brown eyes look at me.

"Are you all right, Lukas?" a voice asks.

My eyes open. A woman is above me, locks of black hair falling across her face. She brushes them aside.

"Nadie? Is it you?" I ask touching her cheek.

She clasps my hand. "Yes, Lukas, it is me. Do you remember?"

"I do, I remember everything."

Chapter 2

Huritt smacked the ball, made from deerskin and stuffed with animal hairs, across the field with his stick. I retrieved the mis-hit and showed him a better way to strike the ball with a two hand grip, instead of one.

Huritt adjusted his hands, studied the ball lying on the grass before him, took a back swing and swung with all of his might. The rounded end of the carved wooden stick connected, sending the ball in a straight line, hip height off the ground and disappearing beyond the sloping hill into the distance.

He looked at me, smiling joyfully.

"Wonderful, Huritt," cried his mother, as she walked toward us.

"Mama, did you see that? Lukas is teaching me how to play."

"I did, my love."

Nadie opened her arms as Huritt leapt into them. She lifted him and they kissed.

With Huritt nestled on her hip and his arm wrapped around her neck, Nadie leaned over to kiss me.

"The Chief has asked that you join him," she said.

"Has there been news?" I asked.

"I believe so."

A few days earlier, we had received reports from trappers that English Rangers had been seen in the south. The Chief had sent a team of warriors to scout the southern plains. I figured that it wasn't good news since they returned in only a few days. That would mean they were closer than we thought.

"What will happen?" Nadie asked as we walked back to the Chief's longhouse.

"We will fight. You and Huritt must go to the caves and wait. I will come for you when it is over."

She squeezed my hand and said, "I will wait for you, Lukas."

These words reminded me of her and Rowtag's betrayal.

She must have sensed my thoughts, because she added, "I will wait for you, my love."

The village was frantic, preparing for the forthcoming battle with the captain and his Rangers. The Chief was speaking with several of his warriors when he saw me.

"You need to move Alan," he said.

"Move him where?"

"With us into the mountains. We will wait for the Rangers there."

"Leave the village empty?" I asked.

"Yes, the women and children will hide in the caves. This will be a fight to the death," the Chief said.

"I understand, Chief. I will go fetch Alan now."

"Lukas, you must go speak with the Shaman first," he said.

Upon entering the longhouse of the Shaman, I saw Kitchi, whose face was being painted blood red, with a long black image of a feather below each eye. He saw me and pointed to where the Shaman was waiting for me.

"Sit with me, Lukas," the Shaman said.

"Now?" I asked.

"Before you go into battle we need to talk," he said.

I exhaled and took a seat across from the wise man.

"Has the Moon Flower released you?" the Shaman said.

"It feels that way."

"What can you tell me, Lukas?"

"My memories are coming back, but not at once. It's as if I need a trigger to stimulate them."

"That is the way they regenerate. You will see an image or hear a word. They act like a key unlocking a door into the chambers of your mind."

"That is what is happening," I said.

"With this pending battle with the English Rangers, there is one recovered memory that deserves your attention."

"You are referring to Captain Lovewell's murder of Father?"

"I am indeed, Lukas."

"That memory is still locked away."

"That is what I thought. If that memory is released upon the battlefield you must take care to not let your raw emotion overwhelm you."

"What do you fear?" I asked.

"That you react foolishly. The captain is a trained killer with years of experience fighting and beating more ruthless opponents than you. You stand no chance against him."

"That is probably true," I said. "But if I am to die on the battlefield it will be by his sword and no one else's."

Chapter 3

After my discussion with the Shaman, I heard from Kitchi that the Rangers were close. I looked around and saw the village was nearly empty. A few warriors were tending the fires to make sure they remained burning, at least until the Rangers arrived. If they saw smoke from smoldering fires, they would realize the village was abandoned.

My task was to escort the prisoner into the mountains, where Alan would be detained while we battled the Ranger army. I was not at first concerned upon reaching the longhouse and finding the guards posted at its entrance gone. After all, only a few warriors were left in the village. But when I entered, I saw that the cage where Alan was imprisoned was empty. The ropes that had secured the door had been chopped away.

I ran out into the village yard. Not a soul was left. Alan couldn't have gone far, especially if he was on foot. I quickly mounted Wili and headed south. It didn't take me long to find his tracks. He was heading toward his father. He must have found out about the pending attack.

I saw Alan just as he reached the advancing army. Quickly I dismounted Wili and took cover. I was too far to hear what he was saying, but his gestures and Captain Lovewell's facial reactions told me the story.

Someone summoned a horse for Alan. The Captain shouted orders to the men. Alan mounted the horse and took the lead. He pointed in the direction of the mountains where the Pequawket warriors were hiding. I needed to warn the tribe.

"Come on, Wili, run like you have wings," I encouraged my reliable companion.

Holding tight to the bridle, I glanced to my right and saw flashing through the trees, broken images of the Rangers in full gallop. I would have only a few moments to warn the tribe.

Wili was fully engaged. We bolted through the village, hopefully gaining time because we knew the pathways that wound around the longhouses. Once beyond, we charged up the steep rocky pathway leading to our hideaway.

I dismounted and saw the Chief and dozens of warriors readied for battle.

The Chief asked, "Where is the prisoner?"

"He has escaped and warned the Rangers. They are headed this way now. We must engage. There is no time."

Just as my words were spoken, sounds of hundreds of horses pounding upon the rocky path echoed among the surrounding bluff. They were coming. The Chief shouted his commands.

Chapter 4

The battle would be fought upon this rocky plateau, and there would be no escape once the fighting commenced. To our backs was a towering cliff reaching up beyond our sight. Only twenty paces across was a steep precipice perched high above a scramble of boulders, where a fall meant a bone-breaking death.

We would fight them on foot, first greeting them with a quick volley of arrows as they turned the bend to face us. After that, the battle would be hand-to-hand.

Standing next to me was Kitchi, gripping his knife firmly in his right hand. I squeezed his shoulder, and he nodded. We were at least thirty strong, standing together and poised.

Alan's was the first face I saw. His flushed expression of excitement melted away the moment he saw us. Arrows flew, and one found Alan's arm and sank into his flesh. His horse bucked and skidded, tossing him off. He hit the ground hard. My first instinct was to help him, but I recovered from such a foolish thought as I saw the overwhelming force attack.

Captain Lovewell led the charge. I gasped upon seeing him seated on his mighty horse. He was dressed in his impressive red uniform, adorned with bright gold buttons. He saw me, and smiled. His gold tooth glimmered, looking as large as one of the buttons on his jacket.

I tried to swallow, but my throat felt as dry and coarse as the sands on the African Gold Coast. My mind flashed an image of the Wendigo, salivating at the sight of me.

The captain's shouting of orders snapped me out of my stupor. He pointed his sword at me and charged.

With no apparent concern for his fallen son who was lying wounded, he lifted his sword high, and from the vantage of his horse, sliced down through the flesh of a charging warrior. Blood sprayed and bedlam ensued.

Within the tight confines of the battlefield, the Rangers soon lost their strategic advantage of fighting on horseback and dismounted.

I faced off with a large bearded man. His eyes burned with hatred. He deflected my attempted knife thrust into his belly with the ease of swatting away an annoying mosquito. He gripped my neck hard. I struggled to escape, but dizziness overtook me. My legs started to buckle. I fell to my knees. The light was going dim.

Suddenly the death grip was released, and air rushed back into my starved lungs. The bearded man was lying beneath me with a knife protruding from his neck. Blood sprayed out in a stream. A hand gripped the knife and pulled it out, while another hand helped me to my feet. It was Wematin. He patted my back.

"Are you all right?" he asked.

"I'm good," I answered with a raspy voice.

There was fighting surrounding me. It was warrior against Ranger; a battle to the death.

I saw Alan lying in a pool of blood. He was in agony. I rushed to him. An arrow had penetrated deep into his upper arm. I removed my belt and tied it tight above the wound, and the bleeding stopped.

"You'll survive," I told him.

I was about to rise and rejoin the battle, when Alan gripped my hand and said, "Thank you."

I patted his chest and nodded.

In the moment that it took me to attend to Alan, the battle changed. More Rangers had fallen than warriors. Warriors were now double-teaming single Ranger fighters. Kitchi and Wematin had backed a powerful looking man to the cliff's edge. He peeked behind him, trying not to get too close. This distraction gave Kitchi the moment to kick him backward. The Ranger plummeted straight down. I imagined his body breaking apart on the jagged rocks below.

Small glimmering stones soaked in blood were kicked about as the fighting wound down.

"There will be no survivors," declared the Chief.

Captain Lovewell had not yet fallen. He held off two warriors, who kept darting in and out, away from his knife thrusts. Off to his side, lying harmlessly on the gravel, was his sword broken in two. The captain displayed impressive fighting skills against two seasoned warriors. As his body tired, his eyes turned yellow, like those of the wolf. I stepped in and shouted, "Enough."

The Warriors stopped and look at me, and then at the Chief.

I answered before the Chief could respond. "The captain is our prisoner. He must be punished for the murder of my father. He doesn't deserve the honor of being slain in battle."

"Kill him now," demanded Wematin, covered in the blood of his kills.

"My father's death deserves retribution. I demand it."

The Chief stepped forward, the blood-stained gravel crunching under his feet. He looked at the captain and then at Alan, who had sat up during the pause in hostilities. A few of the surviving Rangers, with minor wounds, also gawked at the scene.

"Take the captain and his son back to the village. We will give Lukas the satisfaction he is entitled to," said the Chief.

"What about the others?" asked Kitchi.

"No survivors," answered the Chief.

The captain and Alan were leashed to a warrior who pulled them on horseback back down the mountainside toward the village. Alan stumbled at the sudden jerk, but regained his footing.

As the prisoners made their way, the surviving six Rangers were forced to stand at the cliffs edge. The men look down at their impending doom and shouted out pleas for mercy.

"Turn around," ordered Wematin.

As they turned, they faced six warriors, each holding a drawn bow with an arrow locked in place. The arrows were let loose and pierced deep into the torsos of the frightened Rangers. The force took each one over the edge, and for a brief moment they were airborne, until we heard their bones break upon the boulders below.

Chapter 5

Father and son were held captive in the same cage where Alan had spent his previous captivity. Guards were posted and warned that if these prisoners escaped, retribution to the warriors on duty would be severe.

The Chief ordered me to interrogate Alan to uncover who allowed his escape. I greeted the warriors at the entrance and just as I was about to step into the longhouse, I heard Nadie calling out my name. I looked around and saw her running toward me.

When she reached me, she was breathless.

"Lukas, I need to speak with you," she gasped.

"Not now, Nadie. I need to question Alan."

"It's about Alan that we need to talk," she said.

"All right, what is it? Do you know who helped him escape?"

She leaned in and whispered, "It was me."

Nadie took my hand and led me to a private spot just beyond the longhouses and close to the maize fields. We sat among a few scattered boulders with tall grasses growing about.

"Please don't be angry with me," she began.

"Why would you release him? It makes no sense."

"It did, Lukas. I sensed vengeful anger from you toward the captain. I was afraid that your emotions would get you killed in battle." She paused, and plucked a dandelion stem growing at her feet.

"I made a bargain with Alan. He agreed that upon his release he would find his father and tell him of our kind treatment, and convince him to turn back, and let us live in peace."

"Oh Nadie, what have you done?" I asked with a sigh.

"But all has turned out well regardless," she said with a slight smile.

"It has, but what am I to tell the Chief? I cannot say it was you who released Alan. He would need to punish you for such disobedience," I said shaking my head.

Nadie rubbed her chin, tilted her head, and said, "Maybe we don't have to tell the Chief. What if we take Huritt and leave the tribe? We can make a life on our own, away from here."

I gave this some thought for a moment. *Maybe leaving the tribe and starting over with Nadie and Huritt would be good for us*, I thought.

"Okay, Nadie. I guess we have no choice. Prepare what we need. Don't share our plans with anyone. We will leave tonight after the punishment ceremony for the captain."

"What will happen to Alan?" she asked with her hand gently on her cheek.

I shrugged, and said, "He must be punished, like his treacherous father."

The Chief still expected me to interrogate Alan to uncover who the traitor was. So I needed to come up with a believable story.

Alan nudged his father awake when he saw me walking into the longhouse and approaching their cage.

"Hello, Alan, Captain," I said, passing the warriors guarding them.

"What do you want?" Alan barked.

"I've come to talk, that's all."

The captain stood and reached his arms in between the thick wooden bars. "Come closer, Lukas. Let me wrap my hands around that skinny neck of yours."

"Settle down, captain, save your energy. You will need it soon," I said.

"What do you want?" Alan asked again.

"Your evil ways have come to an end," I said to the captain.

"Don't be so sure of yourself, Lukas. I'm not that easy to kill," he said.

"You and your Rangers have decimated the lives of countless peaceful natives. You will finally pay for these crimes."

The captain stepped away from the bars of the cage and turned his back toward me.

"You also must answer for the murder of my father."

The captain quickly turned back around and faced me.

"Your father?" he asked, apparently unaware of the crime.

"You murdered him," I said emphatically.

The captain furrowed his forehead. It seemed he was trying to recall the event.

"Eight years ago in Beverwyck, my father and I met you and another soldier on the road as we were traveling back home. We were transporting a supply of beaver pelts and you ordered us to stop. A shoving match ensued and you shot my unarmed father in the chest with your musket."

"Perhaps you are mistaken. How can you be sure it was me?" he asked.

"Your gold tooth," I said, opening my mouth and pointing.

"Is it true, Father?" Alan asked.

"I suppose it's possible. But so what, I am sure he deserved it."

"And you deserve what's coming to you," I said with relish, turning away.

"Don't you want to know how I escaped?" Alan yelled after me.

"It really doesn't matter now, does it?" I said, exiting the longhouse.

Chapter 6

____

A large raised platform was built in the center of the village. It stood well over the tallest man's outstretched reach. A few braves using ladders were finishing tying up sturdy logs to one another. One long pole rose straight up from its center, and a neat array of logs leaned against it. The captain would be tied to the pole and burned alive.

Nadie and I were sitting nearby watching Huritt play with his friends. We were careful not to even whisper of our plans to leave after tonight's ceremony.

"You still haven't told me what Alan's punishment will be," Nadie said.

"He will be scalped, and made to run the gauntlet," I said.

"What's a gauntlet?" Huritt asked.

"It's nothing you need to know about," Nadie told him.

I agreed. A child Huritt's age should not witness the brutal punishment of a prisoner running in between two lines of warriors, who beat him with sticks and smashed him with stones. Usually after the first pass through, they were wounded so severely with injuries such as a crushed skull, or broken limbs, that death could be just moments away.

Our plan was not to wait for the gauntlet. After tonight's burning we would sneak away under the cover of night. The full moon was still weeks away, and that, along with the persistent cloud cover, would provide us an undetectable escape.

Earlier in the day, I had taken Wili for a ride in order to stash essential supplies at a hiding spot in the forest, which we would retrieve later that night.

As the sun was close to setting, Nadie and I took Huritt for a last walk around the village. Memories, both wonderful and sad, flooded through my mind. This was where Nadie and I first fell in love, and also where Rowtag died.

I asked Nadie if we could go to the pond for one last look. She agreed and allowed Huritt to run ahead.

"I think I will miss this place the most," Nadie said.

I agreed, as it always provided me with a sacred site for meditation and reflection. As we approached, I saw Huritt speaking with the Shaman under the willow tree.

"Ah, Lukas, Nadie, I've been waiting for you," said the Shaman.

Nadie discreetly turned her head to offer me a frown. I returned the confused expression.

"You knew we were coming?" Nadie asked.

"Please sit. Huritt and I have been speaking about your big trip tonight."

I was stunned. "How do you know?" I asked.

"I am Shaman," he simply said.

"Will you stop us?" I asked.

"This is your decision, not mine," he said.

I smiled and placed my hand over my heart.

"But we must speak about tonight's ceremony. Nadie, please take Huritt back to the village. What I need to say to Lukas is not suitable for his young ears."

Nadie looked at me with concern, but I told her it was all right.

The Shaman waved to Nadie and Huritt as they disappeared beyond view.

"The captain has a long dark history with you?" the Shaman asked.

"He does."

"That's why you must also be a participant in tonight's ritual."

"Participate? What do you mean?"

"Evil can be destroyed through fire. But the flames alone do not complete the task," he said, and allowed a moment to pass, letting the statement sink in.

I swallowed hard, anticipating his next words.

"The captain represents the Wendigo in human form. You, Lukas, are his counterpart," the Shaman said, rising to his feet and standing over me.

He offered his hand to pull me up to stand alongside him. He held me tight with his hands on my shoulders and looked deep into my eyes.

"Lukas, to eliminate this evil you must imbibe the Moon Flower and meet the Wendigo inside the flames."

I tried to pull loose from the Shaman's grip, but was unable to break free.

"There will be a great struggle and you may be consumed in the flames as well," said the Shaman.

"I cannot do this. I am only one man. How can I fight a battle against evil?"

"You are not alone. You will lead an army of the seven generations that have preceded you and labored for a relationship with the Great Spirit. You have been chosen as the one to defeat evil and pave the way for seven generations yet to come. This will be your legacy."

I exhaled. "I must tell Nadie. She needs to know," I insisted.

"The journey begins now. She will be fine."

"I'm scared," I said and started to shake uncontrollably.

"Come with me, Lukas, it is time," the Shaman said and took me by my hand.

Chapter 7

The Shaman led me up an unfamiliar mountain path. For an elderly man, he still moved well up the steep incline. Just as I was about to ask our destination, he stepped off the path, kneeled down and turned his body sideways. He fit his skinny frame through a crevice in between two large boulders. He signaled for me to follow through this previously undetectable entrance to the cave.

Daylight barely filtered in, which made it hard to make out details of the damp cavern. The Shaman quickly started a fire with a flintstone that he carried with him. He placed a bowl down next to the burning logs. From a gourd, he poured water into the bowl, and removed a few seeds from a pouch tied to his belt. It was the Moon Flower.

The Shaman placed the crushed seeds into the water to create the mixture for me to drink. He looked up and pointed to a bed covered with bison furs and said, "Lie down, Lukas."

On my back I noticed upon the cave's ceiling a spider web of cracks spreading across its surface. Water from mountain runoff crept through the slivers and dripped onto the cave floor, where small puddles reflected back images of the ceiling.

"It is prepared, Lukas," he said handing me the bowl.

The familiar gritty brown liquid created a perfect greenish spiral. I looked at the Shaman who offered an encouraging nod and kind eyes.

"Will I survive?" I asked.

"I do not know, Lukas. You are fighting an evil that spreads its hatred through men who do not honor the Great Spirit. They exploit the powerless, the weak, for their own riches. I know you have witnessed this."

The Shaman lifted a fur and placed it around my shoulders. I sat cross-legged, holding the bowl. I tried to steady my nervous hands in order not to spill the mixture out of the bowl.

"The Wendigo has found the captain as his vessel just as the Great Spirit has chosen you. You and the captain have not crossed paths by accident, Lukas. This is the battle that I have foreseen. The first time I saw you, I recognized you from my visions. That is why I allowed you, a white man, to consume the Moon Flower."

This sent my mind into a tumultuous retrospection of the past four years. How could I make sense of the Shaman's words?

"All will become clear on the other side. Now drink, Lukas, the time has come for the final battle."

I lifted the bowl to my lips and swallowed.

Chapter 8

As the warm Moon Flower trickles down my throat, slowly filling my body like a river of thick honey, I observe the cracks in the stone ceiling begin to shift in opposing directions and scream in screeching pain as stone scrapes against stone. Dirt and dust, trapped for eons, are released and shower down upon me.

My body lifts from the fur-layered bed and I float upwards. Massive stones supporting the mountain split open. I rise between aged earth, while twists of mighty roots rip away from dirt and stones and fall beneath me.

The mountain screams as it is torn apart. At last the gash opens to the sky and I fly beyond the wounded mountain into the stormy sky. Thunderbolts explode and black clouds release a warm rain that washes off the layers of dirt and earthen debris from my body.

Violent skies subside to a peaceful silence. Clouds evaporate and expose a clear view of the heavens that surround me. Unheard words accompany images of ancient faces. They are my ancestral army of seven generations. I am not alone.

Images of Mother and Father come to me. I hear a voice. It is Father's.

"Fight in the name of those who have paved the way before you, and lead the charge for those yet to be born."

Darkness washes across the heavens and extinguishes the starlit night. My body floats in its emptiness, until a small ember dancing in the distance draws me toward it. As I approach the captain's funeral pyre it spontaneously explodes into an inferno, sending its flames into the heavens, igniting the dormant stars.

I look up to the raging fire consuming the captain. The flames rejoice in appreciation of the burning man.

I settle to the earth and walk unseen among the peoples of the tribe.

The captain's blue eyes find me in the crowd. His once shiny tooth is now a stream of melted gold dripping down his lips. He calls to me.

"Lukas, is this what you want?" he shouts over the cracking sounds of the raging inferno. It is indeed what I want, but it is not enough.

I am back on the mountainside battleground where the Pequawkets defeated the Rangers. Standing at the end of the circular gravel plateau is the captain.

"You think you can defeat me?" he asks, bending down to one knee and scooping up a handful of gravel soaked in blood.

"You are not the captain," I say, watching the blood seep between the fingers of his clenched fist.

He tosses away the bloody stones and walks toward me. With each step his limbs grow beyond human form. He rips off his Ranger uniform with blood-stained claws. I stare breathlessly at its skinless chest cavity exposing a black, beating heart. The face of the handsome captain shifts into a dog-like snout covered in brownish course fur. I look up to the creature, towering before me with its golden eyes and black wet nose, fangs dripping in a thick black gunk and tremendous elk-like antlers crowning its hideous head.

The Wendigo reaches for me with its bony appendage-like arm. I barely avoid its grasp by scrambling backward toward the cliff's edge. Could this, what the Shaman called the final battle, be over so quickly?

Another swipe from the Wendigo and I will be done for. What will happen to me? Will I transform into one of its walking dead, roaming the earth, feasting on the blood of humans?

The Wendigo lifts a long arm high into the stormy sky and swings it at me. Jumping backward allows me to avoid the claws dripping in blackish grime from being buried into me. But I run out of cliff and tumble off the edge. As I hurtle headfirst toward the jagged rocks below, I close my eyes in anticipation of my final demise.

Chapter 9

---

y eyes opened upon the familiar peaceful setting under the willow tree that shaded the pond. The Shaman was sitting there, waiting for me.

"Why am I here?" I asked taking a seat across from him.

"There is only one way to destroy the Wendigo," he said, and pointed to my knife.

I took out my blade and studied it.

The Shaman explained, "This is the knife that was bequeathed to your father by your grandfather. You are now the seventh generation to receive this. It is with this weapon you will kill the Wendigo."

The silver blade shone in the morning light. A door opened in my mind and flashed a memory of seeing this knife sheathed to Father's belt. I gripped it hard, imagining driving it through the Wendigo's ribcage and into its evil heart.

"But that will only slow him down. Wounds heal within moments," the Shaman said sensing my thoughts.

What impossible task is the Shaman about to impart? I wondered.

"To destroy it, you must cut out its heart and bring it back to me. I will encase it in this stone container," he said, showing me two sections of carved stones that when assembled together formed an enclosure. "I will bind it closed and hide it deep in the caves far from the curious hands of man."

I nodded my understanding.

Darkness consumes my vision. A beating vibration like a heartbeat pounds away in my mind. I feel the Wendigo's presence, yet I am bodiless, nothing more substantial than my thoughts.

"You cannot destroy me, Lukas," says the Wendigo.

Its words are deep and resonant, not human like, but surprisingly easy to understand. I dare not respond, for fear of being put under its spell.

"Do you think that knife of yours can do me harm?"

The darkness lifts, and I am in the cave where Rowtag and I were once attacked by the wolves. Standing before me, hunched over in the tight space, is the Wendigo, its long angular antlers scraping away eons of caked-on sediment from the cave's stone ceiling.

There is no escaping him in the confines of the cavern. He pounces, wraps a claw around my body, and lifts me toward his open jaw. In his mouthful of sharp fangs and wet black tongue, I see my certain doom.

In desperation I drive the knife deep into the Wendigo's lecherous tongue. He screams an ear-piercing cry and drops me. I fall, hitting the stone floor hard enough to jar the knife from my hand. It bounces out of my reach.

Scrambling to my feet, I stretch for the knife and grab it. The Wendigo recovers from my strike and smacks my body, sending me hard against the wall. The impact bruises my back, but I am able to maintain a grip on the knife.

I lunge at the monster again. With my left hand, I grab an exposed rib, which allows me to pull myself against its torso. I flip the knife around to point the blade downward, and thrust it through its ribs and deep into its black, beating heart. The Wendigo bellows a blood-curdling screech that echoes off the cave walls, and collapses. I squeeze my left hand through its ribcage, grip onto its devil's heart and with my knife, cut it out.

The stone-cold black heart lies still in my hands. Lying just as still, spread across the cave floor, is the Wendigo. I stand up, slip the knife into its sheath tied to my belt, and walk into the darkness of the cavern, holding the beat-less heart of the Wendigo.

Chapter 10

My eyes felt heavy as I struggled to awaken. I was back in the Shaman's secret cave. It was just as it was before my Moon Flower journey. The gentle array of cracks spreading across its rock ceiling were restored. I propped myself up on my elbows and saw the Shaman.

"What happened?" I asked.

"Ah, Lukas, you're awake," the Shaman said, with a warm smile.

"Is the Wendigo dead?"

"You have completed your task, Lukas," he said, holding the stone box bound closed with braided rope.

"What's in there?" I asked.

"The last remnant of evil," said the Shaman.

"Is it from the Wendigo?"

"You cut out its heart, Lukas."

The Shaman's words sounded strange.

"I don't understand. How is this possible?"

"You have done what was required," he said, and placed the box down on a stone ledge.

"His heart is in there?" I asked, pointing.

The Shaman nodded. "The box will be buried deep in these caves."

As I rose to my feet, I felt pain in my back.

"Why does my back hurt?"

"You must have been injured fighting the Wendigo."

"I have no memory of what happened."

"Only those trained as Shamans recall their spiritual journeys. But as you can plainly see, and apparently feel, the trip occurred," he said, patting the box and pointing to my back.

"Now wait for me here," the Shaman said, as he picked up the box and disappeared into the darkness of the cavern.

Chapter 11

I stood kicking at the burnt remains of the platform. I imagined that intermingled among the black and gray ashes being blown about through the village by the brisk wind, was the remains of Captain Lovewell.

Perhaps a peaceful life could return to the Pequawkets. But even with the captain gone, and his Rangers defeated, there was a feeling that this was not the last violent encounter with the English.

"More soldiers will return, seeking vengeance," said the Chief, affirming my thoughts as he joined me.

I nodded and kicked at a burnt log. "It's just a matter of time, I'm afraid."

"But you got what you wanted," the Chief said. Putting his arm around my shoulder, he looked into my eyes. "Your father's murder has been avenged."

I inhaled deeply and felt the aching bruise on my back, which left no doubt in my mind of the reality of the battle against the Wendigo in the spirit world.

As I watch the Chief walk back to his longhouse, I saw Huritt running toward me. I bent over and caught him as he leapt into my arms, which caused me to twinge in pain.

"Lukas, are you injured?" Nadie said as she approached and noticed my awkwardness in lifting Huritt.

"I'm fine, it's just a bruise."

Nadie and I were soon surrounded by many of the tribe. I handed Huritt to Nadie and raised my arms, asking for their attention.

"Captain Lovewell is dead. His soul has been extinguished in the flames."

There was a collective acknowledgment of heads nodding and men, women and children hugging one another.

I put my arm around Nadie and continued, "Now that he is gone, Nadie, Huritt and I will be leaving the tribe. We will head west to the people known as the Onondagas. They live in an area of many lakes, and administer a treaty among five tribes, known as the Great Peace."

Resounding cries of regrets filled the air. People huddled around us, begging us not to go. As Nadie and I tried to address their concerns, Kitchi pulled me aside.

"Will we ever meet again?" Kitchi asked me.

"Perhaps not in this lifetime, my friend," I answered.

"I wish you a safe journey. You will be missed," he said, and wrapped his arms around me.

Never known for his warmth, Wematin took me by both shoulders and pulled me in tight. "You are a true Pequawket warrior. I am proud to call you brother," he said with a surprising display of affection.

As I thanked Wematin, I saw the Chief walking toward me.

"I have a special gift for your farewell," the Chief said. It was a wampum belt that he said was made by several of the elder women of the tribe.

It was a beautiful design of small shells, bound together to form a belt, that I draped over my shoulder. "It is lovely," I said.

"Your adventures will be shared in our songs, Lukas," the Chief said, smiling. "Your story will be told to our children and to our children's children. You will never be forgotten."

Nadie brought my attention to dark clouds forming in the west. "We should leave soon so we can make camp before the storm is upon us."

"Give me a moment, Nadie," I said, as I spotted the Shaman.

With only a wisp of smoke rising from the ashes, the Shaman was staring into the charred remains of the ceremonial fire. I stood alongside the holy man and asked, "Is it really over?"

"As long as its heart remains hidden away," he said.

"What will happen if someone discovers it?" I asked.

"Each incarnation of the Wendigo becomes more powerful than its predecessor. It learns to evolve from its previous form. Pray to the Great Spirit that this never occurs."

"I will pray," I assured the Shaman.

Chapter 12

With evening and the storm clouds approaching, we made camp. I tied up Wili and Nadie's horse, Sage, to a sturdy branch. Though we were not in a cave, we did have cover from a large stone precipice that would protect us from the coming rains and possible dangerous lightning.

With Huritt asleep, Nadie leaned her head against my shoulder. We said nothing for a while as we sat and stared into the campfire.

"What will happen to us?" she asked, breaking the silence.

"Nadie, why do you keep asking me this same question?"

"I need to hear you reassure me that all will be well. That we will find this tribe you speak of and make a new life for our growing family," she said rubbing her belly.

"What do you mean, growing family?"

"I am with child," she said looking at me.

I jerked my head back and looked at her belly, then into her eyes.

At my stunned look, her brow furrowed. "Are you not happy?" she asked.

"Nadie, I couldn't be happier. This is wonderful," I said, and gave her a kiss.

I smiled as I watched over Nadie and Huritt as they slept. I observed her belly rise and lower with each breath and wondered about our child forming within her. With luck we would find the Onondaga village before she gave birth. Delivering a child was one survival skill I had not yet learned. With thunder booming in the distance, and a heavy rain pounding the forest floor, I couldn't help myself from falling asleep. I had a vivid dream about Father. We were walking together along the North River.

"You have done well, Lukas," Father said.

"I have avenged your murder. The captain is dead."

"Violence only begets violence," he said sternly.

"But your life was taken from you. You were taken from Mother, and from me."

"You may feel good about your triumph over evil. But this is not over, Lukas. The Wendigo will return."

Shaking my head, I said, "Only if his heart is found, and the Shaman will make sure that never happens."

Father pulled me close to him and whispered into my ear, "The heart has already been found."

A powerful thunderbolt struck a nearby tree, waking me from my dream. A large oak was cut in two. Flames and embers exploded and danced into the starlit night. I heard over the persistent rain, a horse approach along the road to the east. I tucked myself behind the damaged tree and prepared to defend my family from the danger.

It was hard to make out the rider in the darkness, until he called out my name.

"Lukas, is that you?"

It was Kitchi. I exhaled a long breath and stepped out from behind the tree. "What are you doing here?"

He dismounted and walked up to me and said, "Alan has escaped."

"Again? How did he manage it this time?" I asked, shaking my head.

"We don't know. He was under guard by several warriors. They claim he just vanished."

"Do you know where we went?"

"He was seen riding south."

"Is that why you are here? Just to tell me about Alan."

"There is one more disturbing piece of news," he said.

"Which is?"

"He has stolen the Wendigo's heart from the Shaman's cave."

"That's not possible," I said, clenching my fists in anger.

"All I know is what I saw, which was the Shaman running into the longhouse yelling that Alan had taken the heart."

"So what do you want me to do about it?" I asked.

"The Chief has sent me to bring back Nadie and Huritt to the tribe."

"And I assume he wants me to track down Alan and retrieve the heart?"

Kitchi nodded and said, "The Shaman says you are the only one who can do it."

Chapter 13

I figured that since Alan had nowhere else to go, he would probably end up at Castle William and Mary. It was the closest English fort and he could tell the Governor what happened to the King's Rangers and more important, how his father, Captain Lovewell, was burned to death.

But how did he know of the Wendigo's heart, and how in the world did he escape? The only possible way would be if the Shaman had something to do with it.

Only the Shaman could remove a prisoner undetected by the guards, and I told no one about the Wendigo's heart sealed in a stone box, hidden deep in a secret cave. But why would the Shaman do this? He knew that the Chief would choose me to track Alan and retrieve the heart. Hopefully, once I found and spoke with Alan, I could figure this out.

Wili and I followed the riverbank of the Piscataqua River. On a late afternoon, of the second day, the sweet smell of the ocean told me that we were close to the fort. Moments later I saw it and it was just as I remembered. The gates were open, wagons were bringing in supplies and English soldiers were milling about.

With my history, along with what Alan was now probably sharing with the Royal Governor, Benning Wentworth, what happened back at the Pequawket village, it would be foolish to enter the fort. Certainly my crimes, according to English law, would see me hanged.

While I contemplated my next move, Wili drank at the river. I stroked his neck in his favorite spot, and he leaned his head against me.

Out of nowhere I heard a scream. It came from the forested area to the west of the river. I tied up Wili and ran to investigate.

Sitting against a skinny white birch tree was Alan. His face was as white as the bark. The stone box was open, and sat in two pieces on his lap. In one hand he held a knife, which I presumed he used to cut open the bindings holding the parts together. His other hand was pointing in front of him. I followed the direction of his finger and I saw the Wendigo. He was looking directly at Alan. I stepped further back out of its line of sight.

The Wendigo stepped toward Alan, bent his massive body down to lift him up in both hands and grabbed him with outstretched arms and lifted him over its head. He opened its large jaw and I saw the familiar black slime dripping in between its ash gray fangs. Alan was looking directly into the Wendigo's mouth.

I leapt forward and attacked. I stabbed the Wendigo on the meatiest part of its body, its horse-like thigh. It howled in pain and dropped Alan, who fell hard to the ground. Black blood oozed from the gash. The Wendigo looked at me with a fearful glare. *Was it afraid of me?*

Without hesitation I lunged again, striking the Wendigo in its belly, opening a gash that released a swampy-green bile. It fell to its knees, screeching in pain. I stepped behind the large creature, grabbed its elongated jaw and slit its throat with a deep cut that nearly severed its head.

It collapsed face down on the earth, motionless. It took a great effort to push its repulsive body over, in order to expose its chest. I buried my hands deep inside the creature's chest cavity and cut out its heart. With its still beating organ in my hands, I returned it into the stone container.

"Lukas, is that you?" asked a groggy Alan.

"Are you all right, Alan?" I asked.

"I think so. What is that?" He pointed to the motionless Wendigo crumpled on the ground.

"That is the devil, and you almost resurrected it," I said, returning my knife to its sheath.

"I've never seen something so hideous," Alan said, getting to his feet.

"Why did you take the heart, Alan?"

"I don't know, your Shaman just gave it to me. He said that there was something magical in the box that would give me great powers. That I could be even more powerful than my father."

I shook my head and said, "The Wendigo is pure evil. Your father was under its spell, and you would have been too."

"Then why did the Shaman give this thing to me?" he asked pointing to the box in my hands.

"That is what I am trying to understand. Perhaps it's because I needed to kill the Wendigo in the physical world."

"What does that mean?"

"Doesn't matter," I said, shaking my head.

"You have saved me more than once, Lukas. I have been a fool chasing after power like Father. What do I do now?" he asked, despondently.

"Well, you can walk through the gates of the fort. I'm sure you will be welcomed. Or, you come back to the Pequawkets with me."

Alan jumped forward so quickly, I thought he was about to hit me. Instead he hugged me and said, "Thank you, Lukas. I want to go with you."

"Are you sure, Alan? These are your people," I said gesturing to the fort.

Alan shook his head. "I have seen what my people have done to the natives, Lukas. I do not want to be a part of that. I choose to go with you and accept the consequences of my decision."

I patted Alan on his back, grabbed Wili's bridle, and said, "Very well, Alan. Let's see what the future has in store for us."

Chapter 14

In the two days it took to return to the village, Alan and I had many hours to talk.

"I imagine that growing up with your father was not easy," I said as we headed north along the trail.

Alan nodded and pursed his lips. "I was always trying to find a way to please him. But he complained constantly that I was not strong enough, or smart enough."

"What about your mother?"

"She died delivering me in childbirth. I was raised by various women, most of whom I don't remember."

"I'm sorry, Alan, I didn't know."

Alan stopped walking, and looked at me. "There's something I don't understand about you, Lukas," he said petting Wili on his neck.

"What's that?"

"My father murdered your father and has committed countless atrocities against you and your people, yet you have always offered me kindness. Why is that?"

I rubbed my chin and put my hand on Alan's shoulder. "Maybe it's because I sense something different in you than in your father. You're a good person, Alan, and you deserve a chance to live a life based on your own merits."

Tears rolled down Alan's cheeks. He embraced me and said, "Thank you, Lukas. You truly are a warrior."

As we approached the village, I glanced over to Alan and took note of his fair skin, blond hair, and blue eyes, and wondered how accepting the Chief and the rest of the Pequawkets would be. Of course I was also not of the same blood of the tribe, but unlike my friend, I had proven my valor.

Anticipating my concerns, Alan asked, "Is it a good idea for me to just ride into the village? I don't think I'll get a warm welcome."

"Probably not. But I'll make sure no harm comes to you."

Indeed, the warriors who spotted us first started to whoop and holler at the sight of Alan. To protect him, I had Alan walk behind Wili as a way to block the warriors from throwing stones. I shouted orders to them not to touch him. They obediently backed off.

"Stay close," I told Alan, who was shifting his eyes back and forth, scanning the gathering crowd.

Familiar eyes of friends gave me curious looks. I returned their suspicions with a smile and a nod and continued through the meandering pathways to the Chief's longhouse.

Waiting for me at the entrance were Nadie and Huritt. I ran forward and embraced them.

"Thanks to the Great Spirit," Nadie said squeezing me tight.

She looked at Alan and asked, "Why is he here?"

"I'll explain, but let me speak first to the Chief and the Shaman," I said lifting the stone box from the saddlebag.

Nadie looked at the container in my hands and followed Alan and me into the longhouse. All eyes watched us as we walked toward the Chief's berth. Standing alongside the honored elder, was the equally respected Shaman, and the warriors, Wematin and Kitchi.

I nodded a greeting and handed the stone box to the Shaman, asking, "Can we keep this safe?"

The Shaman took it and answered, "Indeed we can."

"Why have you brought him here?" asked Wematin with disdain.

"Alan seeks to join the tribe," I said.

A collective gasp of shock rose from the gathering, and then blended into indistinguishable conversations. The Chief raised his arms for silence, and with a flip of his hands, dismissed the onlookers from the inner circle.

With the curious returning to their daily tasks, I described the events leading up to the Wendigo's resurrection and my repeated slaying of it. During my recitation of the battle I noticed the Shaman nodding his approval.

"You have done well," the Shaman said.

"It was you who released Alan and gave him the Wendigo's heart," I said.

The Shaman glanced over to the Chief and then back to me, and slowly nodded.

"I figured as much. Perhaps you can share your reasoning with me?"

"What you did in the spirit world, also needed to be done in the physical world, Lukas. There was no other way to be sure that the Wendigo would not return."

The Chief interrupted, and said, "You two can have your conversation at a later time. Tell me, Lukas, why have you brought the captain's son here?"

"Alan is a victim of the captain as much as we all are. He deserves a chance of living a life in peace. He is here to honorably ask for acceptance into the tribe."

All eyes shifted from me to Alan. He impressed me by bowing his head in respect.

"The council will discuss and decide," said the Chief who rose to his feet and walked down the center pathway of the longhouse, with his long and colorful robe fluttering behind him.

Alan and I turned to watch his departure. When we looked back, Wematin stepped forward, took Alan by the wrist, and twisted his arm behind his back.

"What are you doing, Wematin?" I asked.

"Until a decision is made, Alan will remain a prisoner."

"This is not necessary," I insisted, and put a hand on Wematin's chest, forcing him to halt.

Kitchi gently touched my forearm and said, "It's all right, Lukas."

I dropped my arm and allowed Alan to be taken away.

Chapter 15

It has been six months since the slaying of the Wendigo and the recovery of its heart. Nadie gave birth to a girl last week. We named her Wawetseka, which means beautiful, a perfect name for my darling little girl. She looks like her lovely mother with a skin color that favored mine.

After all our planning to leave the tribe and head west, the Chief convinced us to stay on with the Pequawkets. He forgave Nadie for her disobedience in releasing Alan before the great battle with the English rangers on the mountainside. With this resolved, a great burden of guilt was lifted, and we were pleased to remain with the tribe.

Even Alan was accepted and made a home with the Pequawkets. He learned to speak the language, and while he did not have warrior potential, he proved himself valuable as a teacher of English to the young boys and girls.

As for my quest of seeking a connection with the Great Spirit, I spent many hours under the willow tree speaking with the Shaman. He told me that a warrior's life is a constant journey of seeking out one's purpose.

"Never forget the seven generations that have come before you. They have provided all of who you are today. It is your legacy to make sure what you have learned in this lifetime is passed forward to the seven generations yet to come. Starting with your daughter Wawetseka, teach her what you have learned on your journey. She will carry forward your collective wisdom on to the next generation."

The Shaman left me under the willow tree to contemplate his words. The Great Spirit had blessed my life with Nadie, Huritt and Wawetseka. I was fortunate. But I also knew that deep in the cave, sealed in a stone container, was the black heart of the Wendigo, which if discovered, could be unleashed upon man once more.

About the Author

Moon Flower is the second novel by Author Neil Perry Gordon. His first, *A Cobbler's Tale,* follows the struggles of a family of Jewish immigrants as they try to survive the ravages of World War 1, while the father attempts to build a life in New York's bustling Lower East Side.

Born in the Bronx, Neil Perry Gordon is the eldest son to Elaine and Walter Gordon. At the age of seven years old, Neil's family moved from the Bronx, to the suburban community of Rockland County. Neil graduated as the first high school class from the Green Meadow Waldorf School in 1976. Shortly after graduating in 1980 with a Bachelor's Degree in Marketing from Pace University, he moved to south Florida and started a drapery business. In 1990, he relocated back to New York and still operates his business, Decorating with Fabric. He has two adult sons, Samuel and Maximilian. Website: https://www.neilperrygordon.com/